the girl *you* LOST

bookouture

Also by Kathryn Croft:

The Girl With No Past
The Stranger Within
Behind Closed Doors

KATHRYN CROFT

the girl *you* LOST

Bookouture

Published by Bookouture

An imprint of StoryFire Ltd.
23 Sussex Road, Ickenham, UB10 8PN
United Kingdom

www.bookouture.com

ISBN: 978-1-910751-71-8
eBook ISBN: 978-1-910751-70-1

ACKNOWLEDGMENTS

Thank you so much to the whole Bookouture team for believing in me and for making this book the best it could be. Keshini Naidoo, Olly Rhodes, Kim Nash, Claire Bord, Lydia Vassar-Smith and Natalie Butlin, you have made me feel part of the family and I appreciate all your support! I particularly have to thank Keshini for her superb editorial skills and Kim for being an amazing publicist.

As always, my gratitude goes to my fantastic agent, Madeleine Milburn, and her whole team, particularly Cara Lee Simpson and Therese Coen, who work extremely hard and are always there to answer my silly questions!

My friend, Jonny Garland, thank you once more for supplying invaluable factual information – I really appreciate you giving up your time to let me talk your ear off!

I need to give a special mention to Carolin Lotter, Catherine Nicholson, David Treweek and Chris Walker for all your help with factual information on working in the media industry. Thank you!

To all the Bookouture authors: it's so great to be in contact with you and thank you for your amazing support. It's lovely to know we all understand what a lonely job writing can be!

Once again, my husband, family and friends continue to be a huge support and I am truly blessed to have you in my life.

And finally, to all my readers – thank you so much for buying (and hopefully enjoying) my books. I especially appreciate anyone taking the time to write to me and share their thoughts. Your support is very much appreciated!

For Oliver, our rainbow.

PROLOGUE

It had been easy to get him alone. He'd played right into her hands and all she'd had to do was flash a smile at him. Laugh at his jokes. Pretend to be interested in his words.

But now they were in his flat, in a part of town she barely knew, and if she wasn't careful, her control would slip away.

'This is your home?' she asked, glancing around, taking in the sparse furnishings and bare white walls. This place was a show home, with no sign that anybody lived here.

He nodded, pulling her towards him, his hand sliding down the back of her skirt. His skin was cold and she smelt whisky on his breath as he leaned towards her, his mouth fumbling for hers.

For a moment she let him kiss her; it was a small sacrifice to make in return for finding out the truth. And the truth was what she would get tonight, no matter what it took. She had vowed to herself that before this day was over she would have an answer.

'Tell me what you meant the other day,' she said, pressing her body against his, feeling how hard he was under his jeans.

'Huh? What?' He was distracted. And drunk. Not a good combination.

'You started to tell me something. Remember?'

He took his hand from her skirt and placed it under her shirt, rubbing her breast. She tried not to flinch. She had deliberately worn a low cut denim shirt, too many buttons undone, flashing just a small section of her bra. But her effort had been unnecessary; he wouldn't have cared if she was dressed in a bin liner.

'Forget that,' he slurred. 'Come in the bedroom.'

She would have to do as he asked. Following him, she prayed things would not have to go too far. She couldn't bear the thought of his naked body on top of her. No, she couldn't let that happen.

The curtains were drawn in the bedroom, only a sliver of soft street lighting shining through a tiny slit in the middle. He was digging in his pocket for something, finally pulling out his mobile and tapping on it.

'Damn it. Battery's dead. Fuck. Can you give me your phone?'

'Why?' she said. 'Who are you calling?'

'Nobody. Just let me check something.'

Reluctantly she handed her mobile to him, waiting to see what he'd do.

'I want to film you,' he said, pointing her phone at her.

She stepped back towards the door. 'What? No. Why? Stop it. Give my phone back.' She lunged forward, trying to make a grab for it, but he whipped his arm back.

His smile dropped. 'Take off your clothes.'

Sitting on the bed now, he kept the phone pointed at her. 'It won't be the same as using my camera, but you look so good I need to capture you. I can send it to my phone after.'

The thought of him having any piece of her, even just on film, filled her with horror. 'Wait. Tell me first. Tell me what you meant. And stop filming.' At least it was her phone; she would just make sure she deleted the video the second she got it back in her possession.

He let out a heavy sigh, proving he knew exactly what she was asking. 'Anyone would think you're using me. That's not nice, is it? I want something in return. Come on, play fair.'

His words were jovial but there was something in his expression, the deep lines etched on his forehead. He would not take rejection well. Perhaps she could play along for a few moments longer, let him think he was having his way.

Slowly, she undid the last few buttons on her shirt, trying to ignore the fact that he was still filming, rubbing his crotch. His eyes remained fixed on the phone screen; he was clearly more interested in watching her that way than in the flesh.

'That's it,' she said, removing her shirt and placing her hands on her hips, trying to show she was still in control. 'That's all you get until you talk.'

Ignoring her, he lowered his arm. 'Take everything off. And stay there. Come on, you're wasting time. I'm losing my patience.' He shook his head and his stare became cold, hard and unfamiliar.

That was when she realised she had made a terrible mistake. She had underestimated him. There was no way he was letting her leave until he'd done what he wanted to do.

'That's it, I'm out of here,' she said. There had to be a better way to get the truth from him. Clearly this was not going to work. She began to pull her shirt back on but within seconds he had sprung up and was forcing her onto the bed, tugging at her skirt.

'I've wanted you for ages,' he said, his body weighing down on her, stopping her moving.

She struggled underneath him, but it was futile. Turning away, she wanted to scream but it died in her mouth. And then she noticed the heavy glass lamp on the bedside table. She couldn't give up now she had come this far. 'Just tell me what you meant the other day.'

A smug grin spread across his face, but he didn't answer.

Trying to produce a flirtatious smile, she was unsure she was pulling it off. 'It doesn't have to be like this. Wouldn't you prefer it if I enjoyed myself too? Let you do whatever you want to me? Isn't that better?' It was a risk. He clearly got off on the idea of using force.

But he barely moved. 'Come on then, what are you waiting for?'

She swallowed the lump in her throat and reached for his penis, stroking it, fighting nausea. 'You like this, don't you?'

His eyes glazed over and he raised his head, staring at the ceiling. 'Yeah, that's good.'

'Will you tell me now?'

He looked down and laughed, and she realised she probably wasn't going to get anything out of him after all. She would have to think of a new strategy, one that started closer to home.

But then he opened his mouth and spoke, an unfamiliar name falling from his lips, seconds before he yanked up her skirt and lunged towards her.

And that was when she reached for the lamp and smashed it into his skull, repeating the action until his grip finally loosened.

ONE

Eighteen Years Ago

I stare at my baby as I hold her in my arms and can't believe we've produced something so beautiful. She may have arrived years too early but I wouldn't change a thing. I only hope Matt feels the same. He seems out of his comfort zone, but then so am I. Sometimes I watch him holding her nervously, as if she is china that will break in his hand, but the smile on his face speaks louder than any of his doubts. They have all gone now, vanquished by our beautiful Helena.

As soon as I put her back in her cot she resumes crying, but I have to leave her, that's what the midwife said. I can't keep rushing to her with every shriek. So I leave the room and close the door, carrying the baby monitor with me, Helena's cries following me out.

Matt is on the sofa, surrounded by a pile of textbooks, his brow creased in concentration. I watch him for a moment and my heart swells with pride. He will be a doctor one day and we will live somewhere with more than three rooms. Helena will have her own bedroom and he will have somewhere to work in peace.

He looks up and smiles. 'Hey.' His eyes flick towards the screeching monitor.

I look around but there's nowhere to put it. The kitchen and living room are one open plan area and Helena is in our bedroom, the only other room apart from our cramped bathroom.

'Sorry,' I say. 'I'm sure she'll stop soon.'

He must sense my panic because he puts his books aside and stands up, crossing over to me and pulling me close. 'Hey, it's okay, she's just settling in. Getting used to us. This must be strange for her. I mean, one minute she's comfortable in here,' he rubs my stomach, still swollen from pregnancy, 'and the next she has all this to deal with. Us. Two parents who don't know what the hell they're doing!' He looks around the flat. 'And look at our surroundings. I mean, this place is bad enough for us, let alone a baby.'

'It's not that bad,' I say, gazing at the tiny room. The yellowing wallpaper is peeling from the walls and the carpet is threadbare, but at least it's our home. Most of our friends still live with their parents, so we're lucky to have our own space. And South Ealing's not a bad place to live.

Matt sighs. 'I just wish I could afford something better for us. I will, soon, I promise. Once I've finished medical school and got a job, we'll be fine. We'll laugh about this.'

'Well, it's better than living separately with our parents,' I remind him. 'At least we're together. A family.'

Matt chews his bottom lip. It's a habit I've noticed him doing a lot lately. 'How weird does that sound, eh? A family! At our ages.'

He doesn't need to tell me how strange this is. I am nineteen and he is twenty-two, much too young to be calling ourselves a family. But Helena has changed everything.

I pull back. 'You don't regret it, do you?'

He takes both my hands and gently squeezes them. 'No, never. I mean, I know I freaked out at first, but … I was just … I don't know. Scared? But now she's here, I wouldn't have it any other way.'

'Even if she makes it difficult to study?' I say, holding up the baby monitor. Helena is still crying but somehow I have become used to it, it is only harmless and reassuring background noise, nothing to worry about.

Matt puts his book aside and leans forward. 'Tell you what, why don't I call Mum? Ask her to take Helena to the park for a bit? Some fresh air might help settle her.'

'Do you think she'd mind?' Even as I ask this, I know the answer. As much as she had reservations about us having Helena, Miriam dotes on her granddaughter and we'd be lost without her support.

Matt gives me a look that says, *What do you think?* then reaches for the phone.

Less than an hour later, Helena is in her pram, cuddled up to her toy rabbit, ready for her visit to the park. She is already calmer, as if she knows she has a treat in store.

'I'm so glad you called,' Miriam says, her eyes fixed on the baby. 'You know, I might be busy with work but I could help more often. Don't be afraid to ask. You're both young, you'll need time on your own. And a baby shouldn't come between a couple, it should only make you stronger.'

'Actually, Mum, I just need to study,' Matt says, but his mother ignores him, disappearing through the door with a sing-song goodbye.

'Did you mean it about studying?' I say, as soon as the door clicks shut.

'Why, what did you have in mind?' Matt flashes that smile, the sexy one I haven't seen for a while now, and I feel myself melt. For the first time since our baby was born I need him, right now, there is no time to get to the bedroom.

We lie together, naked on the sofa, our clothes scattered over the floor. I listen to the sound of Matt breathing and realise I don't want to move. Ever. I want to draw out this moment, stretch it as far as it can go like a rubber band, even though I know eventually it will ping back.

I kiss his chest. 'That didn't feel different, did it?' I have to ask, I have heard stories about things changing down there after childbirth.

'No, no. 'Course not. Everything's great. Everything's fine.'

And it is.

Until the phone rings and our world is shattered forever.

'What? Slow down. Tell me again. I can't understand you.'

I grip Matt's arm as he speaks into the phone. I don't need to ask who the caller is, I already know. And I also know something is very wrong.

'Oh, shit, oh fuck. Have you looked everywhere? Are you sure? Call the police. Now. I'm coming down there.'

He slams down the phone and grabs his jeans. 'Don't panic, Simone, but that was Mum. She's saying she can't find Helena. I'm going to the park now but stay here in case the police come. She's calling them now but they might need someone here, I don't know. Fuck! Shit!'

'What … what do you mean she can't find her? What's happened?' I am still naked, and freezing cold now, but can't seem to move.

Matt's words blend into each other and sound like a foreign language. The only thing I catch is that Helena is missing. Something about the toilets in the park. And Miriam getting sick. None of it makes sense. It is all wrong. She can't be missing. It's impossible.

But slowly it starts to sink in and I fall to the floor, my knees cracking against the carpet. I can't feel any physical pain; it is masked too deeply by my inability to breathe. Clutching at my chest, all I can focus on is how I've let Helena down. I'm supposed to be her mother, to protect her, even when she's out of my sight.

I scream these thoughts to Matt and he pulls me up, cupping my face in his hands.

'We'll find her," he says. 'You've got to stay calm.'

I'm too numb to respond and all I can do is listen as he yells instructions at me and rushes from the flat.

And that's when I know this is real.

TWO

Now

It is a strange sensation, being certain that someone is following you. Until now I don't think I've experienced it, but it's unmistakeable; feeling eyes on you, but the heaviness lifting the minute you turn around. Knowing nonetheless that someone is watching.

Five minutes ago I slipped into John Lewis, even though I don't need to buy anything. I just want to be sure. It's lunchtime and I'm due back at work in half an hour and still need to eat, but now I am unnerved. I only came out for some fresh air, to escape the stuffy studio, but now I wish I'd stayed there.

I turn around and there she is. The same young woman I spotted as I left work. The same woman I noticed behind me at the top of Oxford Street. This could be coincidence but I also noticed her this morning by Tottenham Court Road station.

She is following me.

Do I know her? In my job I come across a vast amount of people, but I'm not one to forget a face. Or much else. Matt says my memory astounds him; that my brain somehow stores up even the most trivial of details. He says I should have his job, that it would be a godsend for a GP to have my gift. But I'll leave that up to him; I'd be no good delivering bad prognoses to people. I don't have his ability to remain detached.

I am calling her a woman but she is barely that. I cannot guess at her exact age but she can't be much more than twenty. This should make her less threatening, but it doesn't.

I steal secret glances at her and see she is studying the box of a coffee maker. She is tall and thin, dressed in leggings and a short leather jacket, a turquoise scarf wrapped around her neck. The edge of a long grey t-shirt hangs underneath her jacket but it can't be keeping her warm. On her feet she wears black Converse boot trainers, the bottoms bright white.

Thoughts of Helena try to invade my head. Would she dress this way? But I have to push these destructive contemplations away. I can't let myself think of her now, not here, in the middle of John Lewis, in front of my newly acquired stalker.

Picking up a set of brushed silver cutlery I have no interest in, I try and work out what to do. I could approach her and ask if I can help her. Show her I'm not disturbed by the huge coincidence of seeing her here as well as outside my work. Or I could ignore her, make a speedy exit out of this shop, get back to work and forget this silliness. Sometimes my imagination runs away with me: it is a hazard of the job. And of my past.

Before I have a chance to choose an option, she appears next to me and taps my arm. It is not a gentle tap, but a fast and urgent demand for attention.

'Excuse me?' Her voice is surprisingly soft.

Now that she is barely centimetres away, I realise how pretty she is. Her dark brown eyes are huge and shiny and her long hair is almost black, straightened to within an inch of its life.

'Yes?' It's all I can think of to say, despite my earlier plan.

Her eyes dart to the left then right before she focuses on me again. 'You're Simone Porter, aren't you?'

So I was right. She must know me from a story we've covered. But whatever she wants can't be good, otherwise why would she follow me away from work when she could have asked to see me there? She could have emailed me, like other people needing my help do.

'Yes.' My voice is wary now. 'Can I help you?' I glance at my watch, hoping she'll take the hint that I'm pressed for time.

She checks behind her, reinforcing my belief that whatever she wants to tell me won't be something I'll want to hear. 'Can we talk? Away from here?'

'What's this about? Who exactly are you?'

She places her hand on my arm and I flinch. She must notice because she apologises and immediately steps back, almost knocking into a row of neatly stacked boxes of kettles. 'I just … really need to talk to you. But not here.'

'You'll have to come and see me at work, I'm afraid. The network gets funny about things like this.'

The young woman sighs and shakes her head. 'No, no, it's nothing to do with your work.'

I am not expecting this and am thrown off guard. 'Then … how do you know me?'

'I don't … not really … ' She stares at her trainers.

'Look, I'm sorry but I have to get back. If it's important, call me there, okay?' I turn away but feel her eyes boring into me.

'Simone?'

I know I shouldn't turn back. I should keep walking as if I haven't heard her; she won't know and it doesn't matter anyway. This obviously wasn't important. Perhaps she does know of me from my work and wants to ask if I can get her in the door. That's what happens when you work in TV. But despite this, I look around and her eyes have grown even larger, imploring me to listen to her, to take her seriously.

'I need to talk to you. It's about your daughter.'

The air is sucked from me and I clutch the nearest shelving unit to stop myself falling. 'What?' I say this, even though I have heard every word as if it's been delivered through a loudspeaker.

'Now can we go somewhere else? Please?'

We sit in a coffee shop located on one of the back roads behind John Lewis, away from the bustle of Oxford Street. I simply let her lead me here, storing my questions for when we are away from the crowds, out of the cold January air. There aren't many people in here, and just the right amount of noise to stop us being over-heard.

'Tell me what you know,' I say, unable to stop my voice shaking. I reach for my coffee – black with an extra shot – but my hand trembles so I place my cup down again.

'I've shocked you, haven't I?' Her lip curls at the side, but I can't tell whether she's being apologetic or enjoying my confusion. Whichever it is, she seems more relaxed now.

'What do you know? And who are you?' My words are sharp, but I am on edge. What is she about to tell me?

With the straw that's protruding from her glass of Coke, she stirs her drink, the ice clanking against the sides, her eyes fixed on me. 'I just need to be sure it's you first. Please, just humour me and I promise I'll tell you everything.'

I dig in my bag and find my purse, pulling out my driving license. I hesitate for a moment, unsure what I'm doing. I usually think carefully about things, weighing up the pros and cons of every situation I find myself in, but today there is no time. I hand her my license and she stares at the picture. It's almost ten years old and my hair is different now – shorter and wavier than it was – but it's unmistakably me. Hair can change, even skin tone, but eyes always remain the same, de-spite the passing of time. So why is she taking so long to give it back to me?

'Thanks,' she says eventually, sliding it across the table. I grab it quickly and stuff it in my bag, not bothering to slot it into its place in my purse. 'So you work in TV?'

Trying to hide my frustration, I answer her. 'Yes, I'm a field producer for News 24. I've been there for twelve years. But you know this already, don't you?'

The girl – for that's what I've realised she is – shuffles in her chair, at least showing me the courtesy of looking uncomfortable. 'Yeah. Sorry. I just need to be sure it's you.'

The door is thrown open and she jerks her head up, her eyes following the new customer as he heads to the till.

'Surely you saw me on the channel website? That picture's fairly recent, so you can't still have doubts. Now tell me. What do you know about … my daughter?' The words almost choke me. It's been too long since I've said them out loud. 'And who are you?'

She puts her glass aside and stares at me with her dark, wide eyes. 'My name is Grace Rhodes. And I, um, have information about your daughter.' Her voice is hesitant, and for the first time I feel her confidence slip.

'You've said that already. What information? What do you know? And why should I believe you?' My guard is up. I have been fooled before by people claiming to have information about Helena. Not for a long time, not since she was a baby, but that doesn't mean this girl isn't playing a nasty trick, or just wanting attention. In my line of work I have come across all kinds of disturbed people. There is no limit to what humans are capable of.

'I know that eighteen years ago your daughter was abducted in a park. She was only six months old.'

I grow cold, even though I am seated next to a warm radiator. 'That doesn't prove anything. You could have found that out online. It's public information.' Even to me my voice sounds frail.

She nods. Is she giving up so easily? 'You're right, I don't have anything concrete yet. Not really. I wish I did.'

I can't work her out. I know this is a game, but what does she want? 'If you don't have proof then you're wasting my time.' I stand up, determined to reach the door even though I doubt my unsteady legs will get me there.

'Please, wait.' She rises from her chair and grabs my hand. Her skin feels warm. 'I know this is hard for you, but please, you have to listen to me. Just hear me out. And then you can decide whether or not to walk away.'

They say mothers have strong instincts; something innate that will help them protect their children. Well, I am no longer a mother, but looking at this young girl now, something compels me to give her a chance.

'What do you know about my daughter other than what's already public knowledge?'

'Mrs Porter. Simone. I just need you to know I'm not some crazy person spinning you a line.' She sits down again and I do the same.

'Show me some ID at least. You've seen mine, haven't you? Now I want to see yours.'

She reaches into her pocket. 'All I have is my student ID. Here.' She slides it across the table.

Picking up the card, I stare at the picture. It is definitely the girl I'm talking to, and it says her name is Grace Rhodes. But how do I know the ID is real? The black font stating City University London looks authentic enough, as does the red coat of arms, but it is probably a form of ID that's easy to fake.

'Don't you have anything else? A driver's licence?'

She shakes her head. 'I haven't started driving yet. I keep meaning to have lessons but I'm always so busy studying. I'll get to it, though.'

This seems like a reasonable excuse. However, I am still unsure whether this girl is genuine, so I need to keep listening. Keep letting her talk until she spits out what it is she wants. Because there is always something, isn't there?

'Go on,' I say, keeping my eyes on her, searching for proof of deception. 'You're telling me Helena's alive? What do you know about her? Where is she?'

She looks me directly in the eye. 'She's alive, I swear to you.'

I am numb as she says this. I've had psychics and palm-readers and all sorts of supposed clairvoyants telling me these words before, but nothing has ever come of it. We have never found Helena. I remain quiet and let her finish.

'I … I can't say what happened. I don't know … she doesn't know. But she's fine. She's okay. She's been okay, I mean.'

Now I feel the air being sucked from my lungs once again. I can't hear any more of this. I need to get away from this girl. For years after Helena went missing I got my hopes up every time someone said they had information, but all it ever turned out to be was false leads or lies. And with each occasion, I was ripped even further apart. 'I have to go now. Back to work. My lunch hour's nearly over.' I stand up, ready to bolt.

She stares up at me and her mouth gapes open. I realise she was not expecting me to react this way. Perhaps she thought I'd fall to my knees and beg her to take me to Helena.

'But … I … '

'Listen, do you think you're the first person to do this? Come up with some crazy story claiming to know where my daughter is? I mean, what do you want anyway? Money? Is that it?' I thrust my hand in my purse and pull out a twenty-pound note, throwing it towards her. It flutters slowly to the table and she ignores it, staring at me with her huge eyes. Other people turn to us; I have spoken too loudly, piqued their curiosity.

I leave the money on the table and pull my bag onto my shoulder. Glancing at her as I turn to leave, I notice her cheeks glisten with tears.

'Just let me show you something,' she says, her voice barely more than a whisper. She reaches into her pocket and for a second I am certain I can see the blade of a knife as she pulls out her hand. But then my mind focuses and I realise what I am looking at.

A soft blue velvet rabbit.

Helena's toy.

'Where did you get that?' I say, unable to take my eyes off it.

Grace hands it to me, and with shaking hands I grab it. 'So I'm right. It's hers, isn't it? Your daughter's? I needed to know if it was.' she says. None of her words make any sense.

Sitting down again, I study the toy, trying not to let my emotions overwhelm me and cloud my judgement. What would I do if this were a news story I was covering? I would tell the mother there could have been millions of these toys made that year. Matt bought it in a charity shop but I have no idea of its origins. All I know is that as young as she was, Helena loved her rabbit. And it was with her when she was taken.

As I continue to examine it, stroking the soft material between my fingers, I know this is my daughter's toy. I lift it to my nose and breathe in the fabric, but the scent is unfamiliar: a washing powder I've never used.

'What's going on? Tell me. Now! Where did you get this?' My voice is too loud and once more people turn to stare at us.

Grace's eyes widen and she takes a deep breath. 'It's my toy. I've had it since I was a baby.'

Only once before have I felt the ground fall from beneath me. When Helena disappeared. But now I am experiencing it again, with the same shortness of breath and fear that my heart will stop beating.

'What did you just say?' I need her to repeat it because surely I have misheard?

She tells me again. 'This toy belongs to me. I've had it since I was a baby.'

'But ... so ... '

Grace sucks in a deep breath. 'I need you to help me, Simone. I think I'm your daughter and I need you to help me find out what happened to me.'

THREE

I stare at the girl sitting before me, my heart thudding in my chest. If I were an objective bystander I would urge myself to leave. To get out of this café and as far away as possible from this girl who is claiming to be my daughter. But I remain where I am.

She is tall, like me, but that means nothing. Her hair is dark like Matt's, and even though both of us have brown eyes, so do the majority of people. None of this tells me anything, so all I have to go on is my instinct, which, because of the rabbit, is now telling me to hear her out. If nothing else, I will just listen to what she has to say.

'I know this is difficult,' Grace says, stirring her Coke again. 'I just didn't know what else to do. I had to find you and tell you what I know. I need your help.' Her eyes plead with me.

I tell myself I can do this. I can listen to what she says, let it wash over me as if I am interviewing someone for a news story. That is all I have to do. And then I can walk out of here, go back to work, and one day recount the story of the crazy girl who claimed to be my daughter.

'Tell me everything,' I say. I am doing well so far, no emotion escapes into my words. Outwardly, I am calm and detached.

She lets go of her straw and looks around, scanning the faces of the other customers, and I wonder why. She is jittery and on edge, and this is only one of several reasons not to believe her. Surely I am the one she should be nervous of?

'I always felt different,' she explains. 'You know, a bit out of place, like I didn't really fit anywhere. I mean, it's such a cliché, but it's the only way I can describe it. But I never really thought for one second that my mum … I mean, she's not my mum, is she? But I'll call her that for now, it will just be easier, until I've told you everything.'

She pauses, and I wonder if I'm supposed to speak at this point. But what would I say? That I'm struggling to allow myself even the tiniest hope that she is Helena? I've been burnt too many times, so what happens if I dare to hope this time? But what's becoming clear is that whether she is or isn't, this girl – Grace – actually *believes* she is my daughter.

'Last week,' she continues, 'a family friend, well, more a friend of Mum's, accidentally let something slip about her not being my real mum.' She flicks back a strand of hair that's fallen across her cheek. 'He was drunk, and I don't think he meant to say it. When I pushed him about it a few days later, I managed to get your name out of him. I looked you up online.'

She stops again and watches me, and I can sense her desperation for me to speak. But I am speechless. It is all so far-fetched, I keep expecting someone to jump out of nowhere and tell me I've been pranked.

'Look, this is crazy,' I say. 'The man was drunk. He probably remembered the story about my daughter and used it to try and get to your mum for some reason. You can't take what he said seriously.' But as I say this I look down at the rabbit I'm still clutching, and know that there is something more to this. The police kept details of the rabbit private so it wasn't mentioned in the media.

'Tell me everything he said. Word for word. Leave nothing out.'

She inhales a sharp breath then begins. 'His name is Lucas. Lucas Hall. He went to school with Mum's brother, my uncle.

They were best friends. But Uncle Daniel had a brain tumour and died recently so Lucas came to the house to visit Mum. I guess to check how she was doing.'

'Had you met him before? This Lucas?' I am doing what I am trained to do: ask questions to get to the heart of a story.

Grace shakes her head. 'Not until that day. I'd heard about him. He owns a posh restaurant, in west London, I think, but he never came over. Uncle Daniel used to talk about him a lot.' She pauses and I urge her to continue.

'That day he and Mum were having a glass of wine in the kitchen when I turned up to visit her. She doesn't normally drink but she said they were celebrating Uncle Daniel's life. The thing is, they were really close. Mum was a lot older than my uncle so I guess she mothered him a bit, looked after him.'

All the while she talks, painting this picture for me, I cannot believe I am part of her story. These people are strangers to me; how can any of them have anything to do with Helena?

Oblivious to my thoughts, Grace continues. 'Mum got called out. She's a home carer and one of her ladies needed urgent help with something. She told Lucas that I'd keep him company until she got back. But after a couple of hours Mum still wasn't home, so he ended up opening another bottle. I kept trying to hint that I had uni work to do, I mean, I didn't even know the man, but he wouldn't leave, he just kept on downing the wine.'

'Were you drinking as well?' I have to ask this; her answer could put a different slant on things.

'No, I don't drink. I'm too busy studying to cloud my mind with alcohol.' It is the third time she has referred to how studious she is, and I can't help thinking she's deliberately focusing on this point.

The café door opens and once more Grace's eyes flick to the latest customer walking in. After a second she relaxes and continues her story. 'He started talking about Uncle Daniel. Saying what a good man he'd been, how he'd have done anything for Mum. How they all would. Then he got a bit creepy. He started flirting with me, telling me how pretty I was. It was awful. I told him to cut it out and he seemed offended at first, but then he started laughing. I don't know, maybe he was trying to make out he didn't care that I'd shot him down. But then he told me I was better off with Ginny for a mum than that teenager. I asked him what he meant but he shut down, said it was the alcohol talking. He left before I could question him further.'

I listen to what she tells me, organising the words so I can make sense of them. I still don't understand how she has concluded that she is my daughter.

'Look, Grace, I admit that what this man, Lucas, said is strange, but it's not evidence that you're … Helena. Perhaps he was just annoyed with you for rejecting his advances?'

She sighs, clearly frustrated. 'Wait. I saw him again. I found out from Mum … Ginny … that he was going to a bar last night and I went there. I caked myself in make-up and wore a short skirt and that was all it took.'

I am filled with horror. Whether or not this girl is Helena, I feel an overwhelming urge to protect her. She is the same age as my daughter would be now. 'What are you saying? You didn't …'

She stares at her empty glass and doesn't look at me as she speaks. 'I eventually got the truth out of him. He gave me your name.'

And now I am torn. Surely her story is too elaborate to be false? Or maybe that's exactly the point. Isn't the truth always simpler than a lie? For now, I will continue to hear her out, until I find out what she really wants, because I'm waiting to hear what that is.

'Look, if this is all true then we need to go to the police. Now.'

She startles at this, as if I have punched her in the gut. 'No, we can't.'

'Yes, Grace, we have to. If this Lucas was telling anywhere near the truth, then it needs to be investigated.' I am doing well. I am detached, acting as if I am not involved in this. I will just help this girl, whatever it is she wants.

She begins to cry then, her chest heaving with each sob. 'I know, but please, we can't. I just need you to help me. I need to know if it's true. If I'm your daughter. If my whole life has been a lie.'

'There's no other way, Grace. Can't you see that? We need to tell the police.'

When she looks up at me her eyes are wild with fear. 'We can't,' she says, her words barely audible, 'It's Lucas … He's dead … It was an accident. And I'm the one who killed him.'

FOUR

Did you have a normal childhood? Parents wrapping you in love, protecting you from the outside world, yet still somehow managing to teach you independence?

Well, I had all this. And more. A comfortable house, no siblings to fight with – but that was okay with me – any toy I wanted, within reason. And I have to add the 'within reason' part because I don't want you to think I was spoilt.

I'm telling you this because I'm not the cliché you will want me to be by the time you've finished my story. You will need to think I was neglected or abused, that none of what came later was my fault. It is the only way you will be able to sleep at night: to feel there is a clear distinction between human and monster, a line so wide that you will never meet anyone who has crossed it.

Sorry to disappoint you, but my childhood was normal in every way.

So how did I end up like this; drowning in hideous secrets and foul acts?

The problem was not family or environment or school.

The problem was within me.

Years later, he told me we were cut from the same cloth. That's why we did what we did, driven by the compulsion within us. Life was to be experienced, he said, the only limits were those inflicted upon us by narrow-mindedness and fear. Our own and that of others.

Did it excite you? he asked, after the first time. Did you feel as if your blood would burst from your body? That no feeling would ever match up to it?

I tried to still my shaking limbs, to hide the fear I was drowning in.

But what was I truly frightened of? What we had just done, or the fact that I had liked it?

FIVE

In my line of work I hear all kinds of things. But never before have I sat face-to-face with a person telling me they have killed someone. I want to run away from Grace, or whoever she is, back to the safety of work. But then I become conscious once more of the blue velvet rabbit I'm still clutching. And now she has said the words, I am caught up in this. There is no way for me to erase Grace's statement. Or to forget that she has Helena's rabbit. Whoever she is, she knows something about my daughter.

I see it clearly as she recounts what happened: the man bearing down on her, pinning her to the bed, tugging at her clothes. I feel the desperation she must have experienced. The fear. And the panic after she smashed the lamp into his skull.

'We're going to the police. Now.'

She shakes her head so vigorously that her hair fans out on either side, whipping the air. 'No, wait, please. I just need to … Will you come with me to his flat? It's in Embankment. Not far. I need to get something.'

And that's when she tells me that he was filming her, with her mobile phone, and that she forgot to get it when she rushed out of the flat, but that she had grabbed his keys, which he'd left in the lock. Once again, it sounds unbelievable, like the script of a film. But I remind myself of all the news stories I've covered that seem far beyond the realms of possibility.

I shake my head. I can't get involved in this.

'Please, Simone,' Grace says. 'Come with me and then I'll do whatever you want. I'll go to the police, do a DNA test, anything. Please, just do this for me. I can't let Mu ... Ginny see it. Or know about it.'

And then I do what I should have done as soon as she approached me. Without a word, I stand up and head to the door, not looking back as I pass the window and make my way back to Oxford Street.

It is only when I reach the end of the road I realise I am still holding the blue rabbit. Helena's rabbit. I turn around and head back towards the café; I don't want this toy and all the questions it brings. I need to give it back to Grace. My daughter has gone; I lost her eighteen years ago and have spent these years trying to come to terms with that. I don't want anything to do with this.

I see Grace as she is leaving the café, walking in the other direction with her head down. My legs carry me towards her, unconsciously. I keep my distance because I don't want her to know I'm following her. I need to see where she's going, to know what game she is playing.

Stuffing the rabbit in my bag, I pull out my phone and call work. Abbot answers and I am relieved to hear his voice. 'I've had an emergency,' I tell him. 'A family thing.' This is not untrue. 'Can you cover for me for a couple of hours? I'll be back as soon as I can.'

As I knew he would be, he is full of concern: asking if I'm okay, and if there's anything he can do, but stopping short of pushing me to tell him what exactly has happened. Abbot is more than a work colleague; in the years we've worked together I have come to think of him as a good friend.

Keeping my eyes on Grace, I thank him and disconnect the call. When I slip my phone back in my bag, my fingers brush soft velvet, and my heart aches with the memory of Helena and the last time I saw her toy.

I follow Grace as she heads along Oxford Street, towards Tottenham Court Road. At first I wonder if she is going to my work, but she crosses the road and heads down into the Tube station. I increase my pace to avoid losing her, and get my Oyster card ready in my hand before I reach the ticket barriers.

She heads towards the southbound Northern line and when she boards the tube to Morden, I am certain I know where she is going. She told me Lucas's flat was in Embankment, only three stops from here.

I jump on the train in the next carriage, only just making it before the warning beep starts, and watch her through the glass on the adjoining door. I try to analyse her expression. Is she disappointed that I wouldn't play her game, angry perhaps? But I can only find resignation written on her face.

My suspicion about where she is heading is confirmed when she stands up before we get to Embankment and heads to the doors. What am I doing? I walked away from her, refusing to buy into what she's said, yet here I am, following her. It's not too late to stop whatever this is. I can get off at the next stop, cross the platform and get on a Tube back to Oxford Street. And then later I will sit down to dinner with Matt and tell him what a strange day I've had. What would he think of what I'm doing?

But as the Tube grinds to a halt, I walk towards the doors, as if my feet are making the decision for me. I step onto the platform, keeping my eyes on Grace as she blends into the crowd, and vow to call Matt as soon as I've seen what Grace does next.

It is hard to keep up with her once we exit the station. Her Converse trainers allow her to take long strides, while my mid-heel Mary Jane shoes only slow me down. But I can't lose her, not now.

I have to know, one way or the other.

I have time to think as I follow her. There must be some truth in what she has said, otherwise why would she come here? But then I know nothing about this girl, this could be where she lives, for all I know. I should have asked more questions: about her mother, about her. What about her father? She made no mention of him. I am already too far involved in this to turn back now. This time, it is my own story I am investigating. I don't know what I believe, but the presence of the rabbit means I must continue on.

For twenty minutes Grace continues walking, the crowds thinning out the further we get from the station. Grey clouds have formed in the sky so it is only a matter of time before rain showers down on us. But this is the least of my worries.

Finally she turns into a quiet street and heads in the direction of a purpose-built block of flats. It is far from run down, but its characterless grey concrete façade makes me feel uneasy. I stop where I am; I have no idea what to do next.

When she disappears inside the building, I realise the choice has been taken from my hands. There is bound to be a secure entry system, so there is no way I will be able to follow her inside. As well as this, I have no idea which flat she is going to and there are three floors.

But despite this, I edge forwards until I am standing outside the main doors where Grace stood only moments ago. And then I am pushing at the door, surprised to find it unlocked.

The communal entrance hall is basic, with no lift, only an uncarpeted staircase. From here I have a full view of the ground floor corridor. Grace is not here and she wouldn't have had time to open a door or wait for someone to let her in, so I head up the stairs, my legs feeling heavier with each step I take.

When I reach the second floor, she is there, disappearing into the flat at the end of the corridor. She no longer seems nervous, and doesn't check to see if anyone is around to see her.

It's not too late. I can still walk away. I repeat this mantra in my head, but it does no good; within seconds I am outside the flat door, and finding it unlatched, push it open as Grace spins round, her mouth hanging open when she sees it is me.

'Fuck! What are you doing? You scared the hell out of me!' She flattens her palm against her chest, as if she's trying to slow her heartbeat.

Stepping inside, I curse myself for being so stupid. I have no idea what's going on here, and what I am about to become involved in, but it's not good.

The flat – whomever it belongs to – is immaculate. I recall Grace's story, and find it hard to believe that the events she recounted took place here.

When I don't say anything, Grace fills the silence. 'But I'm glad you're here. How did you – ? Never mind.' She steps towards a closed door but stops short. 'I can't look, Simone. I can't. He's lying in there … dead.' She is crying again now, and for some reason, I believe her tears.

I walk towards the door, preparing myself for the worst. With my eyes squeezed shut I fling it open, rooted to my spot in the hallway. But when I open my eyes again, I am staring at a freshly made bed. And nothing else.

I step further in and take in the room: white walls, a built-in oak wardrobe, a spotless beige carpet. But no one is here, living or dead. And there are no lamps on either bedside table.

I turn round and Grace is right behind me, brushing past me to get in the room.

'What the –? I don't understand.' She rushes round to the other side of the bed and kneels down to check underneath it. 'But … he … I … ' Her words fall away. She stands up, staring at me, her eyes wide and wild.

Finally I speak. 'Look, I don't know what the hell is going on, but I'm walking out of here now, and I don't want to see you or hear from you again. Ever. Whatever game you're playing stops now.'

But she is not listening. She sits on the bed, smoothing her hands over the crisp white duvet. 'I don't understand,' she mumbles. 'He was dead. I know he was. I … I killed him.' Her body trembles.

'There's no body here, Grace. You didn't kill anyone. There's no blood. Nothing.' I turn away but then remember something that doesn't add up. Reaching into my bag, I pull out the rabbit. 'Where did you get this?'

'I told you. It's mine. I've had it since I was a baby. You have to believe me, Simone. You have to help me. There's no one else I can go to.'

I walk out of the bedroom. I cannot hear any more of this. But within seconds she has followed me into the living room.

'Please. We just need to talk about this. Work out what's happened. I'm not lying to you, Simone. I was here last night with him and he was … dead.'

'There's no body!' I repeat, shouting this time. 'What do you want from me?'

Before she can answer, there is a crash from somewhere in the flat. There is no time to think anything, to worry or assess the situation, because seconds later someone throws open a door and hurtles past us, knocking Grace to the floor in his rush to get out. I only see the back of him but it is definitely a man, dressed in a grey jacket and black trainers. That is all I can work out.

I freeze, unable to react. But then I hurry to Grace and help her up. She too, is too dazed to move. 'Who was that?' I finally manage to say. 'Was that Lucas?'

She shakes her head. 'No. I don't know who it was but it wasn't him. It definitely wasn't him.'

I ask how she can be sure when he pushed past us so quickly, but she ignores me and turns to the door, staring at it as if it will provide answers.

I check the hallway, but he has gone, and I have no desire to catch up with him.

'Whoever that was … he heard us,' Grace says. 'He heard every word we said. And now he knows that I … killed Lucas.' Her words blend with heavy sobs so I struggle to make out what she says.

'But I keep telling you there's no body here. You couldn't have harmed him. There'd be evidence of it like blood or some sign of a struggle. But there's nothing.' I try to make my voice soft, but rather than stopping her tears, my words seem to cause her to erupt into even more, her breathing fast and shallow.

'It doesn't make sense. It just doesn't make sense.' She repeats this over and over until I think she'll never say anything else again.

'Grace, you need to calm down. Come on, we should get out of here.'

She lets me guide her towards the front door but then stops. 'Wait. My phone. We need to find my phone.'

I don't know how or when it became *we* but I feel compelled to help her now, and just by being here I have become tangled up in something. I need answers. Despite the danger we now seem to be in, I have to help Grace. 'Come on then,' I say. 'I'll help you look. You check out here and I'll check the bedroom. I think that's best. But we need to be quick in case that man comes back.'

She nods and walks to the front door, turning to face the room. I can only assume she is retracing her steps; reliving whatever happened here last night. I don't know what it was, or if it did involve someone's death, but something took place here. Something has disturbed this girl, whoever she is.

There is no evidence in the bedroom to suggest anyone ever lived here. I open the doors of the giant built-in wardrobe but there are no clothes inside; only four wire hangers, jangling from the force of the door being opened. It's the same story in the chest of drawers and bedside cabinets: all empty.

I sink to my knees and peer under the bed, but there is no mobile phone here. There is nothing but more immaculate carpet, and not even a speck of dust anywhere. I lift up the duvet and examine the crisp white bed sheet. It smells of fabric freshener and there is no sign anyone has slept, or done anything else, in this bed.

This can only mean one of two things: either Grace is lying about this Lucas and what she did to him, or somebody has done a good job of hiding the evidence. But blood can't be permanently removed; the police would be able to find any traces of it, no matter how minute.

I turn towards the door. In another room, I can hear her rooting around in drawers or cupboards. 'Grace?' I call, 'what colour were the sheets when you were here last night?'

A moment passes before she reaches the bedroom. 'Um, white I think.' She eyes the bed. 'But these can't be the ones. There was blood all over them.'

I don't know why I've asked her this; there was surely no other answer she would give me. 'Okay, well, your phone's not here. We need to get out of here now. If you're telling the truth then we're in someone else's flat.' And whoever that man was, he could be calling the police right at this moment.

But Grace doesn't move.

The urge to leave this place is now stronger than ever. 'Look, I don't know what's going on but I can't be part of this. Stay if you want, but I'm not hanging around.'

Grace watches as I walk past but then grabs my arm. 'Please, Simone, can I come with you? I'm scared. I don't know who that man was but he knows about me now. I can't go home. They'll find me. And he must have my phone.' She begins to shake.

Once again, a strange urge to protect her overcomes me, and against my better judgement, I give in. 'Okay, let me think. We need to get out of here and then we can decide what to do.' It occurs to me that I am making decisions for her, taking control, like a mother would. Even though I still don't know if I can trust her, she seems helpless at this moment and somehow I have warmed to her.

It is a relief to step outside. The cold air brushing against my cheeks helps me think, helps me reach a decision. I stop by an iron railing and dig in my bag for my mobile.

'What are you doing?' Grace asks, her eyes widening.

'I need to make a call.' I quickly add that it is not the police I need to speak to. Not until I know what's going on.

She shakes her head. 'Not here, though. We need to get away from this place.' Turning away, she stares at the building, hunching her shoulders as if she has only just become aware of the temperature out here. Pulling out a pair of black wool gloves from her pocket, she slips them on.

We walk for several minutes, rain starting to pelt down, and head back the way we came. I study the faces of everyone passing by. It is unlikely I would recognise the man who rushed from the flat, but it is worth being cautious. Beside me, I can tell that Grace is doing the same, her anxiety returning.

It is only when we reach Embankment station that we stop walking. I delve into my bag and once more pull out my phone to call Matt. I don't expect to get through to him – he will be with his afternoon patients – but I need to give him some warning.

Warning that a girl who has information about Helena will be coming back to the house with me.

SIX

Grace stands in my hallway, making no move to remove her jacket. Even her scarf and gloves remain fixed in place, a silent testament to how out of place she must feel here. I turn up the thermostat and take off my own coat, wondering if she'll follow my lead. But she doesn't; she simply stares around her, taking in the contents of my house.

Perhaps I should feel nervous, letting this stranger into my home, but I don't. In fact, I feel as if I have the upper hand. Grace is in my domain now, so she is the one who should feel anxious. She's got to be wondering if she can trust me not to call the police. After all, aren't I just as much a stranger to her as she is to me? I should call them, but what would I say at this moment? There is no evidence that Grace has done anything, and no proof other than the rabbit that she's Helena.

As I watch her, I see that her shoulders have dropped, her posture less defensive now we are no longer in public.

'Come through to the kitchen,' I say. 'It's always warmer in there.'

She follows me through the hall. 'You've got a lovely home. It's massive. You should see Mu – Ginny's place, it's quite big, but like a matchbox compared to this.'

In the kitchen I look around and try to see the house through her eyes. It is a four-bedroomed Victorian terrace in Fulham, which is deceptively spacious, but I never think of it as being excessively large. Matt and I are not the type to flaunt money or possessions. We just wanted somewhere we would be comfortable. Somewhere we could grow into, if we could ever bring ourselves to do that.

'Do you have other children?' Grace asks, as if reading my thoughts.

I swallow the lump in my throat and motion for her to sit at the table. 'No ... we thought about it, but I just couldn't. It would have felt like replacing Helena. I couldn't do that.' I'm surprised how easily I'm able to say this to Grace.

Taking a seat at our huge farmhouse table, she doesn't reply, but nods.

'Would you like something to drink?' Even as I ask, I am aware of how ludicrous it is for me to be offering this stranger a drink in my home. As if we are friends catching up after a long absence.

'Anything cold,' she says, 'I'm not keen on tea or coffee and haven't had any for ages. Not since I last visited Mum.' She doesn't bother correcting herself this time and the word hangs in the air, full of silent accusation.

Neither of us speaks while I pour Grace a glass of orange squash, but I'm conscious of her presence, of her eyes studying my every move. Is she analysing my features, searching for similarities? Or is she silently mocking me for allowing her into my home? Nothing about her body language or expression suggests this, but I cannot give her my trust too easily. The silence is not a comfortable one, but neither is it threatening. Just like with Grace herself, I don't know what to make of it.

I put her drink in front of her and she takes a sip, all the time gazing around the kitchen.

Joining her at the table, I sit across from her so I can study her face.

'I called my husband when we were at the station. Matt. He'll be home in a couple of hours. He's seeing patients this afternoon.'

She becomes alert. 'So … he's a doctor?'

'Yes. A GP. His practice is not far from here. Fulham Palace Road.' As soon as I've said it I regret my words. I shouldn't be giving her personal details about us. Not when I still don't know who she is or what she wants.

'I don't know it. Actually, I've never been to Fulham properly before. I mean, I've passed through, but don't know it at all.' She clutches her glass in her hands but makes no move to lift it to her mouth. 'Does he know about me? What did you say to him? Do you think he'll believe me?'

She fires so many questions at me I barely know where to start. 'I didn't say much. I just left him a message saying I need to speak to him when he gets home. But the minute he gets in I'll need to talk to him before you see him. To explain what you've told me.' And then I remember Lucas's flat and the story Grace has fed to me. How can I tell this to Matt? I need to make sense of it myself first.

Grace squirms in her chair. 'But you can't tell him about Lucas. Please. No one else can know.' The panic is back in her voice.

'No, I won't tell him that. Not yet anyway.' I don't add that I am determined to figure out what's going on and uncover the truth of what she is telling me. For now I will let her think I am going along with her. It is the only way to catch her out if she's lying.

She thanks me and I watch her and wonder if she really could be Helena. It is possible that my daughter – if she is still alive – could look like the girl before me. They are the same age and her hair is close in colour to Matt's. I need to find out more about her.

'When's your birthday?' I ask.

'Seventh of December.'

'Helena was born on the first of December,' I say. 'A week before.' I speak these words but have no idea what it all means.

Grace shuffles in her seat, clearly as unsure as I am how to explain what we've just discovered.

'So you don't live with your mum?' I say, changing the subject. I try to sound casual, as if I am just asking friendly questions.

She shakes her head. 'It's my first year at university and Mum didn't want me to but I insisted on getting a room in the student halls. Liberty Hall. It's nice. I did miss her a lot. But that was before I knew anything …' She trails off and I am sure she is remembering something painful.

I probe further and she tells me she is studying journalism. 'It's similar to what you do, isn't it?' she says, a proud smile on her face.

Nodding, I tell her my degree is in journalism and agree that it's a coincidence. But is that all it is? I ask her where her mother lives and her eyes narrow, her head slanting sideways.

'Ewell. Why? You're not going to—'

'To be honest, Grace, I don't know what I'm going to do. I mean, what am I supposed to do with this information? Everything you've told me? What happens now?' I don't know why I'm asking her this, because either she has no idea or this is part of some elaborate hoax.

Shaking her head, she puts down her mug. 'I don't know. I hadn't thought beyond finding you and … asking for help. There's no one else I can turn to.'

Hearing these words again, I begin to soften. What if she *is* Helena? I can't send her away and take the chance of never finding out. And then my mind is made up. The first thing I need to do is find out for sure if she is my daughter. I can't decide anything until I know that.

'Well, when Matt gets home I think we should talk to him about doing a DNA test. Just so we can be sure.' I study her face but she doesn't seem shocked by my suggestion.

'I agree. We need to do that. Even though I already know. I knew for sure the minute I saw your picture on the Internet.'

Her readiness to go through with a DNA test puts me at ease, before it occurs to me that the results may not be ready for weeks.

Grace stands up and stretches. 'Can I use your bathroom, please?'

I point her to the downstairs toilet, grateful that she won't be set loose upstairs on her own. I don't want her out of my sight.

When she comes back I am making a selection of sandwiches. I haven't had lunch and she probably hasn't either so she must be hungry too. She offers to help but I tell her it's fine, and while I finish making them she walks to the french doors and stares through the glass.

She only moves away when I place the plate of assorted sand-wiches in the middle of the table and tell her to help herself. She leans forward to take one, biting into it without checking what the filling is. So she is not like me. I am very picky when it comes to food.

I don't reach for a sandwich myself; now that I've made them I realise I can't face any food. There is too much I need to know. 'What's your Mum – Ginny like?'

If she is surprised by my question, her face doesn't show it. 'She's, um … I don't know. It's hard to describe people, don't you think? I mean, especially the ones we're closest to.' Her eyes flick down and she begins pulling apart her bread. 'Or at least think we're closest to.' When I don't speak, she continues. 'But she works hard. She's been a good mum, always there for me, sup-porting me through uni. She's clingy but I can understand her overprotectiveness. Well, now I can. It all makes sense. She was scared of me being taken away like she took me away from you. That must be what happened, mustn't it?'

'What makes you so sure Lucas wasn't lying to you? Why are you so convinced Ginny isn't your biological mum?' As I ask this I wonder if Grace and Ginny have a strained relationship. Perhaps there are problems at home that have caused Grace to so readily believe Lucas.

Grace stares at me for a moment. 'I can't tell you any more than that. It's just a feeling I have. But I just want to know the truth. Don't you think it's a very strange thing for a friend of hers to say?'

'I don't know. But if – and I do mean *if* because I still haven't decided what to think – this man Lucas was telling the truth, then we can't jump to conclusions about your … Ginny.' This is something I've learnt in my job. Things are not always as they appear.

'But why would he lie? Anyway, at least I can avoid her for a while. I'm not due home until half term and that's ages.'

'What about your dad?' I ask. 'Where is he?'

Grace shakes her head. 'I don't know my father. He left Mum the minute he found out she was pregnant. I've never even seen a picture of him.'

It is all too convenient. 'Do you know his name, at least?'

She stares at the table before answering. 'All I know is that his name was Colin. They met in a pub and were only together a few weeks. Mum doesn't like to talk about him. I think she's ashamed that he didn't stand by her.'

When she says this I think of Matt, and how, even though we hadn't been together long and were far too young to have a baby, he stood by me and supported my decision to have Helena.

'What about your family?' Grace asks. 'Do you have brothers or sisters? What about your parents? And Matt's?'

I debate whether or not to answer her questions, but decide it can't do any harm. 'Neither of us have siblings. My parents both live in Florida now so I don't get to see them much, and Matt only has his mum left alive. But we visit her whenever we can.'

Grace's eyes widen. 'Is she the grandparent who was looking after me when—'

'Yes. Her name's Miriam.'

'Don't you … blame her for what happened?'

I know it surprised Matt that after my initial shock, I fully supported Miriam. Of course there were times when I wanted to shout at her, shake her or something, but what would I gain from pointing fingers? It wouldn't bring our daughter back to us. And we could both see how it destroyed her. Even to this day, she is a different person, as if the life has been sucked from her body.

I shake my head. 'It wasn't her fault. And she's suffered enough already, just knowing she was the one looking after Helena at the time.'

There is silence for a while, both of us lost in our thoughts.

'Please will you help me?' Grace asks eventually.

As I've been doing since she first declared she is my daughter, I study her face before I answer. Her huge imploring eyes. Her smooth fresh skin. *Is this Helena?* My Helena? Why don't I know? Shouldn't a mother automatically recognise her own child? But the last time I saw her she was six months old and could look like anyone now. Even though the rational part of my mind urges me to let this go, I decide I will help Grace. Perhaps it is my grief for Helena that drives my decision, but whatever the case, I am caught up in this now. And whoever that man in the flat was, he must have seen my face. But still I am unsettled.

'Let's just take it one step at a time,' I tell her. 'We'll do a DNA test then decide what to do.'

Grace's shoulders drop. 'Thanks, Simone. I know how this all must sound. So thank you for helping me. The first thing I need to do is find out what happened to Lucas.' She picks up another sandwich and keeps it in her hand. 'I've been thinking about it and there are two explanations: either I killed him and somebody moved the body, or he didn't die after I … hit him. Which means he's out there somewhere. With my phone.'

Neither of these options is good news. If she has been telling the truth and he is alive then what will he do to her now? And if he is dead, then someone knows she is responsible. Either way, this girl is in trouble.

'Let me just think about all this, okay? Why don't you finish your lunch and then watch some TV or something while I finish off some work stuff? By that time Matt will be home. Nothing's going to happen in the next couple of hours so let's try not to worry too much.'

Grace seems appeased by this and helps herself to another sandwich.

When she's finished, I take her to the living room and she settles on the sofa, taking off her trainers so she can tuck her legs beneath her. I can't help but marvel at the strangeness of this situation.

Back in the kitchen, I boot up my laptop and email Abbot, apologising once again for not being at work this afternoon. His reply is immediate: a message telling me it's no problem and that we should meet for breakfast tomorrow so he can fill me in on what I've missed. We often do this as a way of catching our breath before the maelstrom of our working day begins, but I can't remember the last time we were able to make it happen. I reply that this is a good idea and tell him I'll text him the details later.

For the next few hours I focus on work, trying to forget that Grace is in my living room, comfortably watching TV on the sofa as if she has always been part of our family. I check on her a few times, and the kitchen door is open so from my chair I will see if she leaves the room for any reason.

I am so engrossed in my research that I don't realise it's nearly eight p.m. when I hear Matt's key in the front door. Jumping up, I rush to greet him and usher him into the kitchen so we can talk before I introduce him to Grace. Once he's inside and I've shut the door, I pour him a glass of wine.

'I got your message and tried to call back a few times but your phone went to voicemail and there was an emergency with a patient so I couldn't get home until now. What's going on? Is everything okay?' he says, reaching for the glass.

I pull my phone from my pocket and sure enough, the screen is blank and my battery is dead. 'Just wait here a sec,' I say. 'I need to talk to you, but don't move.' Ignoring his puzzled expression, I hurry out to check on Grace.

The living room is bathed in darkness when I open the door. She is asleep on the sofa, the television muted, its flickering images highlighting her face. She looks like a helpless child. I close the door and head back to Matt, suddenly nervous about how to tell him what's happened.

He is standing at the french doors, so close to them that his breath leaves clouds of condensation on the glass. A wave of sadness filters though me. I am about to change our lives forever; to disrupt the equilibrium we have spent years building up and keeping in place. We have learnt to live with our grief, to keep it contained, but now it is about to erupt again.

'Matt,' I begin, as if starting with his name will make my words easier to digest. 'I think you should sit down.'

He does as I ask, and doesn't need to urge me to speak. I let the events tumble from my mouth, like a news story I have to inform my team about at work. Instinctively, I omit any mention of Lucas, or how we went to his flat, because I haven't got my head around this part myself yet, and when I explain about Helena's rabbit I pull it from my bag and place it on the table, watching as deep lines crease his forehead.

'This is … '

'I know. I mean, I'm almost certain it is.'

'But … how?'

'I don't know how, Matt, but she had it.' I keep my voice low, even though I am sure Grace will still be asleep.

'And she says she's … our daughter?'

'Yes. Well, she thinks she is. But we need to be sure, don't we?'

Matt takes a deep swig of wine. 'I … um, yeah. We need to find out.'

'I suggested a DNA test. That will prove it, won't it?'

He nods but doesn't speak. I haven't seen him this quiet since the aftermath of Helena's abduction.

'So she's in there,' he says finally, gesturing with his head. 'I … this is all a bit of a shock. What are we supposed to do now?'

'I don't think there's anything we can do until we get the test results. How long do you think it will take?'

He thinks about this for a moment before answering. 'I'm sure I've got some swabs upstairs. I can get them sent off tomorrow. It usually takes a couple of weeks but maybe I can call in a favour and get it fast-tracked. Maybe twenty-four hours if they can do it?'

Relief floods through me. I had assumed it would take weeks, but twenty-four hours is no time at all.

Matt takes another gulp of wine, this time emptying his glass. 'But in the meantime we should call the police, shouldn't we?'

I need to tread carefully here. I can't object too heavily and make Matt suspicious. 'I, um, I think we should wait until we know for sure. It won't be long.'

He is too flustered to realise my answer has no logic. 'Can I see her now? Grace, is it? Surely I'll know when I set eyes on her, won't I? Surely we should know our own daughter?'

This time yesterday I would have assumed so, but it's not that simple. I have tried to recognise something in her, to find something tangible to cling to, something a mother should automatically know, but I don't think it's possible. Not when Helena was taken from us before she'd reached her first birthday. We would have seen no glimpses of the young woman she would become. I try to explain this to Matt, but I can see in his face he is hoping it will be different for him.

In the living room Grace is still asleep. Matt stares at her, just as I have done all afternoon, and as if sensing him there, she begins to stir.

'This is Matt, my husband,' I say, when her eyes fully open.

'Oh.' She pulls herself up and looks embarrassed. 'Sorry, I guess I fell asleep.'

For a moment nobody moves or speaks until Matt finally steps forward, awkwardly holding out his hand. 'Hi. Grace. Um, Simone's filled me in.'

As soon as he says this Grace's eyes flick to me, panic once more filling them. I give a discreet shake of my head and hope it is enough to let her know I haven't mentioned Lucas.

It appears to work and she focuses on Matt, taking his hand. 'I know it's all a bit weird,' she says. 'But Simone's promised we'll work it out. We'll find out what happened.'

I decide to leave them to talk alone. If she is our daughter then this is the first time she has met her dad since she was a baby. Or if she is lying, perhaps without me present, Grace will somehow slip up and reveal an inconsistency in her story. Matt and I can compare notes later. 'I'm just going for a bath,' I tell them. 'But I think Grace should stay here tonight. At least until we have a chance to talk more.'

Neither of them objects to my plan, and as I turn to leave, Matt tells Grace he'd like to do the swabs now.

Later that night Matt and I talk in whispers, cuddled up together in bed while Grace sleeps in the spare room next to us. Neither of us say out loud what a crazy, reckless idea it is allowing her to sleep in our home, but I am sure he feels it as much as I do.

'Do you believe her?' I ask. 'Is she telling the truth?'

He kisses the top of my head and exhales a deep breath. 'I don't know what to think,' he says. 'But my gut is telling me no. It's all lies. We lost Helena a long time ago, and this girl is not her.'

SEVEN

Matt leaves early this morning. He has a meeting at the surgery before seeing his first patient and it's one he can't miss. But he takes Grace's DNA swabs with him so soon we will have some answers. I pray he is able to get it fast-tracked; there is no way I will be able to wait two weeks for the result.

Grace is already in the kitchen when I go downstairs, sitting at the table, and I smell toast before I see that she has made breakfast.

'I hope it's okay?' she says, biting her lip. 'Matt said I could help myself. I've made you some tea too.'

I sit down and stare at the plate piled high with overdone toast, drenched in pools of butter. 'That's great, thanks. It looks lovely but I usually just have tea or coffee in the morning.' As I say this, her smile disappears, so I quickly add that I'll make an exception.

Last night I gave her one of Matt's old T-shirts to wear and it swamps her narrow frame. The faded white logo on the front says U2, and I think Matt had it before Helena was born. It is strange to see her in it.

'What's the plan for today?' she asks, biting into a slice of toast.

'Actually, I need to go into work.'

She doesn't try to mask her disappointment. 'Oh, okay.'

I have spent all night wondering what to do with Grace this morning. I suggested to Matt when he woke up that she stay with us until the test results, but he was heavily against it. I can see his point. Whoever she is, she is a stranger to us so we can't just leave her alone in our house.

Thankfully Grace unwittingly solves my problem. 'I have to go to uni, anyway. I missed all my lectures yesterday and it will be a nightmare to catch up. I really hate getting behind.' She reaches for a slice of toast. 'I need to see Mum too.'

This surprises me, and not just because she's gone back to calling her *Mum* instead of *Ginny*. 'But what will you say to her?'

She shrugs. 'Nothing yet. Not until we decide what we'll do. But I can try and get some info about Lucas. I don't think that flat in Embankment can be his only place because there was nothing in it. I also want to find out where exactly his restaurant is. We have to start somewhere.'

I'm not sure this is a good idea but how can I stop her? I have no hold over her, not really. Even if she is Helena. But I can't allow myself to think like that yet, not until we have proof.

And then I surprise myself; my heart and head pulling me in different directions. 'Well, we should meet up after work,' I say. 'Do you want me to come to you? I can meet you at your uni?' It is only now I realise how much I want to help Grace.

She shakes her head. 'Actually, could I come here? I mean, just in case Mum turns up at my place or something and wonders who you are.'

With each ticking minute the situation gets more complicated, but I agree to her request. 'I should be back here by six-thirty so meet me then. I doubt it but it's possible Matt may be able to get the results early. We could know something by tonight.' I know this is unlikely but I want to check her reaction to this news. But her expression doesn't change.

Grabbing a notepad from a kitchen drawer, I scribble down our address and the house and my mobile numbers. 'You might need this,' I say, tearing the sheet off and handing it to Grace.

'Thanks, Simone. I really appreciate this. I know you don't owe me anything, but—'

'Don't worry, okay?' I have to cut her off because I can't easily explain why I'm helping her. Matt's insistence that she isn't our daughter weighs heavily on my mind. He seems so sure, but I cannot so easily dismiss her. Perhaps I'm letting my emotions cloud my judgement, but it is so hard not to want and need answers.

Grace stands up and begins clearing away the breakfast plates. 'I'm going to get a new phone today, or see if I can borrow one, so I'll text you the number when I have it.'

I tell her that's a good idea, but don't mention it's because I want to be able to contact her any time.

'Is it okay if I have a shower?' she asks, once everything's cleared away. 'I need to be quick, though, my first lecture starts at nine.'

''Course,' I say. I have been dreading her asking this; it will be impossible to know what she is up to behind the locked bathroom door.

But I do what little I can, and while she is in there I stay in my bedroom, sitting on the bed so I have a full view of the bathroom door.

By the time I leave the house it is too late to meet Abbot for breakfast. I text him an apology and he replies within seconds, telling me not to worry. That's another thing I like about him: he never gets annoyed unnecessarily. He understands that sometimes things happen.

When I get to work I find him sitting at his desk, staring at his computer screen. He started at News 24 a couple of years after me, but in that time has worked hard to become a field producer, the same role I have. There is no rivalry between us, and although we work on different stories, being able to share ideas with each other has become something I wouldn't want to be without.

We have easily slotted into our friendship, but I know it helps that I didn't know him when Helena went missing. Not many of my friends back then knew how to handle it and they dropped off one by one, out of my world of sorrow. Abbot knows all about it, but he is part of the new life I've built for myself. It also helps that he gets on with Matt and there is no tension between them. My husband is not the jealous type, although Abbot's smooth coffee-coloured complexion and striking blue eyes are enough to unsettle a less confident man.

'I'm so sorry about breakfast, I'll make it up to you, I promise,' I say, sliding into my chair.

'Hey, don't worry about that. Is everything okay?'

I want to tell him what's happened but now is not the time. 'Yeah, thanks for covering yesterday.'

He tells me I don't have to thank him then points to his computer screen. 'Have you heard? That young woman who went missing in Kilburn a couple of weeks ago? They've found her bag. In east London! That's miles from her house.'

I try my best to remain composed, to appear detached. Even though Abbot is the one who's been working on it, I have been following this story closely, and have been dreading news like this. My heart grieves for her family. 'She's only twenty, isn't she?'

'Yep.' Abbot shakes his head. 'God, that seems so young, doesn't it?'

Abbot is thirty-four, so slightly younger than me, but twenty must seem like a distant memory to him. It's not quite the same for me; at that time I was still grieving for Helena, so the memory is as vivid as if it were yesterday.

I try to focus on what Abbot is saying; I make it a rule not to let work and my personal life overlap.

'Mark wants you to take it over,' Abbot continues. 'Is that okay? I'm just knee-deep in this banker story. We keep getting new information by the minute. Corrupt doesn't even begin to describe him.'

''Course I will. It's fine.'

He places his hand on my shoulder and gives it a brief squeeze. No words need to be spoken; we both understand he is offering comfort.

For the rest of the morning I bury myself in the story, acquainting myself with every detail. Her name is Charlotte Bray and she had only just celebrated her twentieth birthday two days before she went missing on the fourth of January. The night she disappeared, she had told her parents she was meeting friends at the pub, but all her known friends have been questioned and nobody claims to know anything about this arrangement. This detail strikes me as odd: why would a twenty-year-old woman feel the need to lie to her parents about what she is doing? But I am getting carried away. It isn't my job to investigate, only to produce the story. I always do this when the events are too close to home; the scar Helena's abduction has left on me will never fade.

Once I've familiarised myself with all the relevant details, I pick up the phone and call Charlotte's mother. I explain who I am and count the seconds of heavy silence before Mrs Bray lets out a deep breath.

'We don't want to talk to any media,' she says, and I can sense her grip on the phone loosening. So I do the only thing I can, and tell her I've been through something similar. I don't provide personal details, only enough to let her know I understand.

Thankfully the risk pays off. 'Will you be on your own?' she asks.

'If that's what you'd prefer.' Once I get there I will try to persuade her that it's in her interest to speak on camera; that her story needs to be told from her point of view. It might not have worked for me, but I don't regret trying.

'Okay, I'll talk to you,' she says, after a long pause. 'Can you be here at three o'clock?'

The Brays live in a three-storey town house off Kilburn High Road. As I expected, a crowd of journalists and photographers have gathered outside, hovering on the pavement, bringing too much noise and commotion with them. I barge past them, pleased that it is me Charlotte's mother has agreed to talk to. I ignore the questioning shouts as I head to the front door.

Pressing the doorbell, I hold my breath and wait. Within seconds, Mrs Bray answers, her eyes swollen red and her cheeks flushed. She is younger than I expected, no more than forty-five, but something like this ages you, fast-forwards time, so inside I know she will feel a lot older.

'Simone?' Her timid voice matches her frail appearance. She is very thin, and I wonder if it is her natural build, or whether her daughter's disappearance has eaten away at her. Her hair is light brown, a good camouflage for the flecks of grey she will not have had the energy to cover. I am not surprised to see that her cardigan and mid-length skirt are also grey.

She doesn't wait for an answer but urges me inside and shuts the door. 'They haven't left us alone since Charlotte's bag was found. I mean, they didn't bother much before, when she first went missing. But now … I know they're all hoping she's dead.

It makes a better story doesn't it?' She swipes at the tears pooling in her eyes. 'Sorry. Please, come through.'

Leading me to the kitchen, she asks if I'd like tea or coffee.

'Whatever you're having is fine,' I say, knowing only too well that doing something even as menial as making a drink will be a momentous task.

'Tea, then.' She makes slow, mechanical movements: opening cupboards and pulling out mugs, flicking on the kettle, as if she is being controlled by something outside of herself.

In the kitchen I study my surroundings and think of Grace. Only yesterday she was doing the same thing in my own kitchen, and I wonder what she is doing now. Is she in a lecture, her mind distracted with thoughts of me, desperate for the test results? Or is she up to something? I still can't fully trust what she's told me, and she hasn't yet texted me a new mobile number.

'I'm so sorry for what you're going through, Mrs Bray,' I say, my attention snapping back to the distraught woman before me. 'Shall I do that for you?'

'Thanks, but I'm fine. And please, call me Tamsin.'

'Will it just be the two of us?' I know she has a husband, but it doesn't sound as if anyone else is in the house.

She drops a tea bag into each mug. 'I'm afraid so. Elliott's at the police station, trying to find out more information. It's driving us crazy. We just feel so ... helpless. I mean, what was she doing in east London? She doesn't know anyone there.' She turns to me. 'I just don't know what to think. Did you feel like this? I can only imagine how awful it must have been for you; your daughter was still a baby. Charlotte is a grown woman, really. Even though she's still my baby girl.'

I move closer to her and place my hand on her arm, speaking louder so I can be heard over the rumble of the kettle. 'It's still awful for you. It's the uncertainty, isn't it? The not knowing. And like you said, the helplessness.'

We both fall silent, each of us lost in our own stories. Tamsin hands me a mug and suggests we take them to the living room. 'We'll be more comfortable in there,' she says.

The sofa cushion sinks so far beneath me that I have to steady myself, almost spilling my tea in the process. Hoping she hasn't noticed, I begin asking questions I already know the answers to. Over the years I have learnt that starting with the basics will put her at ease, and also give me an idea of how honest she is willing to be.

'Does Charlotte live here with you?'

She nods. 'Yes. She's not really in a position to move out. She hasn't decided what she wants to do yet.' A tear runs down her cheek.

I know this is difficult for her, that all she'll be able to focus on is the discovery of her daughter's bag, but I need to get more background information. 'So is she at college? Or does she work?'

'She helps out in our dog grooming business. But it's not what she wants to do. I suppose it's just a stop-gap until she makes a decision.'

I find myself comparing Charlotte to Grace, who seems confident about her career path, despite being the younger of the two.

'I understand this is difficult but could you tell me about the last time you saw Charlotte?' This is always one of the hardest parts to relive: realising that you said goodbye or waved your child off without knowing it could be the last time you saw them, without cherishing that sacred moment.

Tamsin leans forward and places her mug on the glass coffee table. She doesn't sit back afterwards, but remains huddled, her elbows resting on her knees. 'I've told this time and again over the last couple of weeks, but it doesn't get any easier.'

'I know, I'm sorry.'

'No, it's okay,' she says. 'This is important. I've got to keep Charlotte in people's minds, haven't I? That's what the police liaison woman said. Anyway, it was Saturday evening and she'd been a bit restless all day. I didn't notice at the time, but looking back, it's so clear. She couldn't seem to focus on anything. She helped me set up my new mobile phone, but she was distracted. Normally she likes doing things like that, but this time it seemed like an inconvenience. I asked her what she was doing that evening and she said she was staying in.' Tamsin lets out a heavy sigh. 'Then I didn't see her until she came downstairs just before eight, dressed like she was going clubbing or something. I was surprised because she'd only just been out for New Year's Eve, and again on her birthday.' Her voice begins to shake.

'What exactly was she wearing?' I sound like a police officer now. I don't really need to know how Charlotte was dressed but it helps to paint a picture in my head.

'A dress I told her was too short. But she's twenty, how could I stop her? She's her own person, I can't control her. All I can do is guide her.' Her eyes flick up to the ceiling as she remembers, and more tears pool in her eyes. 'It was one of those sleeveless vest type dresses. Green and sparkly. Pretty, if you can get away with it, and Charlotte could.'

A picture of this woman's daughter floats into my head. Wavy red hair, large green eyes. She is a pretty girl. I look at her mother now and decide she would have been stunning at the same age. Even grief hasn't erased every trace of the woman she once was.

'She said she'd decided to meet friends at the pub,' Tamsin continues. 'I'm a terrible mother. I didn't … didn't even ask which friends or which pub.' She erupts into loud sobs, and I move closer to her and wrap her in a hug. I know we are strangers, but we are bonded by our stories.

'Can I ask *you* something now?' she asks, when finally her tears subside.

I reach forward and pick up my mug of tea. 'Of course. Anything.'

'How do you live with it? How do you get through each day?'

I haven't wanted to talk about Helena in detail, but I give in to the desperation on Tamsin's face. She needs to know she is not alone. 'I didn't. Not at first. But, Tamsin, it's been over eighteen years. I suppose the pain just sits beside me, whatever I'm doing. Like a constant companion. It's just part of my life now, part of me. But please don't think your story will be the same. There's every chance Charlotte will turn up, you have to just cling to that.'

She nods and grabs my hand, squeezing it tightly. 'Thank you. I'll try.'

For over an hour we continue talking, and by the time I leave we have scheduled an interview for tomorrow afternoon. It will mean working through the night to get everything ready, but I want to do this story. I feel as if it belongs to me, that Tamsin Bray's pain is also my own.

It is almost five o'clock when I get back to the office, which doesn't leave much time before I need to be back at the house to meet Grace.

'Simone, I'm glad you're back.' Abbot is still sitting at his desk, in the same position I left him in, and for a second I wonder if he's moved at all since this morning. He turns to face me. 'How did it go? Did Tamsin Bray agree to do an interview?'

'Yes, it's all sorted for tomorrow. I just need to write everything up for Hayley. Mark told me she'll be covering it.' I log on to my computer and tap in my password, not bothering to shield it from Abbot's view.

'Good,' he says. 'I'm glad you got it. Not that I ever doubted you would. People never say no to you, do they?'

But Tamsin's trust came at a price, I think, but don't say. I had to bare my soul to a stranger. 'I can't take any credit for this one,' I tell Abbot. 'Anyway, look who's talking – you're the smooth-talker around here.' This is true – Abbot always seems to get his way.

We both laugh but Abbot stops before I do. 'Hey, do you fancy a drink tonight? Blow off some steam? Make up for standing me up at breakfast? I've been flat out on this banking story, I'm even dreaming about the man!'

An image of Grace appears in my head and I glance at my watch. 'I'm really sorry but I have plans tonight. But soon, okay?'

'Sure,' he says, turning back to his computer. 'Guess I'm not that much of a smooth-talker after all, eh?'

'I'm just immune to your charms,' I say.

By five-thirty I am ready to leave. Meeting Grace this evening won't leave me much time to get everything ready for the interview tomorrow, but I will work at home tonight and come in early to catch up.

I am home by six-fifteen, grateful to have a few minutes to get my thoughts in order. Grace still hasn't texted me a phone number, but perhaps she couldn't get hold of one.

I set up the laptop in the kitchen and wait to see if Grace turns up. I still haven't heard from her so have no idea what to expect now.

But as I wait, I realise I am hoping to see her. I want to hear how her day at university has gone, how it went with her mum. Perhaps I am deluding myself, getting carried away with the idea that she could be Helena, but for years I haven't allowed myself to entertain thoughts of seeing my daughter again. It is an unfamiliar feeling, as pleasurable as it is terrifying.

Realising I haven't spoken to Matt all day, I call his mobile, even though I doubt he'll be able to answer. He does, though, and the first question from my mouth is whether he has had the results yet.

'No, not yet. But they've put a rush on it for us. You know I'll call you the second I hear anything. I'll hang around here for a bit, just in case. Where is she now?'

'She's due here any minute.' I poke my head around the kitchen door to see if I can see a silhouette through the glass of the front door. But there is nobody there.

Matt sighs. 'Is that a good idea? Shouldn't we wait until the results before we see her again?'

I'm about to object and defend my decision when I remember that Matt doesn't know the full story. He doesn't know how much this girl needs help. Whatever might have happened with Lucas, there was still a man in that flat who heard what we were talking about. 'Well, it's not for long,' I say. 'I just wanted to ask her a few more questions.'

'Okay, I just don't want you to get your hopes up, that's all.'

I reassure him I'll be fine, then we say goodbye.

It's nearly six forty-five now and there is no sign of Grace. There are any number of innocuous reasons she might be late, but uneasiness creeps through me as the minutes tick by.

To begin with, I am consumed with thoughts of Grace and Helena, which makes it hard to get my head around doing any work. But eventually I open my laptop and start preparing for the Brays' interview tomorrow. I am so lost in the story that by the time I look up from the laptop it is eight-fifteen.

And there is no sign of Grace.

EIGHT

I need to start somewhere near the beginning, to help you under-stand, don't I? Not that you ever truly will – because what would that make you if you did?

I knew things far too young. Sex was never a taboo subject in our house, a dirty conversation to be avoided at all costs and frowned upon by tight-lipped parents. No, I knew all about it by the time I was five; none of this 'the stork brought you to us' bullshit. I knew exactly how I had come about, and this thing adults did fascinated me. So by eleven years old, I was already experimenting with girls in my class. Ha, I don't even think they knew what they were doing, but for some reason many of them let me do what I wanted.

Perhaps I was charming, I don't know. But even as I got into my teens and eventually left school, all I felt after these experiences was empty, like a deflated balloon. Too much, too young? Maybe. But now I was cursed, sex had become mundane, a function to fulfil, and I was deeply unsatisfied.

Are you astounded by my ability to self-analyse? Well, don't be. A lack of self-awareness is not my problem. My issue is being unable to stop the heavy compulsions within me. I have tried, I really have.

When I was sixteen I watched The Accused *with Jody Foster. My parents had rented it from the video shop and unable to sleep one night, I snuck downstairs and, with nothing else to entertain me, pressed play. Do you know the film? I'm sure you do. Perhaps it made you feel uncomfortable to watch? Perhaps your natural human instinct kicked in and you had to turn away, unable to be a witness to the poor woman's horrific attack? But not me. I couldn't tear my eyes away, and I felt my body stiffen with excitement. I felt alive.*

I rewound that part four times that night, my desire for it never lessening, until every moment was etched in my brain.

But in the cold light of day, I felt floods of shame. I really did. And I vowed to never think about it ever again.

I did well for some time. I listened to music, played football on Sundays. Smothered my compulsions.

Until I met a man who changed everything.

NINE

'I can't say I'm shocked,' Matt says.

He has been home for less than a minute but already I have filled him in on what's happened, my voice betraying how disappointed I am, how desperate I was to believe Grace, despite myself.

'I've tried to make excuses for her but there are none,' I say. 'She has both my numbers. She even knows which surgery you work at. There's no explanation other than she was trying to con us.'

Matt hugs me and pours us each a glass of Pinot Grigio. 'I know it's upsetting. And to be honest, at work today I started to imagine that it could be true. Hope, even. Especially as she so readily agreed to the DNA test.' He shakes his head. 'But now I guess we have our answer.'

I take a sip of wine and stare through the french doors. The garden looks so grim in winter. 'But what do you think she wanted?'

He shrugs. 'Maybe money? I mean, I know she didn't ask for anything but perhaps she got scared off once she'd met us and realised we weren't easily fooled?'

I tell Matt it's possible, but I'm not convinced. I have also thoroughly checked the house and nothing is missing, not even a pair of earrings.

I turn back to face him. 'What about the rabbit? How did she get Helena's rabbit?'

We both fall silent, no easy answer occurring to either of us.

'I think we should call the police,' Matt says eventually.

I know he is right, but something tells me to put him off, to give Grace just a bit more time. 'Can we do it tomorrow, though? They'll probably need us to go down there and make statements and I don't think I have the energy tonight.'

Matt reluctantly agrees and then makes a suggestion. 'Listen, it's too late to cook now, shall we go out to eat? Take our minds off it all? How about that new Italian place near the station?' I know he is just trying to distract me, and I appreciate his effort.

'Okay. I just need to get changed.' As I head to the hall Matt's phone pings, stopping us both in our tracks. His friend at the lab told him he would email the results as soon as they came in, and even though it hasn't been twenty-four hours, perhaps this could be it.

Matt pulls his phone from his trouser pocket, his eyes flicking back and forth as he reads the email.

'Is it the results?' I ask, preparing myself for the worst, even though I'm not sure I even know what the worst scenario would be.

He shakes his head. 'No. Not those results. It's a patient. She has terminal cancer. It really didn't look like it at all. Poor woman. She's got three kids.' His face pales and he shakes his head as he slips his phone back in his pocket.

'That's awful,' I say, stroking Matt's arm. No matter how much he insists he's learnt how to detach from the job, moments like this convince me it's not always that easy. 'Look, shall we just eat here? I can rustle up something quickly.'

He pulls at his tie. 'Actually, I'm not that hungry. Maybe later? I just need to do some work.'

'Will you let me know the second the results come through?' I ask, even though I know he will.

'Of course. But Simone, please don't get your hopes up. I really don't think this girl is Helena. I don't know how she got the rabbit, but she's not our daughter. I can feel it. I know that doesn't make sense, but I think we would know if she was ours. And this disappearing act, well, it just proves she's up to something, doesn't it? Otherwise why hasn't she come back? She must think we've got the results by now and have messed up whatever she was planning.' He pulls me towards him and wraps his arms around me, squeezing tightly.

I open my mouth to object but quickly reconsider. Of course Matt is sceptical. He doesn't know the whole story, he wasn't there to see the fear in Grace's eyes when we were at Lucas's flat. He knows nothing of the man who knocked her down.

'Let's just see what happens,' I say. 'We'll know soon, won't we?'

'And we'll get through it together,' he says, rubbing my back.

When he's gone upstairs, I sit once more in front of my laptop and bring up Google. It is nearly nine p.m. and I need to know what's happened to Grace. Whether or not she is Helena, she has started something now and I want answers. It might be different if she hadn't told me about Lucas – easier to dismiss her as a fraud – but I have an uneasy feeling about that man in the flat.

Grace's student ID was from City University and I'm sure she told me the name of her halls of residence, but can't recall what it was. I type the university into the search box, and check the names of the student accommodation, to see if anything rings a bell. When I see the name I know it is the one. Liberty Hall. That's definitely where she said she lived. A further search tells me it's near Angel station. I shut the laptop and grab my bag from the table.

At the bottom of the stairs I shout up to Matt, telling him I need to go back to work, that I've forgotten something and need it urgently.

He appears on the landing and peers down at me. 'But it's late. And dark. Is it that important?'

'I'll be as quick as I can. I left my notes for an interview behind and I need to write up the report tonight.'

'I'll come with you, then."

'Don't worry, I'll be fine. And Grace might turn up. If she does, text me and I'll come straight back.'

Matt nods. 'Okay, but don't be long.'

It takes over an hour to get to Angel and I feel guilty as I head out of the station. I never lie to Matt, not even small ones, and it doesn't sit well with me. Up until now I have been able to tell him everything, but I assure myself I am doing this for us. To get to the truth, whatever it is. If Grace is our daughter I will encourage her to be as open with Matt as she has been with me. The three of us will need to get through this together, and how can we do that with a lie hanging over us?

And if she isn't Helena then I will go straight to the police. I'll tell them everything, including what she told me about Lucas.

Using Google maps, I find Liberty Hall and stand across the road, staring at the building. It is larger than I expected, with a modern light brick façade and huge glass doors, and I have no idea how I will find Grace in the mass of students that must live here. I haven't thought this through in any detail, but I am used to formulating plans on the spot.

Through the glass doors I see a reception area with bright orange sofas and an unmanned desk. It is long past office hours so I'm not surprised to find there are no staff around, but this will only make it harder to find Grace. The only thing I can do is wait for a student to come in or out and then ask if they know her. Although it's past ten p.m., for many students their night will only just be beginning. So I stay in my position across the street, in the doorway of a mobile phone shop, and wait, folding my arms against the cold.

Ten minutes pass before a young man appears in the lobby. He is dressed in loose-fitting jeans and a hoodie and I assume he is a student. He crosses to the reception desk and dumps a huge rucksack on it, bending his head down to rummage in it. This is my chance.

Crossing the street, I stand by the door of Liberty Hall, the bright lighting inside providing me with a good view of the student. He is still busy searching in his bag and doesn't notice me for a moment. Finally, he lifts his head, heaves his bag onto his back and makes his way towards me.

'Hi, sorry,' I say, once he's opened the door. 'Could I just ask if you know Grace Rhodes?'

His thick dark eyebrows knit together and I wonder if he is startled by my abrupt question. He scratches his unshaven chin. 'Um, what does she look like?'

'Tallish. Long dark hair. Pretty. She's studying journalism.' Even as I say this I know it could describe a number of people. But I don't know enough about Grace to give a more personal description.

The student shrugs. 'Not sure. But go in if you want.' Holding the door open, he steps aside to let me through.

Part of me is pleased I have got in so easily, the other half annoyed at the lack of security for Grace, and my protectiveness towards her takes me by surprise. Thanking the student, I head towards the lift he has just come from, not looking behind me in case he suddenly realises he's made a mistake letting in a stranger.

In the lift I see this building has five floors. I press the first floor button and prepare myself for the task ahead.

On the first floor there are doors on either side of a long corridor, making this hall of residence feel more like a hotel than anything else. I feel a stab of sadness that I never got to fully live the student life. Having Helena so young stalled my plans, and then after her abduction it took me years to be able to focus on studying and get my degree. I lived with Matt, so never got to experience what Grace is doing now.

At the far end of the corridor I see what looks like a communal kitchen, and excited voices drift from inside. Feeling like an intruder, I head towards the noise, preparing a speech in my head.

'Oh, hi,' a young woman says when I knock on the door. 'Can I help you?'

There are three other students in here and they fall quiet and watch me, probably annoyed at my intrusion. I give each one a cursory glance before explaining that I'm looking for Grace Rhodes.

'Oh, yeah, she's on the second floor,' one of the other girls says. She looks me up and down, but I ignore her judgemental stare.

'Oh, I thought this was the second floor?' I smile, pleased at my quick response.

'I'm always doing that,' one of the girls says. 'They all look the same, don't they?'

And then they resume the conversation I have interrupted, forgetting I exist.

On the second floor, I am still clueless as to which room is Grace's, but I start at the first one, number eleven, and rap my knuckles against the door. There is no answer, so after a few seconds I move on to number twelve.

There is no sound from inside but the door suddenly opens a fraction and a girl's face peers through the narrow gap.

'Hi. Sorry, I'm looking for Grace.' This time I don't mention who I am, just in case this girl has already met Ginny.

She stares at me for a moment. 'Her room's next door. But she's not in. I've just tried her.'

'Oh. Do you know where she is?'

The girl shakes her head and opens the door wider, allowing me to see her more clearly. She is barely five foot tall and looks as if she may have at least one Chinese parent. She's dressed in jeans and a red jumper and has a sweet, pleasant face.

'No,' she says. 'The last time I saw her was this morning. She was just coming home as I was leaving for a lecture and she said to tell our tutor she'd be a bit late. She needed to get changed. But then she didn't show up for it. Come to think of it, she didn't show up for any yesterday either.'

'So the two of you are friends? Did she mention she'd lost her mobile?' I ask.

'No. I've been trying to call her all day but it's switched off. We were supposed to meet up to study at lunchtime but she didn't turn up for that either. Do you … have you seen her? Are you a friend of hers?' She frowns. It's not hard to see I am a lot older than Grace, so her theory is unlikely.

'Actually, I'm a friend of her mother's. Ginny.'

She nods. 'Oh yeah, I've met her a few times. She's really nice.'

I try not to show any emotion at these words. Whoever this Ginny woman is, she might have been bringing up *my* daughter, keeping her from me. 'Yes, she is. Actually, it's Ginny who sent me. She's worried she hasn't heard from Grace and just wanted me to check on her while I was in the area. You know, make sure she's okay.'

The girl visibly relaxes. 'To tell you the truth, I *have* been worried. It's not like her to miss classes. She loves uni. But I just thought maybe some family stuff had happened.'

Hearing this, I become convinced that something isn't right. Grace seemed so desperate for my help, so why would she now disappear? I need to get her mobile number from this girl, but I'm concerned it will blow my cover story. Any friend of Ginny's would be able to get Grace's number from her.

I focus on her friend once more. 'Okay, well if you hear from her, could you ask her to call me? Actually, I'll give you my number, so maybe you could let me know if she doesn't come back in a few hours? If you're still awake, that is. A text is fine.' I fumble in my bag for a pen and paper and scribble down my number. 'What's your name, by the way?'

'I'm Jasmine,' she says, taking the piece of paper.

'Well, thanks, Jasmine. I appreciate your help.'

'Wait,' she says, as I turn to leave. 'I, um, actually have Grace's key. We weren't supposed to but we got a copy cut of each other's just in case there was an emergency. Do you think we should check her room?'

For a second I wonder if I've heard Jasmine correctly. She has known me for less than a minute yet is full of trust. I almost want to tell her to be more careful but rarely do things fall so easily into one's lap so I take this opportunity, even though it feels wrong, an intrusion into Grace's private world. But I remind myself she could be in trouble and needs my help so this is justified. If nothing else, the story about Lucas shows how troubled Grace is.

'I think that's a good idea.' It is hard to keep the eagerness from my voice.

Jasmine rushes inside to fetch the key while I wait in the corridor, and less than a minute later we are standing in Grace's room, staring at chaos. Clothes are strewn over the bed, drawers hang open and the floor is littered with books and papers. I let out a gasp.

Jasmine chuckles. 'Oh, don't worry. It's not been broken into or anything. Grace is always this messy.'

I smile at the irony; breaking in is exactly what I'm doing now.

'What's through there?' I ask, pointing to a door in the corner of the room.

'The bathroom.' She steps over an open shoebox to reach it and peers inside. 'Just in case,' she says. When she turns back she shakes her head.

A wave of sadness washes over me. If Grace is Helena then I should have been here before. I should have helped her move in, shared her excitement at being independent, cried tears over the emptiness she would leave behind.

'Is there anywhere you think she could be?' I ask, snapping out of my melancholy. 'Perhaps with a boyfriend or something?'

Jasmine shakes her head. 'There's nowhere I can think of. And she doesn't have a boyfriend. Grace is too picky for that. She won't just settle for anyone. And when she's not in lectures she's with me or at her mum's. She takes her studying seriously, you know. Wants to work for a newspaper. But you must know all this.'

I smile and keep to myself that I know very little about Grace. 'I think I'll leave her a note. In case she comes back late and you don't get to speak to her.'

'Okay,' Jasmine says, bending down to pick some clothes off the floor.

On the desk by the window I find some printer paper and a pen and begin scrawling a note. It is difficult to know what to write, as anyone will be able to read it, so I only get as far as writing her name. If I ask her to call me, Jasmine will wonder why I'm not asking her to call home. Exasperated that I don't quite know what to write, I simply scrawl *Call home, your mum's worried about you. Simone x.* Only Grace will recognise the double meaning behind my words.

And then I notice a set of keys by Grace's laptop. They can't be for this place and I wonder if they are for Ginny's house. Checking that Jasmine's not looking, I grab the keys and thrust them up my coat sleeve, clutching the fabric to keep them in place. Once more I have crossed a line, but I'm only doing what's necessary to get to the truth.

But having the keys is no good if I have no idea where the woman lives. All Grace told me was that her house is in Ewell. Glancing around the room, I realise it won't be hard to find something with Grace's home address on.

'I'm just going to tidy these papers away quickly,' I tell Jasmine. 'Ginny would never forgive me if I left the place like this.'

Jasmine frowns but then starts gathering the pile of books from the floor. 'It won't take long if I help. I'm always telling her, but she can't seem to organise herself.'

I begin tidying the desk and within seconds I have found a mobile phone bill, registered to an address in Ewell. Checking that Jasmine is occupied, I pull out my phone and quickly snap a photo of the address, making sure Grace's phone number is visible. If she's been telling the truth about Lucas then it won't do me any good, but I need to find out.

Ten minutes later the room is as tidy as we can get it, without intruding too much, and I let out a heavy sigh. I have been lucky so far, but I'm waiting for my luck to run out.

'Okay, I'll go now,' I say, heading towards the door. 'But don't forget to text me later, even if you don't hear from Grace.'

Jasmine nods and follows me out, locking the door behind her.

As soon as I am away from Liberty Hall, I check the photo I took and dial Grace's number.

But the phone is switched off, and it doesn't give me an option to leave a message.

* * *

It is past midnight by the time I get home. Expecting to find the house in darkness, and Matt asleep, I am surprised to find him in the living room, sitting on the sofa with the fire lit. I kneel in front of it to try to warm my frozen hands, and turn to him, praying for some news. He shakes his head and there is no need for me to question him. The test results have not come through and Grace has not shown up.

He gets up to make us tea and when he comes back we both sit together on the sofa. 'You were gone ages. Did you write the report there?' he asks, sipping his tea.

'It's not quite finished,' I say, avoiding an outright lie. 'I don't think I'll get much sleep tonight.'

He nods slowly. 'This business with Grace is crazy, isn't it? For years we hear nothing, not even a sniff from the crazies, and now this.' I wonder if he is beginning to believe Grace is telling the truth, but he soon puts me straight. 'I just want to know what she wants. Are we sure it's not money?'

'But she hasn't asked for anything,' I say. *Except my help.*

'Not yet, at least,' he says. 'I think she must have realised we're not the type of people who will fall for this kind of thing. We're stronger than that, aren't we?'

He pulls me towards him and I sit cradled in his arms. We have been through so much, it's hard to believe we have survived it. And then, just as we've managed to accept and live with our tragedy, this happens.

'Let's see what tomorrow brings,' I say, and Matt squeezes my hand. It is what we said to each other in the time following Helena's abduction, when our strength ebbed away. *Fresh hope for a new day.*

'I love you,' he says, kissing my forehead and then my lips. Despite my thoughts being a million miles away from anything physical, I warm to his touch. I escape into the moment when he unbuttons my shirt and strokes every part of my body. And I relish every second of it just being the two of us and nothing else, because I know it will be fleeting. Somehow, the feeling that Grace is our daughter is now stronger than ever.

An hour later I am upstairs in bed, the laptop balanced on my legs, while Matt watches television downstairs. I manage to write the report for the Brays' interview tomorrow, but my mind is distracted, crowded with thoughts of Grace.

I try Grace's mobile several times, but get the same message. Jasmine hasn't texted, so even though it is late, I send her a text, asking if there is any news. There is always a chance she is still up. But when fifteen minutes pass with no reply, I can only assume she is asleep.

I shut down the computer and open my bedside drawer, pulling out the set of keys I took from Grace's room, jingling them to check they are real. Tomorrow I will use them to find out more about Grace.

If Grace is Helena, then Ginny Rhodes is tied up in her abduction. This faceless woman could have stolen our daughter from us, robbed us of the lives we were meant to live. I will never get those years back, no matter what happens now. Anger wells inside me.

Tomorrow I will pay Ginny Rhodes a visit.

And I will get answers.

TEN

The atmosphere at the Brays' house is tense this afternoon. Hayley Shaw, our News 24 presenter, tries her best to put Tamsin and Elliott at ease, but, as is to be expected, their bodies are rigid as they sit on the sofa and robotically answer questions.

I sit to the side of them in an uncomfortable armchair, and occasionally Tamsin glances across at me, her eyes desperate for reassurance. The police liaison officer, a short, friendly faced woman, stands by the window, but it is me Tamsin seems to need. I nod each time she catches my eye, silently urging her to keep going. It will soon be over and this interview will gain them important exposure.

As I watch Tamsin, her eyes red and her cheeks glistening with tears, I remember how it feels to be sitting there, words spilling out you pray will make a difference. The desperate hope that whoever took your child will take pity on you and suddenly see the devastation they have caused. But this is a pipe dream. People who do things like this aren't capable of feeling emotions.

Elliott Bray seems to be holding it together, and I admire him for keeping his composure. When Helena was taken, Matt could barely utter a word. There were moments when I wondered if we would make it, if we would ever be able to communicate again. But perhaps it is different when your child is an adult. Not easier, just different.

'This is not like Charlotte,' Elliott says. 'I know she hasn't done this voluntarily. She would never put us through this pain.' His tone is firm. 'I know everyone says that, but it really is the truth. Surely finding her bag proves she's been abducted?'

When Hayley brings the interview to a close, I help her and our cameraman Rob pack away. I tell them I'll see them back at work, and when they both offer me a frown, I quickly explain that I have some errands to do.

'Thank you,' Tamsin says, once Hayley and Rob have left. 'I don't think I could have done this if you hadn't been sitting right there with us. It just helps knowing you understand.'

I nod and we both fall silent with our thoughts, until Elliott lays a hand on his wife's shoulder, giving it a soft squeeze before he tells her he's heading back to their shop. I'm glad they have each other; I don't know how Tamsin would cope without his support.

I think of Grace, and how I need to visit Ginny Rhodes as soon as possible, but I know without her mentioning it that Tamsin needs me to stay a bit longer. I wonder what she would think if I told her what happened yesterday. It's been twenty-four hours since Grace first approached me, but it seems impossible that so much has taken place in that small amount of time. And, now she is missing, I have more of a bond with Tamsin. We are both worrying about missing young women, and even if Grace isn't Helena, I have begun to feel responsible for her.

The police liaison officer excuses herself to use the bathroom, and Tamsin waits until she's disappeared upstairs before she speaks. 'Can I ask you something?' she says.

'Of course. I hope you know that. Anything.'

'We've been discussing hiring a private detective. What do you think?' She looks down at the tiled floor, as if she is ashamed of her suggestion.

'I think it's a good idea. Matt and I hired one, but with Helena being a baby it was hard for him to find anything. All he had to go on was the park where it happened. The difficulty is that babies don't leave much of a trace. I mean, it's not like they use credit cards or mobile phones.'

Tamsin nods. 'I just feel like people will think we don't trust the police. Do you think that's what they'll say? Because it's not that at all, I just want to find Charlotte.'

I think carefully about what I say next. I cannot let Tamsin know that I feel let down by the whole system. By everyone. Nobody could find Helena for us, or give us any answers, so I can't put my trust in anyone. I have seen plenty of cases where the police have helped victims since then, but it's hard not to focus on my own story. 'I think you have to do everything you can to find your daughter. That's all that matters.'

Tears slide down Tamsin's cheeks and she makes no attempt to wipe them away. 'Was he good, though? The one you used? Would you recommend him?'

An image of Mark Hunter forms in my head. His kind, serious face. His assurances that he would find our daughter. I had immediately warmed to him. He seemed to care about Helena, and didn't treat us as just another job he had to do. But I was so distraught at the time, perhaps I would have trusted anyone. It has all become a fog now, and I only remember snippets of conversations. Futile conversations that got us nowhere. I had let Matt deal with him after the first few meetings; I couldn't bear the disappointment when I had pinned my hopes on this man. But still, I am convinced he tried his best.

'Well, it was a long time ago,' I tell Tamsin. 'But he was quite young so there's every chance he's still working. I'll get his details from Matt for you. He dealt with it all.'

She lets out a deep sigh. 'Thank you, Simone. For everything. You won't forget us, will you? You'll keep Charlotte in your thoughts?'

'Of course I will.'

Outside the Brays' house, I sit in my car and call Abbot. I am weighed down by guilt that I am asking him to cover for me again, but he takes it in his stride.

'I wish you would talk to me,' he says, lowering his voice. 'I know something's going on – this isn't like you. You never miss even a second of work.'

'I know. And I will explain. As soon as I can. I just need this afternoon to do something ...' I trail off, wanting to explain, but not able to form the words. 'How about we meet up this evening?' Abbot lives in south west London, in Putney, easily accessible from Ewell. It's also only a ten-minute drive from my house. 'I could come to yours? We can talk then.'

'Perfect,' he says. 'I'll be home by seven tonight, so any time after that?'

I thank him, wishing I could tell him how much this simple arrangement means to me.

Next I call Matt, to check if he's heard any news about the DNA test, but it goes straight to his voicemail. And then for the tenth time today, I try Grace's mobile again, already knowing it won't ring. I stare at the Brays' house before I drive off, and picture them inside, Tamsin folded up in her husband's arms, inconsolable.

In just over an hour I am in Ewell, following my Sat Nav through unfamiliar roads. It is a strange area: not quite London, but not exactly Surrey either. School hasn't yet finished for the day so the traffic is light, and as I turn into River Way, I begin to feel nervous. I tell myself to treat it as just another news story, but there is so much at stake, so much I don't know about. Still, I keep going; I have come too far to turn back now.

Number eighty-seven is a semi-detached 1930s property and I park across the road and watch for signs of life. I have no idea whether Ginny Rhodes will be at home; Grace told me she works as a carer, so her hours are probably irregular, but I have already decided if she's not here I will stake the place out until she turns up. I can't risk using the keys yet when she could be back any moment. There is a red Renault Clio parked in the driveway but it could belong to anyone. I know nothing about this woman; I am fumbling along with a half-formed plan, out of my depth.

Taking a deep breath, I step out of the car and wrap my coat tighter around me as I cross the road and head towards the house. My mobile pings and I scramble to grab it from my pocket. It is Jasmine, apologising for taking so long to get back to me but saying Grace still hasn't come back. I send a reply thanking her and asking her to keep me updated, adding that I promise to do the same if I hear from Grace.

But as I slip my phone back in my pocket, foreboding engulfs me. Disappearing for one night is one thing, but Grace missing another day of lectures makes me certain something is wrong.

At Ginny's front door, the bell chimes and echoes when I press it and I take a step back and wait. Through the glass panel in the door, I see a figure appearing and hear shoes click-clacking against wood.

My body turns cold when she opens the door and says hello. I am connected to this woman somehow – this stranger – if nothing else, the rabbit is proof of that, and it's not a good feeling. I search her face for signs of Grace, but see none. Her hair is light brown and curly, her skin several shades paler than Grace's. I remind myself this doesn't mean anything. Grace's father – if it's not Matt – could be her mirror image. Ginny looks older than me and wears a baggy jumper over fitted bootcut jeans.

'Hi,' I say, flashing a bright smile. 'I'm sorry to just turn up like this but are you Ginny Rhodes? Grace's mum?'

She frowns, unable to recognise me, puzzled by what could have brought me here. 'Yes. Can I help you?'

'I'm Hayley, Jasmine's mum.' My colleague's name is the first one that comes to me, but as soon as I say it I realise I could be making a huge mistake. There is every possibility that Ginny has already met Jasmine's mum, or that she might at least know her mother is Chinese. And even worse than this is the fact she might know exactly who I am. If she abducted Helena then perhaps she has been following my life, keeping tabs on me to make sure I remain at a harmless distance?

I wait for recognition to cross her face but thankfully the frown remains. 'Grace's friend at uni?' I continue.

Finally she smiles back. 'Oh, yeah. Jasmine's a lovely girl.'

'Thanks. Well, I met Grace the other day and she mentioned you're a carer?'

'That's right.' She makes no move to invite me in and the frown is back now. Perhaps she is puzzled about where my question will lead.

I persevere with the story I concocted on the drive here; I have started now so I will see this through. 'I should have called, but I was visiting the area because my mum's about to move here. To a retirement property. And I thought it would be good to meet you and see if you would consider caring for her. I'll visit at least three times a week but I live so far away and I'd really like someone to see her every day.'

Ginny's frown disappears. So far, so good. 'Well, I work for an agency,' she says. 'So you'd have to go through them. But, do you want to come in? One of my ladies has just moved in with her son so I do actually have some free time.'

Once I'm inside, she closes the door and leads me through the hall to the kitchen. I don't take in much of the house; I am too busy staring at Ginny, trying to match her up with the snippets of information Grace revealed yesterday. *Clingy*, I think she had said. But that's not surprising, if this woman stole her from us. She must constantly live in fear that it will catch up with her.

'I've just boiled the kettle, would you like tea or coffee?'

I ask for coffee, even though having a cosy drink with this woman is the last thing I want to do. She seems kind and pleasant, but isn't that what they say about the worst kind of people? Isn't it always the ones you least expect that turn out to be the perpetrators of atrocities?

'Please, have a seat. Make yourself comfortable.' She gestures to the round, glass kitchen table and I sit down, my posture too straight against the high-backed chair.

While Ginny fills our mugs I study my surroundings. This is a normal kitchen: neat and clean, with a lingering odour of cleaning products. But I will not be fooled.

For a few minutes I talk about my mother, sticking as closely as possible to the truth. I describe her in detail, and only leave out the fact that she is more active than I am and retired to Florida with my father.

'Well, Jean sounds like a lovely woman,' Ginny says. 'I'd be happy to take her on, but you'll need to go through my agency, Angel Carers. Just tell them I was recommended to you and they'll get it all set up.'

Once again, I have the feeling that this is almost too easy. There is nothing about her words or behaviour that suggests she mistrusts me. And this makes me feel uneasy. I thank her and tell her I'll let her know as soon as we have a moving day.

When she frowns, her eyes squinting at me, I realise I may have messed up. 'Don't you want to know what the cost is?' she asks.

I curse my carelessness. 'Oh, yes. Silly me. But it doesn't matter. I just want Mum to be in the best hands.'

She laughs and takes a sip of tea. 'I'm just used to it being one of the first questions I'm asked. Anyway, the agency charge according to the needs of the person. But it will probably be around twenty pounds an hour. I know that sounds a lot but I do my best for all my ladies and men. And of course the agency need to take their cut. Which is a lot more than mine.'

Relief floods through me. I haven't done any permanent damage. 'That's fine. And I'm sure you do your best for everyone. Grace is such a lovely girl, she must have learnt it from you.' I lift my cup to my mouth but only take a tiny sip. The coffee is too strong and leaves a bitter taste in my mouth.

Ginny blushes. 'Thank you. I'm probably so dedicated because of my own mum. She doesn't quite need care yet but I often think about if, or when, she will. I wouldn't want just anyone looking after her.'

I search Ginny's face for sincerity and find it straight away. Her eyes light up and I can tell she is picturing her mother. But I won't let this throw me off track. I am here for a reason.

'In fact, I'm off to visit her this evening,' Ginny continues. 'She lives in Portsmouth so it's a bit of a journey, but I have a day off tomorrow and she does love me staying the night.'

I snap to attention. So Ginny will be away all night. Once again things are falling into place with little effort on my part. 'Does Grace come home much?' I ask. I am confident now to broach the topic.

Once again her face lights up. 'All the time, actually. In fact, she was meant to come and see me yesterday, but she texted in the morning to say she couldn't make it. She had an exam she needed to study for. And then today I was working and then going to Mum's. But we'll catch up soon. Life's always hectic, isn't it?'

My blood turns cold. How can Grace have texted Ginny yesterday when she didn't have her mobile? My mind quickly searches for an answer, but all I can come up with is that she lied to me. Or Ginny is lying. Either explanation is as likely as the other. But unless Ginny knows who I am, she has no reason to mislead me. Her lips continue moving and I struggle to make out the words until I force myself to focus.

'Anyway, she said she'd try and come back home in a couple of weeks. Teenagers! They're just so busy, aren't they?'

I nod. 'Yep, Jasmine's the same. Anyway, I'd better leave you to it, I'm sure you've got plenty to get on with.' I stand, leaving my coffee almost untouched.

She sees me to the front door, telling me to give her love to Jasmine, and reminding me to contact the agency. To save me looking up the number she recites it from memory and I tap it into my phone.

I'm about to step outside when she grabs me and gives me a hug. I don't want this woman touching me and it is all I can do to lift up my arms to reciprocate.

By the time I get home it is nearly dark, most of the day gone and evening creeping in. I sit at the kitchen table, checking my work emails on the laptop, not bothering to turn on any lights. My head aches from going over everything on the drive home, but I still have no answers. All I can do is hope tonight brings up something that will help me make sense of it all.

When Matt gets home at six p.m. I am still sitting here, the coffee I have made myself stone cold in front of me. He turns on the light and I squint as my eyes struggle to adjust.

'Are you okay?' he asks. 'Why are you sitting in the dark? Has something happened?'

I need to compose myself. Matt can't know what I'm involved in, what I'm planning. It would put his career at risk, and everything else he's worked so hard for. 'No, I'm fine. Just had a tough interview today. Charlotte Bray's mother. It just brought it all back to me.'

Matt joins me at the table, pulling his chair closer to mine and reaching for my arm. 'That poor couple. They're in hell now, just like we still are. I just hope they get answers soon.' He kisses my forehead. 'Look, Simone, I need to tell you something and—'

I reel back. 'You've got the results back? Tell me!'

'I'm really sorry. There's been a problem and they've come back inconclusive. Apparently Grace's sample got contaminated.'

I quickly digest what this means. 'But … but we can't do another one! Grace is missing and …'

'What do you mean missing? Why do you say that?'

'I … just meant she didn't come back. So we'll never find her now, will we?' My voices rises, as does my anxiety.

Matt reaches for my arm again. 'But it's possible to track her down. What's her surname?'

'I don't know.' The lie lodges in my throat.

Matt falls silent, shaking his head. I desperately want to tell him the whole truth but I can't get him involved in this. I can't even make sense of it myself. Ginny said earlier that Grace texted her, but according to Grace, she left her phone at Lucas's flat. So either Grace is lying, and is fine, or Lucas or someone else texted from her phone. But why?

Oblivious to my thoughts, Matt continues. 'The simple truth is, if she really is Helena she'll come back to us, won't she?'

He is right.

Unless she can't make that decision for herself.

ELEVEN

'I'm sorry,' Abbot says as he answers the door.

At first I'm not sure what he's apologising for, until I notice he is wearing only his jeans. I glance at his toned chest and wonder how he maintains his physique; I have never known him to set foot in a gym, and all he eats is food that requires no effort to cook it.

'Oh please, spare me!' I say, covering my eyes with my gloved hands.

Abbot steps aside. 'Hey, it's not that bad, is it? I jumped out of the shower to answer the door. Didn't realise it was seven already. Just be grateful I bothered to throw these on.' He tugs at his jeans. And for just a few seconds, Abbot has made me forget what's happened in the last couple of days. Standing here, it could be just an ordinary evening after work.

But I am soon brought back to reality when I remember why I'm here. I brush past him and head straight for his open-plan living room. The flat is small, but it's well-maintained. Besides, Abbot spends so much time at work, he only really needs somewhere to lay his head at night.

Sitting on his sofa, I flop back and let out a deep breath I had no idea I was holding in.

Abbot watches from the doorway. 'I'll just throw on a top and then I think you'd better tell me what's going on. Because I know there's something, Sim.' For as long as we've known each other,

Abbot has called me this; he is the only person who addresses me as Sim.

Moments later, he sits beside me on the sofa and I find myself telling him everything that's happened since Grace approached me on Monday. I recount every detail of our meeting and the conversation we had, and for the first time I speak aloud what she told me about Lucas Hall. It feels good to share this with someone else, even though that person should be Matt. Feelings of disloyalty stir within me but I remind myself I'm doing this to protect Matt.

It is not often Abbot is lost for words, but my story tonight renders him speechless. 'It can't be for real,' he says eventually. 'Can it?'

'That's what I need to find out,' I say.

He questions me further about what Ginny said and then chews his bottom lip, deep in thought. 'I just don't know, Sim. It sounds so dodgy. And I'm someone on the outside so it's probably easier for me to be detached. It just seems so implausible.'

I know he is right, but if there is even a one per cent chance that Grace is my daughter then I need to pursue this. I explain how I feel to Abbot and he assures me he understands.

'So what are you going to do?' he asks.

'That's the thing. I really need your help with something.' I hate dragging him into this, but I'm desperate and am sure he knows I'd do the same for him.

'Uh oh. That doesn't sound good.' He turns to me, a wide grin on his face. 'But you know I'll help you in any way I can. Especially if it's technology related.' He eyes his laptop, which is sitting on the coffee table. 'What do you need?'

'I know it's a lot to ask, but would you come with me to this Ginny woman's house? Tonight? She's away until tomorrow and it's not like we'll be breaking in. I mean, not really.' I reach into my pocket and pull out Grace's key, jangling it in front of Abbot.

He hunches his shoulders and whistles a sigh. 'Let me guess? You took them from Grace's room?' He doesn't wait for an answer. 'But what are you hoping to achieve there? What do you think you'll find?'

I tell him there might be something there to prove that Grace isn't her natural daughter. I have no idea what that might be, but it's a good place to start. All I know is I need to take action because this is driving me crazy. When Helena was abducted I was too distraught to do much, too dependent on police, or Matt, or the private detective. And there was nothing to go on anyway. But this time it's different. There is something I can do.

I hold my breath and wait for Abbot's response.

'Sim, you know you're my great friend, but this is crazy. If we get caught that's the end of our careers or worse. I want to help, but there has to be another way?'

'I know I'm asking a lot but there's no other option. I can't just approach her and accuse her without firm evidence. I wouldn't ask but I'm desperate for answers.'

Abbot is silent for a moment, and I prepare myself to go to Ginny's house alone.

'I know how hard this must be for you,' he says eventually. 'I may not have kids yet but losing one has got to be the worst kind of hell. You've waited long enough for answers.'

'Does that mean you'll come?'

'Okay,' he says. 'But let's go now, before I realise how crazy this is and change my mind.'

In less than half an hour we are in Ewell, parked outside Ginny's house, in the same spot I was in earlier. I have told Matt I am working on a story with Abbot, which is not exactly a lie, so we should have a couple of hours to search Ginny's house. Abbot insisted on driving here and I'm grateful for his kindness. I am too pumped with adrenalin to concentrate on driving. Bathed in darkness, the road has a different feel to it; sinister, too quiet. It's my guilt, I tell myself.

Beside me Abbot drums his fingers on the steering wheel and peers over at the house. 'Are you sure about this? Really sure? Because—'

'I'm sure.' My words may be forceful but I've had no time to actually stop and think carefully about what I'm doing. I feel I'm being pulled along by a magnetic force I have no control over. I am just doing what I have to do.

'Let's do this, then.' Abbot jumps out of the car, and I wonder if, even after his reluctance, some small part of him is enjoying playing detective.

At the front door I ring the bell, just in case Ginny's plans have changed. There are no lights visible anywhere in the house, and the red Renault Clio I saw earlier is no longer in the drive, but I plan on claiming I left something behind earlier if Ginny does answer the door.

'I think we're safe,' Abbot says. 'And there doesn't seem to be a burglar alarm.'

I pull out the key and we both step inside, shutting the door behind us. Not wanting to turn on lights and alert any nosey neighbours that someone's in the house, I use the torch on my mobile to light our way, and Abbot does the same. Just like the street outside, the house has a sinister feel about it when it's shrouded in darkness.

'Where first?' Abbot's voice is a whisper, even though we are alone here, and he heads towards a closed door on our left. I wonder if, now that we are inside, he feels as anxious about being here as I do. But I remind myself why we are here.

'How about you check down here while I have a look up-stairs?' I suggest.

'Okay, but it will help to know what exactly I'm looking for.'

'Anything relating to Grace that might prove Ginny is or isn't her mother,' I say. 'Like a birth certificate or hospital records.' It suddenly hits me that I have no idea what I'm doing. 'I'm not sure,' I admit. 'Just see what's around. Check everything you can.'

Abbot squeezes my arm. 'But don't get your hopes up. We may not find anything.'

I tell him I realise this, and he disappears into the room I assume is the lounge.

Upstairs there are three bedrooms and a bathroom and I begin with the closest door. It appears to be the main bedroom so I assume it is Ginny's. Even in the dim light of my phone torch, it doesn't take long to work out she is almost as untidy as Grace. The duvet lies in a crumpled mound at the bottom of the bed and there are clothes scattered on top of it. Odd pairs of shoes are strewn across the floor and the curtains are half-closed. This woman cares for other people; she is supposed to be organised.

I slide open the mirrored door of the built-in wardrobe and find clothes fighting for space, so tightly packed together that I wonder how she picks anything out each day. Although she has twice the amount of clothes I have, none of them seem glamorous. They are mostly jeans and sweatshirts, dark-coloured T-shirts and vest-tops. There doesn't seem to be anything here that might help me.

Next I check the chest of drawers, but again, I find nothing but clothes and underwear, and the bedside table only contains hair products and make-up. I hope Abbot is having more luck downstairs.

The room next door must belong to Grace; I know this the second I step inside. It has the same smell as her student room – a mixture of perfume and shampoo – only it is tidy. She will have taken most of her things with her to Liberty Hall, but it is worth checking what's left behind.

I start with the small computer desk in the corner of the room. There is no computer sitting on top, only a couple of pens and a dictionary so I check the drawers. The first one is full of scrap paper and notebooks and I dismiss everything after a quick scan. But in the second drawer, the first thing I spot is a small red address book. It strikes me as odd that in this age of technology and social media, someone Grace's age would use this old-fashioned method of storing numbers. But as soon as I open it I see that it isn't hers. The name scrawled across the top of the page says Virginia Rhodes.

I remember Grace telling me that she had tracked Lucas down. This red book in my hand must be how she did it, which could mean she was telling the truth. Why else would she have her mother's address book hidden in her drawer? Slipping the book in my coat pocket, I finish my search of the drawers, but there is nothing else useful.

The third bedroom is a box room, with only a single bed and empty bedside table. There is nothing else in here, so I close the door and after a quick check of the bathroom – which doesn't even have a cabinet to snoop through – I head back downstairs.

Abbot is still in the living room when I get there, sitting on the floor, surrounded by an assortment of folders. 'This is all her paperwork and stuff,' he says, shining his mobile phone torch in my direction. 'Bills and receipts, that kind of thing. I'm checking each one, but so far there's nothing that seems relevant.'

I join him on the floor and stare at the pile of folders.

'She's very organised, though,' Abbot continues. 'Whoever this woman is. Everything is chronological and she seems to keep everything. Including this.' He holds up a yellowing sheet of paper. A birth certificate.

'Is that ... is it Grace's?' I know as soon as I ask that I want Abbot to say no. I haven't fully admitted it, or known it until this moment, but I want her to be Helena. And if there *is* a birth certificate here, then she can't be my daughter.

Abbot shakes his head. 'It's the mum's. Virginia.'

Relief floods through me as I pull it from his hand and study it. It says she was born Virginia Jane Rhodes in 1967. That makes her forty-seven, ten years older than me.

'Don't you think it's strange?' Abbot says, interrupting my thoughts. 'You'd think she'd have a copy of Grace's too. And she's kept all her own medical letters and information, but there are none for her daughter.'

I digest what this means. 'That is weird.' Even odder than the fact she is so organised with her paperwork, but not the rest of her things. 'So there's no red book?'

Abbot frowns. 'What red book? What's that?'

'When Helena was born I was given a red book, for all her medical information. Every mother gets one. And I'd assume someone as careful at record keeping as Ginny would definitely keep that safe.'

Abbot rubs his chin. 'I suppose Grace could have it all,' he says.

'I don't think so. She'd have no need to have it, really.' I stare at the folders. 'Which one's Ginny's medical stuff?'

Abbot slides a green A4 folder towards me.

'I need to take this home,' I say, ignoring the frown appearing on his face.

'What? No, that's not a good idea. It's too risky. Just look at it here. And why do you need this woman's info? It's Grace we need to find out about.'

'But I also need to know about Ginny. Anything I can find out is important. If she really is Grace's mother then there will be evidence of her giving birth in here, surely?' I flick through some of the papers in the folder. 'I mean, it looks like she's kept every single hospital letter going back years.'

Abbot thinks about this for a moment. 'Okay, but look at them here. If she's guilty and she notices this folder's gone – which she's bound to given how meticulous she is with her record keeping – then she'll immediately tie it to Grace, and probably the abduction. She'll know someone's on to her, won't she?'

I can't argue with this so agree and begin trawling through the documents, while Abbot leaves to search the kitchen. By the time I've finished I am familiar with every illness and procedure Ginny Rhodes has ever had. They are all in here.

All except any mention of her ever giving birth to a baby.

It is a relief to be back in the car, driving away from River Way. Abbot always drives too fast, but for once I don't mind; I want to be back at his flat and getting my thoughts in order, working out where we go from here.

My mobile rings and when I see Matt's name flash up I almost end the call. But I can't do that to him, I am keeping too much from him already. He asks where I am and I tell him I'm still with Abbot and we've just got a bit of work to finish off. It's nearly ten p.m. now so I wouldn't blame Matt for being annoyed.

But if he is, he doesn't show it. 'Okay,' he says. 'But don't be too much later, I miss you.'

I know Matt feels bad about the DNA test results, and the fact that we haven't completely agreed about Grace. In over twenty years together I have learnt to read the silent messages in his words.

'Everything okay?' Abbot asks. 'He's not annoyed I'm keeping you from him, is he? Especially at a time like this.'

'No, he's fine.'

'You really trust each other, don't you? I think that's great. Jealousy is ugly.'

'Perhaps it's because we've had so much else to deal with in our relationship, that petty things like jealousy never factor in. I've been with him since I was eighteen, it kind of gives us some security. I mean, I know people can split up at any time, but we've been through so much together.'

We turn into Abbot's road. 'I know,' he says, keeping his eyes fixed ahead. 'I envy you a bit. What you both have. I just never seem to feel that strongly about anyone.'

I laugh. 'I thought you just said jealousy was ugly?'

'Yeah, it is. But there's nothing wrong with a bit of healthy envy. Take it as a compliment.'

Back in Abbot's flat, my mobile rings again, this time with an unknown number. Not knowing who it could be, but hoping it is Grace and not something to do with us breaking into Ginny's house, I am surprised to hear Jasmine's light and perky voice on the other end of the line. She tells me Grace still hasn't shown up, but that she's just received a text from her to say she's gone away for a few days, because she had to see a friend in an emergency. I thank her and hang up, the knot of fear back in my stomach. It is true that fear of the unknown is greater than any other.

Immediately, I try to call Grace's mobile again, but still it is switched off.

'Here you go,' Abbot says, handing me a glass of water. 'You don't look right, what's happened?'

I repeat the conversation I've just had with Jasmine and watch his face crumple in thought. 'Okay, we need to work this out. Sort out the facts so we can try to figure something out.' He takes a sip from his glass.

'All I know is that Grace claimed to be Helena. She had Helena's blue rabbit, or at least one that looked identical, and then she told me she might have accidentally killed someone.'

'Lucas Hall.'

I nod. 'But there was no evidence of that. Nothing to back up her story.'

'So she was probably lying. But why?' Abbot drums his fingers against his glass.

'I have no idea. She agreed to the DNA test but then disappeared.'

'So doesn't that tell you something?'

'Maybe. But what about the man in Lucas' flat? He was real. And what about the missing birth certificate and medical information? Doesn't that back up Grace's story?' I know how I must sound to Abbot. Like a woman desperate to believe her missing daughter has come back into her life. But it's not like that. I only want to know the truth, and I will deal with whatever it is. I would rather live eighteen more years without Helena in my life than fool myself into believing a lie. Before meeting Grace I had gradually accepted that I might never have answers, but now I am as desperate to know what happened to Helena as I was in the beginning.

'Possibly,' Abbot says. 'But we don't have strong enough evidence. We need more. None of this makes sense. She told you she left her phone at that flat, but both Ginny and her friend are getting texts from her. How can we explain that?'

'I don't know for sure. But I'll get the evidence I need,' I say, staring into Abbot's intense blue eyes. 'And I need to start by finding Lucas Hall.'

TWELVE

Have you ever lived with shame? It is a heavy burden, an invisible hand covering your mouth, sucking out your breath, relishing every second of your suffering.

Even though I'd made a vow to myself, and tried to smother any thoughts I had the moment they appeared, I knew I was capable of succumbing. It was like any other addiction – drugs, alcohol, cigarettes – always there, tempting me, trying to get me back in its grip. But for two years I fought against it, working hard at school, excelling academically, while sleepwalking through the rest of my time, numb and filled with self-loathing.

And then at university, everything changed.

Much like the video I'd seen years earlier, the morning I met him was a pivotal moment. How different things would have been if our paths hadn't crossed.

He was a year older than me and we weren't even on the same course, so in a university with thousands of students, the chances of us meeting were slim. But fate brought us both to an empty stairwell that September, and his magnetic pull hooked me.

'D'you know where room 234 is?' he asked, flashing a smile. It was a simple enough question, and there was nothing in it, or his face, that would hint of things to come.

I told him I had no idea. That the whole place was a maze and it would be a miracle if I ever worked out where I was going.

He laughed. 'You'd think it would be next to 233, wouldn't you? But no, why would they make it that easy for us?'

I chuckled then, and nodded my agreement. I had been there for almost two weeks and had spent more time roaming the corridors than doing anything else.

We proceeded to discuss the ways in which they could make it easier for students to find their lecture rooms – try adding signs, he suggested – and then we introduced ourselves.

It was only years later I thought to wonder why, after he'd already been a student there for a year, he didn't know where room 234 was.

That could have been the end of our encounter, we should have gone our separate ways, but that's not what happened.

'It's student night at Harry's bar across the street tomorrow,' he told me. 'You should come.' A flash of that smile again.

This was the first social offer I'd had, and I wasn't going to turn it down. I needed a distraction since my girlfriend, Amanda, had left me. 'You're just not interested in me,' she had claimed, and I couldn't argue with that. I can count on one hand the number of times we'd had sex, and we'd been together for six months.

'Yep, I probably will,' I said, trying to sound casual, as if I already had a busy social life.

He nodded slowly, his eyes searching my face, and I got the sense he could see right through me. 'Well, if you can find the time, it will be great to see you there.'

So that was it: a simple, chance encounter.

That changed my life forever.

THIRTEEN

I am at work by six a.m. the next day, to make sure I'm in before most of the other staff. I hardly slept last night and I'm sure the tiredness will catch up with me by the afternoon. Thankfully Matt was already asleep when I got home, and I managed not to wake him with my restlessness.

Before I left Abbot's flat last night we Googled Lucas Hall. I already knew from Grace that he owns a restaurant, but I didn't realise it was such a popular one in Notting Hill. It's called The Brasserie, and although I have never been there, I have heard people rave about it.

While I wait for Abbot, I pull up the website again and stare at Lucas's picture, as if his face can provide me with answers. According to his bio he is forty, but he could easily pass for thirty-five. His blond hair falls across his face and shiny brown eyes stare back at me. He's not bad looking, but everything I've heard about him has tainted his image for me. And now I picture his actions as Grace recounted them, and wonder if her story could be true. Or was Grace using him, blackening an innocent man's character in order to play her game?

Someone coughs and I spin around to find Abbot standing right behind me. 'Sorry,' he says. 'You were miles away. I've been standing here for ages!' He flicks his head towards my screen. 'Anything interesting?'

'Just checking out Lucas Hall again. I'm going to his restaurant at lunchtime.' I say the words but until now haven't realised this is what I'm planning. 'The chances are he won't be there, but I have to try.'

Abbot flings himself onto his chair and types his password into his computer. 'You mean *we're* going there at lunchtime. I know I was a bit funny about going to Ginny's house but at least we won't be breaking and entering this time. And I won't let you do this alone. Not after everything you've told me. Especially as you don't feel you can tell Matt.'

It's obvious Abbot doesn't agree with me lying to my husband. 'I can't get him mixed up in all this. I have no idea what's going on and I don't want him in any kind of trouble that could affect his career. It's the only thing that got him through losing Helena.'

'Not the only thing, I'm sure,' Abbot says, turning to me and smiling before facing his screen again. 'I'll make us a reservation.'

The Brasserie is full of suited men and women, and I imagine most of them are discussing business, grateful to be out of the office with a glass of wine in front of them and an expense account.

I sit opposite Abbot and while he studies his menu, I glance around me, looking for Lucas Hall. So far I can't see anyone who looks as if they might be management, only smartly dressed waiting staff, gliding in between tables as if they are skating on ice.

'Are you hungry?' Abbot asks. 'I think we'll need to order something.'

Food is the last thing on my mind, but I glance at my menu and tell him I'll have French onion soup. Abbot decides to have steak, and when the waiter comes over he also orders us each a glass of wine.

'I think you could do with it,' he says. 'And you don't have to drive anywhere today, do you?'

'Not right now. But who knows what will happen later? What if we find out where Grace is and I need to get to her? I might need to drive somewhere ...' I trail off, realising the futility of imagining this scenario.

Abbot reaches across the table and pats my hand. 'You believe she's Helena, don't you? In your heart.'

I consider his question. 'I'm not sure. I'm torn, Abbot. Her story seems so far-fetched, but then when I picture her, and how I felt talking to her, I can't help but wonder. I just felt she was being honest. But I'm well aware she could just be a good actor. And I can't explain her disappearance. Sending both Ginny and her friend texts seems to suggest she's fine and just doesn't want me to know where she is.'

Abbot's smile puts me at ease; he will not make judgements. 'Then we really need to find out what's going on, and Lucas Hall is our best chance of doing that. After we eat, I'll go and ask for him, okay?'

I nod, Abbot's kindness rendering me speechless. I am really testing our friendship to the limit with all I'm asking him to do, and I only hope one day I can repay him. But again I am reminded that it should be Matt I'm sharing this with, and my heart feels heavy with guilt.

We talk about the Brays while we wait for our food to arrive. For them today is another day without their daughter. I know that time will make things worse for them rather than easier; it does not heal the pain of a missing child. Instead, each passing day only diminishes hope, and gradually fades the image you hold of them.

The food arrives and I take quick sips of my soup, ignoring the heat as it scorches my tongue. Each time the door opens my eyes flick towards it, and I convince myself every male who enters the restaurant is Lucas. But not one of them turns out to be him. I think of Grace's claim that she killed him and for the first time seriously consider it might be true. But I can't jump to any conclusions yet; I can only go on evidence.

An elegantly dressed woman pushes through the door, bringing a gust of wind with her, and I watch as she heads straight to the bar area, her blazer and fitted midi dress clinging to her slender frame. She begins talking to one of the bar staff and I wonder if she also works here. But then I notice her eyes are red, and she wipes at them with her coat sleeve.

'So, what do you think?' Abbot says, forcing me to focus.

'Um ... I—'

'You haven't heard a word I've said, have you?' He laughs. 'I was just telling you to ditch Matt and run away with me to Vegas. I hear it's quite good for quickie weddings.'

And then, despite the circumstances and the anxiety I've felt since we got here, I too am laughing.

'Seriously, though,' he continues, 'I'm ready to ask for Lucas. Stay here and finish your soup. I'll be right back.' He stands up and heads off to the bar area, and it is only then I notice he has hardly touched his food.

I watch while he talks to a man behind the bar, and smile to think of how Abbot will be charming him. But when the man shakes his head, I know Lucas isn't here.

Finishing my wine, I wait for him to come back, pulling my purse from my bag.

'Two things,' Abbot says. 'Put that away and get your coat on. We need to be ready to leave any second.'

'What? Why?'

'Nobody's seen Lucas since Saturday night. But see that woman over by the bar? That's his wife. And we need to follow her the second she leaves.'

I open my mouth to protest, but realise we have no choice. It doesn't feel right to stalk her, but if she can lead us to Lucas, and hopefully Grace, then I need to do this.

Abbot calls over our waiter and asks for the bill, already counting out some notes he's pulled from his pocket.

'But what if she's driven here? We'll never know where she lives. What if she's not even going home?' My mind is a blur of questions. I also wonder if Grace knew Lucas was married, because she neglected to mention it to me.

Abbot smiles. 'Don't panic. The barman said Lucas lives a short walk away, so if she is going home then I doubt she'll have driven. Let's just wait and see. And be ready to move quickly.'

We don't have long to wait, as only moments later, Lucas's glamorous wife heads towards the door, her eyes still bloodshot.

'Come on,' Abbot says, grabbing my arm.

Outside, we keep our distance as we follow her. She walks slowly, teetering on heels unsuitable for this icy weather, but her bad choice of footwear makes it easier for us to lag behind while keeping her in sight.

As we walk, a plan forms in my head, and although adrenalin is pumping through me, I begin to feel calmer.

'Do you want me to do the talking or do you know what you'll say?' Abbot asks, once more in tune with my thoughts.

I explain my idea and he nods, smiling wryly while he keeps his eyes on the woman ahead of us.

'I don't know whether to be impressed or worried. You're too good at this sleuthing.'

'I'll do whatever I have to, for Helena,' I say. 'At least until I know the truth about Grace.'

The woman turns into Pembridge Road, and by the time we've reached it she is already turning into the next road. We walk faster; we cannot lose her now we're this close. She takes a right onto Pembridge Square and crosses the road. Then she stops suddenly, fishing in her oversized leather bag for something. Seconds later, she is easing up the steps of the house in front of her and opening the door.

Abbot whistles. 'So that's his house. He must be loaded to live here.'

I remember the flat that Grace claimed belonged to him, and once again feel a deep sense of foreboding. If this man has done something to her, something that has forced her to run away, then it won't be easy going up against him. Money gives people a sense of entitlement. And power.

We wait a couple of minutes then climb the steps to the front door. The building is double the width of my house. It is also a far cry from Ginny Rhodes's modest home. Grace mentioned Lucas being friends with her uncle, but I have no idea how they met, or what bonded them as friends.

'Are you ready?' I say to Abbot, reaching forward to press the bell.

She is still wearing her coat when she answers the door, and close up her face is strained and haggard. But despite this, I can tell that on a good day she is an attractive woman. She doesn't say anything but waits for one of us to speak.

'Hi, sorry to bother you,' I say. 'Is this Lucas Hall's house?'

Her eyes widen and she pulls the door further open. 'Yes.' She looks me up and down and then does the same to Abbot.

'I'm a friend of Lucas's. From university. I lost touch with him soon after we left but recently found out he owned The Brasserie.' When she doesn't react, I continue. 'I went there today hoping to catch up with him but they said he might be home?' I gesture to Abbot. 'This is my partner, Abbot Jackson.' I can sense his surprise at how I've introduced him and only hope the woman hasn't noticed it. I also know without looking he is flashing his mesmerising smile at her, and that she won't be able to help warming to him. 'And you must be Lucas's wife?'

She nods. 'Hannah,' she says. 'But Lucas isn't here.'

I try to act surprised. 'Oh. Would it be okay if we came in for a minute?'

Hannah Hall stares at us and I can almost see her lips forming the word *no*.

'Well, there's no point waiting for him. He's not coming back right now.'

'It's just a bit cold out here,' Abbot says. 'And we'd like to leave our contact details for Lucas. Is that okay?'

She watches Abbot for a moment, seeming to mull it over, and then pulls the door open wider. 'Come in for a minute, then.'

The first thing I notice when we step inside is how cold the house is. It's not just the temperature; the cold white walls and bare wooden floorboards make it feel unlived in. Just like the flat in Embankment.

She shows us into the first room leading off the hall and tells us to take a seat. It is a small sitting room and I assume it's not the main one as there is no television, only floor to ceiling shelves filled with ornaments. Abbot and I sit together on the L-shaped fabric sofa, while Hannah Hall perches at the other end, her hands folded in her lap.

'So ... you know Lucas from university?' she says.

'Yes, that's right. Westminster uni. Business studies.' I have done my research.

She doesn't smile, and her stare seems to become harder. I wonder if she suspects I might be an ex-girlfriend. 'But you haven't seen him since you left? Or heard from him?'

'Well, we kept in touch for a couple of years afterwards, but then I moved to Australia for a while and we lost contact.' I haven't planned to say this but it seems convincing enough.

Hannah stares at her hands, twisting her wedding ring around her finger. 'The thing is … I … Lucas … as I said, he's not here right now.'

'Will he be back later? I'm happy to hang around Notting Hill and wait. We don't often get to see London.'

'No,' she says. 'There's no point. He won't be back today.'

'Oh, I—'

'He's gone. Left me.' The words shoot from her mouth and seem to surprise her as much as they do me. 'At least, I think so. He's done this before. Just upped and left when he's fed up. But he doesn't usually desert the restaurant.'

Abbot and I glance at one another. We aren't prepared for this. Although I have given Grace the benefit of the doubt, only a small part of me believed what she told me happened with Lucas. But now his wife is confirming his absence, I have to start taking Grace's story as a possibility.

'Where does he normally go?' Abbot asks Hannah. 'I mean, when he's done this before?'

Hannah shakes her head. 'That's the thing. He normally tells me where he is. In a hotel or staying at a friend's. But this time I've heard nothing. I've called everyone I can think of who might have heard from him, but they're all saying the same thing. Nobody knows where he is. I just … ' Tears trickle down her cheeks and she turns from us and stares out of the window.

Instinctively, I move over to her and pat her arm. 'I know this must be really hard. Why don't Abbot and I try and help? We could ask around, put the feelers out and see what comes up. Abbot's got a lot of contacts.'

Hannah rubs her eyes with the sleeve of her coat. 'Would you? I'd really appreciate it. I know he's a nightmare to live with, but he's a good person. It's just not like him to do this.'

It is strange hearing Lucas described in this way; a complete contrast from the man in Grace's story.

'Have you told the police?' Abbot asks. 'Reported him missing?'

She turns to him and then stares down at her hands, once again twisting her wedding ring. 'No. I … I was … we'd had an argument and I thought he might be punishing me. I assumed the police would accuse me of wasting their time. But now I will do it. As soon as you've gone.'

'I think you should,' I say, for the time being ignoring her contradictory description of Lucas. For Grace's sake, I didn't want to get the police involved, but I doubt at this point they will do much to look for a grown man who clearly makes a habit of leaving his wife. 'And could you write down the names and numbers of anyone you can think of who knows him? That will be our starting point.'

'But I've already phoned people,' Hannah says, the tears back in her eyes.

'I know. It's just to make double sure. There might be someone you didn't think of contacting before.'

She nods. 'Okay. I'll need to get my phone. I'll be back in a minute.'

Once she's left the room, I turn to Abbot but don't speak. I have no idea how far Hannah has gone, or how soundproof the walls are, and at this moment we can't trust anyone. Abbot appears to be thinking the same and he only offers me a small smile and raise of his eyebrows.

Minutes tick by before Hannah finally comes back, her eyes less red now. 'Here,' she says, handing me a sheet of A4 paper. 'All the people I could think of.'

I take it from her, fold it and slip it into my bag. 'We'll make a start on this as soon as possible.'

'Thanks. But I don't hold out much hope.' Hannah's eyes well up again.

'We should get going,' I say, standing quickly.

Abbot follows my lead. 'Um, Hannah, would you mind if I use your bathroom?'

Hannah nods. 'You'll have to use upstairs, I'm afraid, the downstairs toilet doesn't flush. Lucas was meant to be getting it fixed but … well … '

I grab her hand and give it a gentle squeeze.

Outside, I wait until we are almost on Notting Hill Gate before I speak about Hannah. 'So what did you think?'

As always, Abbot knows exactly what I mean. 'I believe her. I don't think she knows where her husband is.'

'I agree. Does that mean Grace is telling the truth? That she really did kill him by mistake?'

Abbot stops walking. 'I don't know, but it doesn't look good.'

'Well, we've got the list of names to check out. We need to know who this man is and what he knows about Helena's abduction. And how Grace's disappearance is tied to him.'

Abbot smiles. 'And we've got this.' He moves one side of his coat aside and reveals a Mac Book Air tucked under his arm.

'What? Where did—'

'When I went to the bathroom I had a bit of a snoop. Found this in the study. It could be Hannah's of course, but no harm checking. I'll take a look at it after work tonight.'

'Wait, are you the same person who told me we shouldn't break into Ginny's house?'

Abbot smiles. 'I figured we've already crossed the line and now I want answers as much as you do. It's the journalist in me.'

'But what if she notices it's missing?'

'There are so many gadgets upstairs in that house I doubt she'll notice it's gone. But if she does she may assume Lucas has taken it with him.'

I don't know whether I want to hug him or smack him for taking such a risk. 'Thanks, Abbot. You always do go above and beyond. That's why you're so good at your job.'

He shrugs and we resume walking, but I sense his embarrassment at my compliment. A vision of Matt floats into my head, and with it a reminder of all the pain we have experienced together. I hate keeping things from him, but I need to protect him, at least until I know what's going on.

Matt is asleep on the sofa when I get home from work. I tiptoe in and curl up next to him, breathing in his familiar scent. Although we have been together over twenty years, and his hair, body and face may have gone through small changes, his smell remains the same, always comforting.

'You're back,' he says, slowly opening his eyes and pulling me closer towards him. 'Sorry, I just needed a nap. So tired.'

I offer to make some macaroni cheese and his face lights up. It's a simple meal but is one of his favourites.

Standing up, I watch as he stretches, his hair ruffled from where he's been lying against the sofa cushion. 'I meant to ask but forgot this morning. Do you remember that private detective we hired when Helena was taken? Mark?'

Matt sits up. 'Yeah, Mark Hunter. Why?'

'I was talking to the Brays about him and said I'd get his details for them. I mean, he was good, wasn't he? Even though he couldn't find her. He did try.'

Matt nods and stares at the floor. 'Yep, he was. But it was a long time ago and there's a chance he may not even be doing the job these days. I don't have his card any more but I'm sure he'll be on the Internet somewhere.'

While I cook dinner, I realise that as well as helping the Brays, Mark Hunter might also be able to help me find Grace. I won't be able to tell him what Grace confessed to me – he would be duty-bound to contact the police – but he may be able to help me track her down.

Leaving the macaroni to simmer, I pull out my phone and click on the Internet browser, typing *Mark Hunter* into the search box. Immediately I am inundated with hits, but a quick scroll down the page shows me that none of them refer to the man I am looking for, and there is no mention of any detective or private investigation agency. Puzzled, I stick the phone back in my pocket and try to bury my disappointment.

All I know is that I won't give up on Grace, even if it's just down to Abbot and me to find her by ourselves.

FOURTEEN

Four days have passed since Grace tracked me down in John Lewis and I am no closer to the truth. In fact, each passing hour seems to throw up new questions, forcing my thoughts to spin in a vortex I can't slow down.

For some reason, Fridays at work are always a frantic rush, and today is no exception. It's as if the news is playing a cruel joke on us: take this to ruin your weekend. Abbot is pulled away all morning to work on a breaking story – a high-profile politician has been caught with a prostitute – so it is lunchtime before I have a chance to speak to him.

He finds me in one of the conference rooms, where I have come to gather my thoughts. 'I picked you up a sandwich,' he says, 'as I know you won't have thought about lunch.' He places it on the table in front of me.

Thanking him, I pull out the chair next to me, but leave the sandwich in its bag. 'Any luck with the laptop?'

'Not yet. It's heavily security protected and is beyond even what I can do, but I've got a friend looking into it. He's good, he'll crack the password quickly.' Abbot sits down and pulls out his sandwich. 'In the meantime, what's our next step?'

I have given this a lot of thought overnight, going over and over what I know and what we should do next. I explain to Abbot there are two things. First I need to cross-reference the list Hannah gave us with Ginny's address book to see if there are any contacts they both have in common. I don't know if it will do any good, but it's all I can think of. I also need to find out more about Ginny. I don't think any of her friends will speak to me about her, but I could contact her manager at work, tell her care agency the same story I told Ginny; that I need a reliable carer for my mum. I may be able to get some information from them.

Abbot's eyes widen. 'Wow, you've clearly done a lot of thinking. Okay, it seems like a good place to start. Listen, I've asked to leave early tonight, so I can start working on those contacts.'

A wave of guilt floods through me; Abbot is so conscientious about his job. 'Are you sure? I was going to do it myself. I really don't want this to interfere with your work.'

He picks up his sandwich but doesn't take a bite. 'It's fine, they owe me some annual leave so I'll just use some of that. To be honest, this is all giving me something other than work to focus on, and that can't be a bad thing, can it?'

'I really appreciate this. Thank you.'

Abbot avoids eye contact and stares at his sandwich. 'You know you don't need to thank me.'

I give his arm a quick squeeze. 'Right, well, after work I'll pay a visit to Angel Carers. They're based in Putney so shall I come to yours afterwards? We can go through whatever we find out?'

Abbot nods. 'Sounds good. And I promise to be fully dressed this time.'

We finish our sandwiches and then I call Tamsin Bray to let her know about Mark Hunter.

'That's strange,' she says, her voice soft and strained. I wonder again if she is always so quietly spoken or whether it's only since her daughter went missing. 'There's no record of him at all? Are you sure you've got his name right?'

I tell her I'll never forget his name and through the silence that follows I can almost touch her disappointment. 'It was eighteen years ago, though, Tamsin. He probably wouldn't have had a website then so that could explain why there's no mention of him. And maybe he gave it up soon after our case?'

'Okay. Thanks for trying. We'll find someone else.' She falls silent, not realising that I am just as disappointed as she is. I had a glimmer of hope that Mark could help me again, but now it's just down to Abbot and me.

Even though I already know the answer, I ask her how she's holding up.

'I've set up a website. Well, a friend of Charlotte's did it for us. FindCharlotte.com. We've already had lots of hits and loads of support from people we don't even know. I don't think it will help us find her but it's nice to know people are thinking of us.'

I tell her it's a great idea and promise to check it out. Before we hang up I make sure she knows I am there for her if she needs anything. I know my words are futile – unless I can find her daughter there is nothing that will help – but I need her to know I care, that I understand the pain she feels.

It is impossible not to think of Grace once I've ended the call, and I try her mobile again. I am so used to it being switched off that I expect nothing else, and I am right again. I know Ginny and Jasmine don't seem to think she is missing but something still doesn't feel right. But I have little to go on right now until I can find out more about Ginny Rhodes. I probably won't learn much from her employer, but it's a start. Picking up my mobile once more, I scroll to Angel Carers and connect the call.

I am in Putney by ten to five, with just enough time to make it to my appointment. The office is a fifteen minute walk from the train station and I almost run there, not wanting to be late and antagonise anyone when I need their help. The manager has already agreed to wait for me to arrive, even though she usually leaves at five.

'Hi,' the receptionist says, when I push through the doors. She looks about my age and already has her coat on. 'You must be Hayley?'

I am about to correct her, when I remember I have had to use this name again. 'Sorry for keeping you back late,' I say.

The receptionist waves off my apology and tells me to take a seat, before disappearing around a corner. The only chairs are by the large front window and it is growing dark outside so I feel as if I'm in a goldfish bowl, on show to anyone outside, while through the window all I can see is the reflection of the room I'm in. The office is tiny, but the plants and flowers scattered around make it feel welcoming.

'Hayley, hi! I'm Cassandra.'

I hear the woman before I see her, her voice loud and deep, echoing through the room.

Standing up, I move across to her and she vigorously shakes my hand. She appears to be in her early fifties, and her dark hair is scraped back in a tight bun. I feel as if her eyes are probing me, already trying to work me out.

'Thanks for meeting me at such short notice,' I say, the smile I offer her genuine, despite my deception.

'Let's go in my office. I've had the heating on in there so it's a lot warmer than out here.' She wraps her arms around herself to emphasise her point.

I follow her through a narrow corridor and eventually she leads me into a small room at the back of the building. Her desk is cluttered with family photos, and behind her chair hangs a large whiteboard, scrawled with names in green pen. I take a seat, but not before I spot Ginny's name with an arrow pointing to the name of someone I assume she cares for.

Cassandra smiles, folding her hands together on the desk. 'So, you're interested in one of our carers looking after your mother, I believe?'

I nod. 'That's right. Her daughter and my daughter are friends, so that's how I heard about her. Ginny Rhodes.' I try not to glance at the whiteboard, and force myself into the role of concerned relative.

Cassandra's eyes brighten. 'Ah, Ginny. She's one of our best. All her clients love her.' She must think my surprise is from her use of the term *clients* because she quickly explains. 'That's what we like to call the people we look after. It lets them know they're important, and it's better than calling them patients, because that's not what they are. And as they're not in care homes, they're not really residents, are they?'

'I agree,' I tell her. 'And I'm sure my mum will be in the best possible hands here. What I'd like, though, is just a bit more information on Ginny. I just want to make sure she's a good match for Mum. Is that okay?'

Cassandra places a hand on her computer mouse and the monitor springs to life. 'Well, it's not really what we usually do, I mean, all our carers are thoroughly screened of course, so the fact they're with us is a reference in itself. But I understand your need for as much information as possible.' She turns to the screen. 'Let me just check some details on our system. We keep detailed notes on all our carers, and although I can't let you see them, it will help me give you a good idea about how well thought of Ginny is.'

I thank her and wait while she taps keys and concentrates on the monitor. She reads for a few moments and jots notes on an A5 pad of paper. Finally, she finishes and turns back to me.

'Okay, well, Ginny's been with us for over ten years and in that time she's had nothing but glowing feedback from all her clients. She's dealt with all sorts of issues, from Alzheimer's to Cystic Fibrosis, and she goes out of her way to learn everything she can about the people she cares for. I can promise you, your mother will be in great hands.'

She places her pen down and waits for me to speak. So this is it. I'm going to get nothing more than a vague account of how good Ginny is at her job. I don't know what I was expecting, but of course Cassandra can't tell me anything personal. All I've managed to learn is that Ginny appears to be a decent person, the description I've just been fed far removed from that of a woman who could abduct a baby. But I remind myself again that you can never know what people are capable of.

'That all sounds great,' I say to Cassandra. 'She seems perfect. I don't suppose there's any way I could speak to any of the people she cares for? Just to get more of a picture of how she goes about caring on a day-to-day basis.'

Cassandra frowns, and I worry I have pushed too far. 'Sorry, we just can't allow that. Our clients are classed as vulnerable, so we can't just let people grill them for details of our carers.'

'Yes, of course. I understand.' My eyes flick to the whiteboard and I focus on one of the names next to Ginny's. Ivy Whitehouse. And next to it is an address. Pams Way, Ewell.

'Can I just ask what you use the whiteboard for?' I know it is none of my business, but I have to try.

Cassandra turns around. 'Oh, that's just to note down any people leaving our care. It's usually because they no longer need help, or because they've moved from our area.'

This is interesting. I now have the name of one of Ginny's *clients*. There is only one thing I can do with this information. I tell Cassandra I'll speak to my mother about Ginny and call the agency to get it all arranged.

She reaches across the desk to shake my hand. 'That's great. I'm sure she'll be very happy with Ginny.'

This time when he answers his door, Abbot is wearing a thick jumper, the collar of a red polo shirt visible underneath. 'Is this better?' he asks, winking at me. 'I've layered up just for you.'

'A great improvement,' I say, pulling off my coat.

'I've had a productive afternoon,' he says. 'Come through and I'll tell you about it.'

We sit on Abbot's sofa with his laptop between us. 'Okay, so I compared Hannah's list with Ginny's address book, and there are only two contacts the same. One is Daniel, Ginny's brother, but that's no surprise as they were friends. The other name is Nicholas Gibbs. Did Grace ever mention him?'

I shake my head. 'No. I've not heard that name before.'

'Well, I Googled him, and this is what I found.'

Abbot slides the laptop towards me and I pick it up and place it on my lap. An unfamiliar face stares back at me. It is a friendly face and the man's smile stretches across it; his shining dark eyes and smooth head make his age hard to guess. I wonder if he is losing his hair or whether he chooses to have it shaved so close.

The website I'm looking at is for a computer games company called Alpha Games, and I pore over the short paragraphs, quickly learning that Nicholas Gibbs created and owns the company.

Beside me, Abbot can no longer control his excitement. 'The guy must be loaded. His company have made some of the best PlayStation games. I've got most of them!' He points to his TV, where for the first time I notice the cabinet is stacked with games.

'Weird. How would he and Ginny know each other? She didn't strike me as the type to be into gaming. And there was no evidence of it in her home.'

Abbot focuses once again. 'I thought the same thing. But I guess they could just know each other through Lucas? Or Daniel, Ginny's brother? You never know how people from different worlds can be brought together.' He reaches for his laptop before continuing. 'Now we've got a lead,' he says. 'We can pay this Nicholas a visit, under the pretext of helping Hannah, and see what we can find out about Lucas. Tomorrow's Saturday so there's a chance he'll be home if we just turn up.'

'But we don't have his address. Hannah only gave us phone numbers.'

Abbot waves Ginny's address book in front of me. 'Lucky Ginny still records her contacts the old-fashioned way then, isn't it?'

I can't help but smile. The book may be able to help me with something else too. Snatching it from him, I flick through to the *W* section and scan the page. There she is. Ivy Whitehouse. 10 Pams Way.

'What are you up to?' Abbot asks.

'Before we meet tomorrow there's something I need to do. I found out from Angel Carers, without them knowing, that Ginny looks after a woman called Ivy Whitehouse. I'm going to pay her a visit and see if I can find anything out about Ginny. I mean, they obviously spend a lot of time together, they're bound to have talked a lot. Which means that this lady's in a good position to know things about her.' I pass the book back to him. 'And I'm in luck because her full address is in there.'

Abbot frowns. 'Sim, are you sure about this? Taking Lucas's laptop was bad enough, but do you think we're going a bit far now? And I doubt she'll tell you that she thinks Ginny's daughter isn't really hers.'

'I know. But somewhere along the line, Ginny might have slipped up with something. I've got to try, Abbot. I need the truth.'

He thinks about this for a moment. Surely he is realising I don't have much choice. 'I guess,' he says eventually. 'Just be careful. You could get in serious trouble for turning up at this woman's house. Especially if she's elderly or frail.'

I tell him not to worry, that I've got it covered. But the truth is I have no idea what I will say to Ivy Whitehouse.

When I get home, I find Matt sitting at the kitchen table. A half-empty bottle of wine sits in front of him and one of our photo albums is open on the table. He looks up before I can ask what he's doing and I see his eyes are swollen and red.

'I wonder what Helena would be like now?' he says. 'And we'd be different people, wouldn't we? We would have had the chance to be parents. That's bound to have changed us for the better.'

I pull out a chair and sit next to him, helping myself to a sip of his unfinished glass of wine. 'Do you remember when I always used to say that things happen for a reason? Every little thing? Well, maybe I don't believe that anymore. It's been eighteen years and we still don't know why she was taken from us. What if we never do?' I am speaking aloud the fear I have always had, but this time I am also worried that my investigation of Grace will come to nothing. She won't be Helena, and where will that leave us?

Matt squeezes my hand 'You would have been a great mum. Do you think I would have been a good dad?'

'The best,' I say, leaning over and cuddling into him. I open my mouth to speak again but think better of it. Because what will come out is the truth about everything Grace told me, and an explanation of what Abbot and I have been doing. And I can't burden Matt with that.

We sit like this for over an hour, sharing wine from the same glass, poring through the old photos and talking about the six months we had with Helena. It is a comfort to us both.

But I don't sleep well that night. My mind is a flurry of ominous thoughts; there can be no happy end to whatever our search turns up. All I know is that I am getting closer to the truth. Of that I am certain.

FIFTEEN

Ivy Whitehouse lives one street away from Ginny Rhodes. I park on a different road, just in case she is anywhere nearby and recognises my car, and tentatively walk along the icy pavement to number ten. It is a similar house to Ginny's, and I wonder what kind of help Ivy needed, and why she no longer requires it.

'Can I help you?' a voice says, before I've reached the front door.

Spinning around, I find myself staring at a woman who can't be more than sixty. She is wrapped in a thick winter coat and her short hair is bright white. She inches towards me, clearly on guard because there is a stranger in her front garden.

'Hi, I'm looking for Ivy Whitehouse.' I take a step back.

'That's me,' she says, reaching into her handbag but keeping her eyes fixed on me.

I explain the story I am now well-rehearsed at: how my mum needs a carer and I've recently found a lady called Ginny Rhodes, through Angel Carers. 'I know she looked after you recently and just wondered if you had time for a quick chat. Just so I can make sure I'm leaving Mum in good hands. I won't keep you long.'

Through narrowed eyes she digests my words, and for a few seconds I can't tell whether she is buying my story or not. But then she speaks. 'I suppose I can spare a few minutes. Come in, then. What did you say your name was?'

'Hayley,' I tell her, suppressing the usual guilt that I'm again using my work colleague's name. 'And please, feel free to call Angel Carers to check I am who I say I am.' I can only pray she doesn't take up my suggestion. Thankfully she heads towards the door, with no mention of making any call, so I follow her in.

She directs me to her living room and we sit on her grey fabric sofa. I study her appearance and still can't see any sign of her needing a carer. She walks and stands without help, and her posture gives no hint of any physical issues. 'Do you mind if I ask what Ginny was helping you with?' I say.

'I had an operation and couldn't get around much for a while. It was only a few months, but even just washing myself was impossible.'

I don't ask what operation she had, I am already pushing ethical boundaries, and if she wanted to offer that information she would have done so. Instead, I ask what she thought of Ginny personally. 'I know she's a great carer, but Mum's the kind of person who needs a bit of companionship too, and I just want to make sure they're a good match for each other. Does that make sense?'

'Perfect sense,' she says, her smile showing me she believes me. 'But I don't think you'll have anything to worry about. Ginny is so easy to talk to, we hit it off right away. In fact, I'd say I got to know her quite well over the last few months.' Her tone becomes perkier as she talks more about Ginny. Once again it all comes back to how well thought of she is.

'That's good to know,' I say, hoping I'm hiding my uneasiness at hearing Ginny spoken of this way.

'Her brother died recently. So sad. I think they were very close.' She shakes her head slowly and stares at her feet.

I feign ignorance and agree that this is awful for her, but I still find it hard to sympathise with the woman when I'm so unsure of her.

'But she never let it affect her work,' Ivy continues. 'She always turned up when she was due, and more often than not, ended up staying longer and just having a chat.'

'Oh, Mum will love that,' I say, picturing just how much my mum would hate having a carer around. She is so independent, she wouldn't even want me having to help her. 'And, she does sound like a lovely caring woman,' I stifle the bile rising in my throat.

'Well, it comes so naturally to her. She's just one of those people. But then she is a mother, so she has experience of looking after others.' She fixes me with an inquisitive stare. 'Do you have any children?'

Her question catches me off guard, immediately transporting me to a different time, a different place. 'Um, yes. A daughter. She's eighteen.' I am only telling the truth.

'How lovely! She's the same age as Ginny's daughter. Grace, her name is. Lovely name.'

But is that her real name? I nod and smile, trying to stay focused on what Ivy Whitehouse is saying. For the next ten minutes she talks about her own children. She has three grown-up sons, all of whom are married with their own families. I only half-listen, desperate to find a way to steer her back onto Ginny, but before I think of anything, Ivy suddenly stops talking, her face crumpling.

'Is something wrong?' I ask. 'Are you okay?'

It takes her a moment to answer. 'Yes … I'm fine. Sorry, I just thought of something I'd completely forgotten until now. It's … no, it's nothing. Forget I said anything. I'm always being told off for gossiping.'

Finally, I feel as if I am about to learn something, but getting it out of Ivy won't be easy. 'Please, Mrs Whitehouse. I just want to make sure my mum's in good hands.'

'Of course she will be. It's nothing to do with her ability to care.'

'Then what is it?'

Sighing, she finally answers, her need to gossip overcoming her. 'Well, it's a bit strange, and I don't know what to make of it. In fact, it was months ago so I'm not even sure I'm right.'

I lean forward. 'What is it?'

She bites her thin lower lip, and her face flushes. 'Yes. I feel bad saying this to you but Ginny and I were talking about our children once. It's a bit hazy but I do remember telling her I had to have a caesarean for all three of mine. I didn't recover well from them and I've always envied women who can have natural births, but I'm sure Ginny said she'd also had a caesarean. I'm sure we talked about how difficult it was for both of us.'

My heart thuds in my chest. If this is correct, and Ginny has had a caesarean, then she will have a scar as evidence she gave birth. But there is something else Ivy wants to tell me and it must be related to Grace. 'Why is that strange?' I ask.

'It's not. Except that another time when we were talking she said she'd had a home birth. Through choice. She told me all the details about it, I'm sure of that, because I remember wondering why on earth she didn't just go to the hospital and get looked after in the right place. I don't know why I didn't put the two together before, but I was a bit fuddled after my operation. But I've probably got this all wrong, and it doesn't take away from the fact that she really looked after me. There's every chance I misunderstood her.'

I nod. 'Yes, I'm sure that's exactly what it is.'

'Yes, that's what happened. There's always a simple explanation for things, isn't there?'

My head spins as I walk to the car. Has Ivy Whitehouse just given me more evidence that Ginny abducted my daughter? Or is she misremembering, somehow mistaken because the conversation took place so long ago, and when she wasn't in the best of health? There is no way to know without confronting Ginny, and it's looking increasingly likely that this is what I'll have to do. But I need more evidence to present to her. I don't want to give her any opportunity to weasel out of what she has done. If she's guilty. I still don't know if I can trust Grace's words.

In the car, I call Abbot to tell him I'm on my way. I fill him in on what I've just found out and he emits a heavy sigh. 'Just get here quickly,' he says. 'I don't know what's going on, but I don't like it. The sooner we track down Lucas Hall and find out where Grace is, the better.'

Nicholas Gibbs lives in Richmond, only a short drive from Abbot's flat. He answers the door with two young children clinging to his legs, and looks even friendlier than he does in his photo. As he is the CEO of his own company, I have been expecting him to be dressed in a suit, but when my eyes focus on his jeans and Lacoste polo shirt, I remind myself it's Saturday. Plus, he probably doesn't need to dress up in his industry.

Abbot steps forward first. 'Hi, are you Nicholas Gibbs?' He asks this even though we already know he is.

He smiles. 'Yes, I am. How can I help you?'

Holding out his hand, Abbot explains that we're friends of Lucas Hall. 'Hannah's sent us,' he adds, when a puzzled frown crosses the man's face. 'Can we have a quick chat?'

Nicholas steps back, his kids both shuffling back with him, and beckons us in. 'Sienna!' he calls, turning towards the house. Moments later a small brunette woman appears, smiling when she notices they have company.

'Oh, hi,' she says. 'Sorry, I wasn't expecting anyone. I must look a mess.' She smooths down her hair, but she is far from a mess. Although she is dressed casually in jeans and a loose jumper, I can tell she has made an effort with her appearance this morning, and bothered to put on a touch of make-up.

'This is my wife, Sienna,' Nicholas says. 'Honey, these are friends of Lucas and Hannah.'

I cringe at the word he uses to describe us.

Sienna holds out her hand and shakes mine first. Her palms are warm and moist, and I'm not surprised if she's running around after two small children. She grabs Abbot's hand next and I notice him jolt slightly at her touch.

'Kids, come on, let's leave Daddy to talk to his friends.' That word again. She ushers the children away from Nicholas, with an apologetic smile when at first they resist her. A pang of envy takes me by surprise. This should have been me, years ago. With Grace. Perhaps with another child too. Instead, my life has taken a different direction, one I try hard to appreciate and make the most of. But sometimes witnessing moments like this threatens to floor me.

Pushing my feelings aside, I focus on the man whose house we're standing in. 'Sorry for interrupting your family time,' I say. 'Two young kids can be a handful, I'm sure.'

'Three actually,' Nicholas says. 'We also have a thirteen-year-old. He's probably holed up in his room. Anyway, enough about me. Let's sit in the front room and you can tell me what's going on.'

As we sit on his black leather sofa, I think of how many different people's living rooms I have sat in over the last few days. And how, despite this, I don't seem to be getting any closer to the truth.

'Now, how can I help?' Nicholas says, looking from me to Abbot, a pleasant smile on his face.

'Well, Nicholas,' I begin. 'We—'

'Please, call me Nick. Nicholas is so formal!'

Surprised by his interruption, I agree, and then tell him we're here because Hannah is worried about Lucas. 'We're just trying to see if we can help her find him,' I say.

Nick's smile disappears, replaced with concern. 'Hmmm. Hannah did call me a couple of days ago,' he explains. 'She was in a state, but I just thought it was Lucas being Lucas. He's not … well, let's just say he's not the most reliable of husbands, as I'm sure you know.'

'Actually, I haven't seen Lucas since university,' I say. 'I was trying to get back in touch with him. Then we found out he was missing. It got me worried so we said we'd help Hannah.'

Nick nods. If he finds this strange, nothing in his expression reveals these thoughts. 'I see. Okay, well, all I can tell you is what I told her. I haven't seen him for several weeks now. To be honest, we've both been so busy, it's been hard to stay in regular contact.'

'How do you know him?' I ask.

'Oh, just through the restaurant. I used to have a lot of business meetings there. I know it's a bit of a trek, but the food is well worth the journey.'

'So you haven't seen Lucas for a while?' Nick asks.

'It's been years. I've been living in Australia so lost contact with most of my friends over here.'

'Yep, that happens a lot doesn't it? I'm not in touch with anyone from uni. Or school actually.' He leans forward. 'Anyway, it is a bit strange. Lucas would never leave Hannah to worry about him, no matter what goes on in their marriage. He at least tells her where he is. I told her to call the police, do you know if she's done that?'

'Hopefully by now,' Abbot says.

'Unfortunately,' Nick says, 'they probably won't do much about a grown man leaving his wife, especially when he's disappeared on her before. But I have some contacts who might be able to help, so I'll get on to them. But please, if you hear anything before me, will you let me know?'

I tell him we will, and give him my mobile number.

When Abbot grills Nick for details about his company, he answers politely, and doesn't lose patience with Abbot's gushing, but I feel that each second ticking by is an intrusion into the man's life. His wife must surely need help with something, and we have taken up enough of his time.

But then I remember he knows Ginny. I want to ask him about this but can't risk it at the moment. And does being acquainted with Ginny also mean he knows something about Grace? But he said that he only knows Lucas through the restaurant, so it is doubtful he will know if there's any truth to Grace's claim. It occurs to me that I can't trust anyone. Since Grace appeared a few days ago my life has been turned upside down, not only because of the conflict I feel about the possibility that she's Helena, but also because I'm lying to Matt and relying on my friend far too much.

'What do you make of him?' Abbot says, as we're driving back to his flat.

'He seemed nice, the complete opposite of how I imagine Lucas to be, so I don't know how they ended up friends. But anyway, I don't feel like we got any further.'

Abbot agrees. 'I know what you mean. It's like we're going around in circles and always coming back to the beginning. But we had to be careful what we said.' He sighs. 'Let's just hope the laptop turns up something. In fact, I'm going to go and see my friend now. Maybe encourage him to move a bit quicker. What will you do now?'

What I want to do is confront Ginny, this time demanding answers, but we still don't have enough evidence. 'I need to go into work. All of this is making me so far behind, I need to get on top of things.' It will also be a welcome distraction.

Abbot drops me back at my car and we say goodbye, arranging to speak later. But as I drive home alone, I feel the heavy weight of the last few days.

I spend a few hours at work so it is evening by the time I get home, and the house is shrouded in darkness. It is only then I remember Matt is going for a meal with some colleagues tonight. The house is cold so I turn on the heating and flick on light switches, anything to help me feel less alone.

I pour myself a glass of red wine, and take it to the living room. The curtains are still open in here and as I head to the window to close them, a flicker of something catches my eye.

There is a man outside. Staring straight at me. I don't recognise his face but something about him is familiar.

And then it hits me. His grey jacket and black trainers. I have seen him before. In Lucas Hall's flat.

Rushing to the hall – with no thought to consequences – I throw open the front door and step outside to get a closer look. But he has gone. If he was even there to begin with.

Later, I sit at the kitchen table and tell myself I imagined it. Perhaps this whole situation is causing me so much stress that I'm hallucinating. And just when I'm trying to comprehend what I did or didn't see, my mobile rings.

It is Tamsin Bray. And she is telling me they have found Charlotte.

SIXTEEN

I went to Harry's bar the next night. I had no idea how seriously he had meant his invitation, so hadn't made up my mind to go until the last second. Maybe he wouldn't be there, but I could easily walk back out again. And at least I would get out of my shabby room for a while.

But he was there, just as he'd said he'd be. He wasn't alone, but then how could I have expected him to be? No, he was flanked by two other students I'd never seen before. They barely glanced at me so I ignored them and tapped his arm.

'It's you,' he said, that magnetic smile back on his face. He offered to buy me a beer, and even though I had early lectures in the morning, I gratefully accepted.

'Wonderwall' by Oasis blared from the speakers, drunken voices in the background singing along, and now I can't hear that song without thinking of him.

We hijacked a table in the corner, and for a while he was the only person speaking. I could tell the other two weren't comfortable with me being there, but couldn't think why. We were all students – weren't we supposed to be sociable? Meeting new people? Too drunk to care? But after a while – and countless beers – we all seemed to forget we were strangers, sharing stories about our lives, and by the end of the night I was confident I had made some new friends.

Perhaps you are wondering why he was so important to me, right from the start, before I truly knew him? It wasn't as if I'd been a loner, desperate for people to like me. I'd had plenty of friends in school, and wasn't bothered about making more at university, but I had never felt an affinity with anyone like this.

Did I recognise something in him that I knew to be in myself? I can't say, but whatever it was, I felt that he understood the core of me. I wasn't to know then the extent to which this was true. That came later. But if it's possible to fall hard and fast for a friend, then that is exactly what I did.

We went back to his house after the bar closed. Just he and I, the other two having left some time before, and I don't remember much after that. Only that the conversation flowed, and everything was so easy.

To this day, I don't recall whether I said anything to him that revealed anything about the real me, but I have often wondered how he knew. He must have known, though. Because from that moment on we were as inseparable as our timetables allowed us to be.

He will say I started the whole thing, and in some way this is true, but if I was the match, then he was the hand that struck it.

But I'm getting ahead of myself. That came months later, when we'd secured an invisible bond between us. When we knew without having to express it that we could trust one another.

And now I need to tell you about Leanne.

SEVENTEEN

'She won't talk to anyone,' Tamsin Bray says.

We are standing in her kitchen, staring out at the frost-covered garden. As I listen to her speak, I initially struggle to understand why she isn't more excited. But as she explains, it dawns on me that for her family this is only just the beginning.

'The police can't even get a word out of her,' she tells me. 'They think she might be in some kind of shock. Traumatised by something. The only thing that's clear is that something awful has happened to her.' Her voice wobbles and tears flood down her cheeks. 'What if she's been … raped?' Tamsin looks at me, her eyes begging for answers I don't have.

'Is that what they think's happened?' I don't want to ask this question, but now that she's brought it up I can't ignore it.

'That's just it. She won't let anyone touch her. And she wears clothes that cover her body completely so who knows what she's hiding? The doctor tried to examine her but she just went rigid and shrieked the place down. And they can't force her, can they?' Again, she throws me that look. 'Not that I want to put her through that. I guess it's her choice.'

'Maybe she just needs time?' I suggest.

This must be the wrong thing to say because suddenly Tamsin is reaching for the back door, throwing it open and rushing outside. I give her a moment then follow her out.

I'm about to apologise when she beats me to it. 'I'm sorry. I just needed some air. This is all—'

'I know. Don't worry. The main thing is, she's back. That's what's important, isn't it?'

She takes my hand and I am surprised how cold her skin is, considering we've been outside for less than a minute. 'Yes. It's everything,' she says.

The Brays' back garden is larger than I imagined it to be. Although it is narrow, it stretches on endlessly, and a paved path leads to the bottom of it, where I can just about see a high fence. Without discussing it, we begin walking, even though neither of us has on a coat.

'I need to ask you something,' Tamsin says, once we've neared the end of the garden. 'I just wondered if Charlotte might … talk to you. If you explained who you are and how you … lost your daughter? It might force her out of herself? I know she needs time but the police need to know what's happened to her, who's responsible. Otherwise, how will they ever stop them doing it again?'

As much as I want to help, I'm not sure this is a good idea. How could I be of any help? I understand why Tamsin is asking me; it has nothing to do with my job, and everything to do with losing my daughter. 'I don't know, Tamsin. I'm not sure it's ethical. I think the police would—'

'The liaison officer says it's fine,' Tamsin says, her tone authoritative, even though her voice is still soft.

But I'm still not convinced. Charlotte was only found last night, by a canal in north London, wearing no coat or shoes, only the tattered green dress she'd gone out in the night she disappeared. Her body was covered in cuts and bruises and she could barely walk. She is lucky to be alive.

'Please, Simone,' Tamsin continues when I don't answer. 'I wouldn't ask if I wasn't desperate. I just need to know my girl's okay.'

It would be easy to refuse if I hadn't lost Helena, if I couldn't imagine exactly how afraid for her daughter Tamsin must be.

'Where is she now?' I ask. Tamsin has asked me to do something momentous. I am not skilled in speaking to victims in this way. I have no idea what I would even say to Charlotte. But I also understand why she needs me to do this, and even though I'm battling my own troubles at the moment, I can't let her down.

'In her room. She's barely left it, but I know she's not sleeping. She's just staring into space.'

We reach the back fence and turn around, retracing our steps back to the house. 'Okay, I'll do it. I'll try and talk to her but I can't promise anything. Please don't get your hopes up.'

Tamsin grabs me, squeezing me so tightly I gasp. 'Thank you so much, Simone. Thank you.'

Charlotte's room is dark and stuffy. The curtains are drawn and she sits cross-legged on her bed, wearing a long-sleeved dressing gown and some loose pyjamas. Her hair is pulled up in a messy ponytail and her face is make-up free, making her look even younger. She doesn't look up, or even flinch, when I come in and sit on the floor opposite her.

'Hi, Charlotte. I'm Simone. A friend of your mum's.' There is no reaction, her eyes are fixed on the carpet. I take a deep breath. 'I don't know if she's told you about me, but eighteen years ago my six-month-old baby Helena was abducted.' I pause to let this register, but her face remains blank. 'I still haven't found her. I know it's very different to what happened to you, but I just really want you to know that I'm here to listen. You can tell me anything you like, or say nothing, it's up to you. But I'm just going to sit here with you for a while. Is that okay?'

Her eyes flicker towards me, but then she goes back to staring at the floor. I am out of my comfort zone here and have no idea if I'm making things worse. 'Helena would be just a bit younger than you now,' I say, picturing Grace. I still have no idea where she is, and whether I can trust that the texts being sent from her phone are really her words. Turning my attention back to Charlotte, I notice her leg twitching, although she still doesn't look at me.

For twenty minutes I sit on the floor and talk to the silent girl. I tell her my hopes and dreams for Helena, how I imagine she has turned out. Then I talk about Matt and how we're stronger than ever, despite our tragedy, how there were many moments I wasn't sure we'd make it, but we're still here. I even tell her about Abbot, how much of a friend he's turned out to be. It is a relief to be speaking this out loud – even though I doubt Charlotte is listening – but I don't mention Grace, or the events of the last few days.

Charlotte remains in her position, never once looking at me.

'Is there anything you can say that will help the police find who did this to you? Don't you want that to happen? So that there won't be other victims?'

Again there is no response. I have given this my best shot but I am getting nowhere. I need to leave her alone now. 'I'm going now, Charlotte. Get some rest, and please remember that you will get through this. That's one thing I've learned. Humans have a remarkable ability to adapt and deal with the most horrific circumstances.' Even as I say this, I am not sure how I would do that if I ever found out Helena was dead.

Closing her door behind me, I head back downstairs to tell Tamsin that, as I had feared, I couldn't help.

Outside in the car, I call Matt to tell him I won't be home for a while.

'But it's Sunday,' he says. 'I was thinking after you visited the family we could do something together.' As busy as we are, Matt and I usually try to keep Sundays for each other, so I understand his disappointment.

Pulling my seatbelt across me, I stare at the Brays' house. 'It's been a difficult morning. Tamsin Bray wanted me to talk to Charlotte, to try to get through to her. Apparently she's not said a word to anyone since she was found. Anyway, I just need to pop into work.' I know Matt understands how important my work is to me; it is exactly the same for him.

'It's okay. We can always do something later.'

Hearing him say this reminds me how lucky I am to have him, and I am about to change my mind and tell him I'll come home when an image of Grace pops into my head. I need to see Abbot urgently and find out if his friend has managed to hack into Lucas's laptop yet. So instead I tell Matt that I'll try not to be too long. I'm doing this for Helena, I think, as guilt floods through me. For our family.

'Would you mind if I go to the pub with Spencer?' he says. 'I fancy a roast dinner.'

It makes me smile that in the midst of everything that's going on, Matt is still able to focus on the small things. I am doing the right thing keeping this from him. ''Course not, go ahead. And don't rush. I'll see you at home later.'

'I love you,' he says, before we end the call.

I stand outside the door of Abbot's building, pressing the buzzer to his flat. Seconds tick by but there is no crack or hiss from the intercom. There is nothing but silence. This is strange. I texted him after I spoke to Matt to let him know I was on my way. He didn't reply, but I know his phone is never out of his reach so he must have seen my message. I press the buzzer again and this time the door clicks open, but he doesn't speak.

'What's going on?' I say, when he answers the door. There are bags under his eyes and he rubs at them, forcing himself to concentrate.

'I'm sorry, Sim, I fell asleep. I've been up all night. Researching. Calling all the people on Hannah's list. I lost track of time and forgot to go to bed.'

I rush forward and pull him into a hug. He is doing this for me and I don't know how I will ever repay him. I bury my head in his chest and whisper a *thank you*.

'Hey,' he says, pulling back. 'It's fine. I'm only helping because there might be a huge story for me to produce at the end of it. You know, I don't want you to think I'm being selfless.'

I laugh then and gently smack his arm. 'Please tell me we've got something to work with?'

He takes my hand and leads me to the sofa. 'We haven't got into the laptop yet, but I did find out some very interesting things about Lucas.'

Finally something to go on. 'How? You mean his friends actually told you stuff about him?'

Abbot smiles. 'I just turned on the charm, you know how I do that, and they were falling over themselves to help me. Thing is, I wouldn't call some of them his friends. More like employees who only just tolerated him. By all accounts, he is not a very likeable man.'

I listen while Abbot repeats the information he has learned about Lucas Hall. According to some, he has had numerous affairs with women, and always seems to dismiss them the minute he's slept with them. I remember Grace's description of the events last Sunday night; it now seems more likely she was telling the truth.

'But nobody knows where he is,' Abbot continues. 'That's our biggest problem. I've been racking my brain but can't think how we'll find him. We really need to get into his computer.'

'Maybe it's time to confront Ginny.' I say. 'We've been focusing so much on Lucas that we're forgetting the one person who, if Grace is telling the truth, is most likely responsible for abducting my baby.'

Abbot leans forward and rests his head in his hands. 'You're right. Plus, there's something else we've been forgetting. Lucas was her brother's best friend, so there's a possibility she knows where he is. Add that together with the missing baby medical records and the C-section mistake she made with that woman she was looking after … we need to catch her out. Get the truth out of her.'

'I've been thinking a lot about it and I can't see how she would know what he's like, otherwise she would never have left him alone with her daughter, would she? And despite what she may have done, she does seem to be a good mother to Grace.' I hate to admit this, but it's undeniable. Grace said nothing that would make me question Ginny's parenting.

Abbot considers this. 'Perhaps. But I think we just have to doubt everyone. Assume everyone is lying, at least until we have evidence to suggest otherwise.'

'And that includes Grace,' I say, more to myself than to Abbot.

'Sorry, but yes. Especially Grace. We still don't know where she is, but neither her friend nor her supposed mother is worried. Something's not right with that, Sim. Especially given how studious she is. I mean, who's this friend she's supposed to have gone to stay with, anyway?'

Abbot doesn't need to tell me this; it's all I have thought of since Grace failed to turn up at the house on Tuesday. 'But let's wait to confront Ginny. We need to see if we can get something to take to her first, other than just an accusation.'

I have to agree here, as this is the only thing stopping me hammering down her door. 'Okay, well, you need to get some sleep,' I tell him. 'There's not much we can do until we get into the laptop or hear from Nick Gibbs. We've hit a dead end for now.'

Abbot yawns, as if the mention of sleep has reminded him he needs some more. 'I'll just have a quick rest. No more than a couple of hours. But call me if you need anything.'

What I need right now is to be at home with Matt, cuddled on the sofa with a glass of wine and a blank mind. I say this out loud and Abbot's mouth twists.

'Go and be with your husband,' he says.

When I pull up to the house my phone beeps with a text. Matt is still at the pub, but says he'll leave if I'm back already. I text back:

Stay, have fun x.

I am already planning to work on the Charlotte Bray story when I get inside. I doubt we will get an interview out of Charlotte herself, but Tamsin and Elliott might be willing to talk to us again. Even so, I need to give them at least a few days alone with their daughter, before the media intrusion resumes.

Stepping out of the car, I am so consumed with my thoughts that I don't immediately notice someone close beside me. Too close. It is only when a hand grabs my arm, forcing me around that I take in what's happening. I stare at the face of a stranger, at the grey jacket, and then it all becomes clear.

It is the man who was in Lucas Hall's flat.

EIGHTEEN

I open my mouth – but to do what? Shout? Scream? It is not yet dark and there are cars driving past and people walking the pavements, so would he risk hurting me out here? Perhaps he plans to force me to go somewhere more secluded with him. I try to control my breathing, keep quiet and wait, but I can't remember what I'm supposed to do. Kick him somewhere it will hurt is the only action that comes to mind. I am debating how best to do this when he takes me by surprise.

'I'm sorry. I didn't mean to scare you. I'm … can we talk? Please? It's important.' He holds up his hands, palms facing me, and takes a step back. His expression is more anxious than menacing, but that does little to calm me.

There is no point pretending he didn't find Grace and me searching Lucas's apartment. I need to find out what he wants. And quickly. 'Okay. Talk.' I force my words to be firm, to disguise the fact that my whole body is shaking.

'I know you've seen me before. But my name's Chris Harding, and I've been looking for Lucas Hall.' He pauses. 'Apparently you have too.' It is only now I notice his slight Irish accent.

Again, I am taken by surprise. 'But … who are you? What were you doing in his flat?'

'Look, I don't really want to talk out here in the middle of the street.' His eyes flick towards the house. So I was right about him being outside the other night. It was a reconnaissance before he made his move.

I shake my head. 'Not in there. But we can sit in my car.' I don't have time to assess how reckless this decision may be, but at least we will still be in view of passers-by.

Once we're in the car and the doors are shut, he turns to me and I study his face. He can't be older than twenty-five and the patchy stubble and dark bags under his eyes hide a pleasant-looking face. Frown lines crease his forehead, showing me he is troubled.

'What were you doing in his flat?' I repeat, more confident now. 'How do you know him?'

He exhales a deep breath and stares through the windscreen. 'I don't know him. I've never met him. All I know is that Lucas Hall was the last person to see my sister. Before she disappeared.'

He turns to me, shaking his head. 'They were seeing each other, or at least Mel thought they were. She told me she had no idea he was married at first, and by the time she did, she had already fallen for him.'

'Wait,' I say, 'slow down. Start from the beginning.' If I'm to understand this fully, he needs to make more sense.

He leans forward, but doesn't look at me as he speaks. 'About six months ago my sister Mel met Lucas in a bar. She was on a hen night for one of her friends, just having fun. She told me she wasn't looking to meet someone. So when Lucas started talking to her she really couldn't be bothered with him. She gave him the brush off. Told him she wasn't interested. But somehow he got her number and kept calling her, trying to convince her to meet up with him.' He sighs and turns to face me. 'I guess his persistence paid off because a few weeks later she had given in and agreed to meet him. She told me he'd grown on her and she thought she really liked him.'

The windows in the car are steaming up, so I turn on the engine and blast the radiator. Chris continues with his story.

'Anyway, they met up a few times and all I know is I got a text from her on the day she disappeared, saying she was meeting up with him that evening.' He pulls out his phone and scrolls through his messages, holding it out to me when he finds his sister's text.

I read her words.

Hey bro, hope you're ok?
Can't meet up tonight as seeing L. Sorry, but I really like him! xx

Handing back the phone, I ask him how he knows for sure she was talking about Lucas. 'The *L* could be anyone, couldn't it?'

He shakes his head. 'She'd told me his name before. Lucas Hall. Mel and I are close, we tell each other stuff. She knows all the names of the girls I've dated, and I know what's going on in her life too. At least I did.'

Forgetting I am somehow part of this, my natural instinct to get to the heart of a story kicks in. 'What's your sister's full name?'

'Melanie Harding. Mel. She's twenty-eight and is a legal secretary. She works hard, she has everything going for her, I know she wouldn't just run away and leave it all behind. She wouldn't do that to our parents. I know people always say that when they lose someone, but I know it in here.' He thumps his chest.

I try to recall if this story has come through to us on the news wire, but her name is unfamiliar. 'Have you been to the police? Reported her missing?'

He nods. 'My parents did. Back in November when she first went missing. But the police spoke to Lucas and he claimed he'd never met my sister. They believed his lies, and we couldn't prove otherwise.' Anger crosses his face now and his hand clenches into a fist. 'We even searched her flat for anything that would link them together, but there was nothing. He was obviously making her keep it a secret because of his wife.'

It is easy to jump to conclusions. Desperation forces us to try and make sense of things, to get answers, no matter how starved of evidence we are. I have done exactly this with Grace. I need to be objective. I believe Chris's story but, just like me, he needs to keep an open mind.

'So how did you know about that flat?' I ask.

'I … I started following him.'

My eyes must widen because he quickly defends himself. 'Well, if the police weren't going to investigate him then I had to do it myself.' I cannot judge him for this; it is exactly what Abbot and I have been doing. 'I found out everything I could about him,' he continues, 'and went to confront him at that flat. I thought he lived there, but now I know different. It's not his home, just some place he takes women to so his wife doesn't know. It makes me sick to think of him bringing Mel there.'

I picture Hannah, how distressed she was when we sat in her living room. She had mentioned him leaving her before, but I wonder if she knows the extent of her husband's infidelity.

'That's when I saw you,' Chris says. 'And that girl. I heard everything. So now I need you to tell me what the hell's going on.'

Now that it is my turn to talk, I have no idea where to start. I don't want to tell him about Grace's story that she is my daughter, but I struggle to remember what we talked about in Lucas's flat, so there is a good chance he already knows. But I will take my chances and explain myself if he confronts me about it. So I only tell him that Grace is the daughter of a friend.

He silently listens and when I've finished he shakes his head, his mouth hanging open. 'I don't get it. I mean, I heard what you said in his flat, but it made no sense to me. Actually, it still doesn't. But what the hell's happened to him then?' This is good, he is not questioning how I know Grace.

I shake my head. 'I don't believe Lucas is dead. There was nothing to suggest it. It's possible she only thought she'd killed him. There's every chance he got up and walked away after she'd run off.' Or she was lying to me about everything.

Chris frowns. 'But why the disappearing act? What could he hope to gain from that? Unless he wanted to frame Grace? Teach her a lesson?'

Until now I hadn't considered this possibility. 'That seems extreme, doesn't it? And how could he frame her if there was no body?' And then something occurs to me. 'Do you think there's any chance he's gone off with your sister somewhere? I don't know, to start a new life maybe?'

'No chance.' He vigorously shakes his head. 'I told you, Mel just wouldn't do that.'

I don't want to tell him that he can't know for sure. I have seen it a thousand times: family members acting out of the ordinary, surprising their loved ones with what they are capable of. Instead, I ask him if he believes without a doubt that Lucas is responsible for his sister's disappearance. 'Perhaps he only lied to the police because he didn't want his wife to find out he'd been unfaithful?'

Chris considers my words. 'I just don't know. He could be innocent in this, but I know she was meeting him that night. He must have been the last person to see her so I desperately need to talk to him. That's all I've got to go on. But from what you've told me, he doesn't sound like a trustworthy man.'

I tell Chris about Abbot and how he's been helping me, and he frowns. 'But, you're married? Or you at least live with someone. I've seen him at your house.'

I explain that I didn't want to get Matt involved because of his job, and Chris seems to accept my reason.

'Okay, well, I'll be careful, but I think we should work together on this,' he says, turning away from me to stare through the windscreen.

He has a point. The more eyes that are out looking for Lucas, the better. 'Fine,' I say. 'Give me your number and I'll call you later.'

He tells me his number and I store it in my phone, then ask him what he's going to do now.

'Think I'll go back to his flat in Embankment. I need to ask the neighbours if they've seen him. I tried the other day but most people were out. As it's Sunday today, though, I'm hoping I'll get more responses.'

His plan sounds like a good idea, and I wonder why I didn't think of it myself.

Watching him walk off, I tell myself I shouldn't be so quick to trust him. I only have his word for it that he is who he says he is, and that his sister is missing. For all I know he could be in on this with Lucas Hall, checking up on me, sussing out how much I know. I will ask Abbot if he can find a way to check the man out.

Once he has disappeared around the corner, I head into the house and stand in the hall, leaning back against the wall, too exhausted by what I've just heard to move. If Chris Harding's story is true, it is just one more reason to mistrust Lucas. One more reason to believe Grace.

A shadow appears at the front door and I am convinced it is Chris Harding, until a key turns in the lock and Matt steps inside. 'You scared the hell out of me,' I say, walking over to him.

'Sorry.' He smiles. 'But who else do you think would have a key?' He closes the door and throws his keys on the telephone table. While he takes off his coat I double lock the door.

'I was just a bit distracted thinking about work, and wasn't expecting you back so soon,' I say, hoping I sound convincing, and that he won't notice I've latched the front door when it's not bed time.

Matt appears to be oblivious and wraps his arms around me. 'We need a break, don't we? When was the last time we gave ourselves a holiday? Florida, about five years ago, I reckon. What do you think? Shall we get away somewhere? I know this business with Grace has been hard, and it's brought up fresh feelings about Helena, so I really think we need to be kind to ourselves. Doctor's orders.'

He is right. But there is no way I can go anywhere now, not when I am on the edge of discovering what happened to our daughter. Especially now I've just met Chris Harding. But as I look at the hope in Matt's eyes, and witness his desperation to escape, I know I can't let him down. 'How about in a couple of months?' I say. 'Work's just so crazy at the moment and there are some things I can't leave dangling.'

I wait for Matt to present a counter argument but he surprises me. 'It's one of the things I love about you,' he says. 'Your dedication to work. To me. To everything you do. A couple of months will be fine, but we need to stick to it. Come on, let's have a cup of tea. I'll tell you what Spencer's been up to.'

And as I follow Matt into the kitchen, I know how lucky I am, despite everything that was taken from us. The guilt that has been my constant companion since this started almost forces me to tell him everything, until I remember what's at stake, and that right now I have no firm evidence to show him.

Later that evening, when Matt is watching a science fiction film I have no interest in, I sit on the bed and call Abbot. There is no answer and I wonder if he's still sleeping. He said he only needed a couple of hours and then he was going to chase up the progress with Lucas's laptop, but tiredness must have overcome him.

Using my mobile, I search the Internet for Chris and Mel Harding, but nothing turns up except Facebook pages for several people with those names.

I'm still holding my phone, contemplating what to try next, when it rings with an unknown number. I usually ignore unidentified callers, but my hand presses the connect call button with no hesitation. It could be Grace.

'Hi, Hayley?' The voice is male, one I don't recognise.

I am about to tell the person they've got the wrong number, when I remember that I have been calling myself by this name. I spurt out a quick greeting.

'It's Nick Gibbs. We met the other day?'

I try to keep the surprise from my voice. 'Oh, hi. Thanks for calling. Have you heard from Lucas?'

'Oh, no, sorry. It's not that.' In the background I hear children's voices. 'Hang on a sec.' The sounds become muffled as Nick sees to his family, and I feel a pang of envy. Moments later he is back, and I focus on what he has to say. 'I got worried after you left, wondering where Lucas could be. I know Hannah's a very private person so it must have taken a lot for her to ask for your help. Anyway, I did some digging around and I have to be honest, I'm a bit freaked out by what I've found out.'

I suck in my breath and ask him what he means.

'Actually, do you mind meeting me tomorrow evening? It will be easier to tell you in person. The kids are here, you know.'

'Okay. Where and when?'

There's a pub near here and it should be fairly quiet on a Monday evening. It's called the White Cross and is practically on the river. Lovely place.'

'Okay,' I say, my mind a whir of activity. Has he found out that Lucas is dead? Surely he would have gone to the police if that were the case? In the background I hear his wife calling so I quickly thank him and end the call.

Checking that Matt is engrossed in his film downstairs, I close the bedroom door and try calling Abbot once more. There is still no answer so I leave a message asking him to call me as soon as he can, and telling him that I need him to check something for me.

I go to bed feeling uneasy and even when Matt joins me, his solid body against mine offers little comfort. So much has happened since Grace came into my life, and now Chris Harding's story adds to my confusion. Can I trust him? This and so many other questions spin around my head.

Where are you, Grace? Who are you?

NINETEEN

It is nearly midday before Abbot returns my call. He is still on leave so I sit at my desk, his empty chair next to me, and don't mention I've been worried about him. 'I've been following Ginny,' he explains. 'Trying to get a sense of her. Plus, I wondered if Grace might turn up there. It just seemed weird that Ginny wasn't worried she'd been missing lectures to go and visit a friend.'

My pulse races. 'And? Anything?' Before he has a chance to answer I hear the words I want to hear. *Grace is there, at Ginny's house. Acting as if nothing's happened.*

'Well,' Abbot says. 'The woman does work hard, I'll give her that. She left home dressed in a carer's uniform and spent the day visiting different houses. I can only assume she was working. Other than that, she didn't go anywhere, and had no visitors.'

My heart sinks, all my hopes evaporating with Abbot's words.

'But one thing's for sure,' he continues, 'she doesn't seem worried about her daughter.' In the absence of a reply from me Abbot asks if I'm okay.

But I am far from okay. Yesterday, after speaking to Chris Harding, I was almost convinced of Grace's story. But now what Abbot has said once again throws her words into question. But if Grace is lying then how can the rabbit be explained? 'Yeah, I'm fine,' I tell him. 'Just taking it all in.'

'I'm going there again today. To Ginny's. I may as well use this time off work to do some good.' He chuckles, but I don't reciprocate. It is hard to find lightness in any of this.

When he asks how things have been going with me, I tell Abbot about Nick's call and he can hardly contain his excitement. 'That's great! This is the closest we've come to getting anywhere, isn't it? What do you think he's going to tell you?'

I tell Abbot I have no idea, but it doesn't sound good. Although I know it's about Lucas, it can't be that he knows his whereabouts, otherwise he would have said so on the phone. It must be serious for him to want to meet up, away from his house.

'There's something else,' I say, and then I tell him about my encounter with Chris Harding yesterday.

'Shit. No wonder you were trying to call me so much. Sorry. Anyway, I haven't heard anything about his sister but I'll check it out, see what I can find out. We both know so many people go missing every day that it's hard to give media attention to them all.'

Abbot and I say goodbye and arrange to meet at his flat after I've seen Nick. For the rest of the afternoon, I bury myself in work, keeping an eye on the clock, anxiously waiting for six p.m.

The White Cross pub is lovely, looking as if it is sitting right in the River Thames, and I can immediately tell it is a family pub, the kind of place it feels safe and right to bring children. There aren't any out tonight, of course, but I can imagine people like to spend lazy summer Sunday afternoons here.

As I walk up the steps to the entrance, my phone beeps with a text message. It is Nick, letting me know he'll be ten minutes late. He writes *Sorry* in capital letters at the end of the text, and I am surprised he feels it necessary to emphasise the word.

Inside, I order a Coke without ice and take it to a round table by a large bay window. There are only a few people in here tonight, and nobody pays me any attention.

I barely touch my drink while I wait for Nick. Instead, I stare out of the window and go over everything Grace told me the afternoon we first met. The blue rabbit is still in my handbag – I have not had the heart to remove it – and I reach inside now and feel the soft velvety fabric. It makes me feel closer to Helena. This is the strongest piece of evidence to suggest that Grace is Helena, or at least knows something about her abduction, and when I think of it, it's hard to see how it can't be Helena's. There may have been thousands manufactured, but details of the toy were never made public, so how can Grace having it be explained any other way?

Nearly twenty minutes pass before Nick walks in, making his way straight to my table. 'I'm so sorry,' he says. 'The kids were fighting and I had to sort it out before I left. I didn't want to leave Sienna to deal with it on her own. She's not feeling well today.'

I wave away his apology. 'I hope it's nothing serious?'

'No, just a cold-type thing – she'll be okay. She just needs to rest. Can I get you another drink?'

I hold up my glass of Coke and tell him I'm fine, watching as he strides to the bar and leans on it while he waits for the barman to notice him.

'I hope you didn't mind me asking to meet here?' Nick says, when he comes back. His glass is filled with what looks like fizzy water and a lemon slice. 'I just don't want Sienna worrying.'

'It's fine,' I say. I don't tell him that it makes a nice change from sitting in people's living rooms. 'What you've found out about Lucas doesn't sound good. Can you tell me what it is now?'

Nick takes a sip of his drink and leans forward, checking around us before he speaks. 'Like I said, I got worried after your visit. The thing is, I don't really know Lucas all that well. I mean, we're definitely acquaintances, but I don't know all the ins and outs of his life. So it got me wondering. Plus, I really like Hannah, she's a good woman.'

I almost beg him to hurry up, to get to the point because the anticipation is almost too much to bear. Will what I'm about to hear shed any light on Grace's story? Will it help me find her? I need him to spit it out.

'Anyway, I got some friends to do some snooping for me, but I wasn't expecting to find out what I did.' He shakes his head and stares into his glass, avoiding my gaze.

I want to ask him who his friends are and how they've managed to find anything out, but there isn't time for that. Plus, I hardly know him and he's already going out of his way to help me so I don't want to push it. 'What did you find out?' I say.

Finally he meets my stare. 'It's probably better if I show you. Stay here, I'll be back in a sec.'

Leaving his drink on the table, Nick gets up and heads towards the door, disappearing through it and out of my sight. Bewildered, I stay where I am, staring at the pub entrance. The only conclusion I can reach is that he has gone to get something from his car.

As it turns out, I am half-right. When Nick reappears he hovers by the door, holding it open for someone. At first I assume he is letting in another customer, but when a young, dark-haired woman steps in, she looks over at me and follows Nick to our table.

Now that she is close-up I notice how much make-up she has trowelled onto her face.

Nick offers her his seat and takes the one nearest to me. 'Hayley, this is Gabby. I think you need to hear what she has to say.' He turns to the girl. 'Gin and tonic, was it?'

She looks up at him and smiles, pulling off her thick Puffa coat. From her bag she fishes out an e-cigarette, inhaling on it as she watches me.

'So you know Lucas Hall?' I ask, trying not to stare at her eyelashes, which are far too long and thick to be real.

She nods. 'But do you mind if we wait for Nick to come back?' She glances at the bar, checking on his progress.

'That's fine,' I say, hiding my annoyance. 'Gabby, is it? That's pretty.'

She eyes me suspiciously. 'Thanks. It's actually Gabrielle, but I don't think it suits me.'

'No, I like it. But Gabby's nice too.' And now it is my turn to check on Nick; this small talk is becoming difficult. I turn around and see him still at the bar, handing money to the barman.

Gabby finishes pulling on her e-cigarette and fishes her mobile from her pocket, seeming to find something more interesting to do on it than speaking to me. With her head down, she doesn't notice me watching her, can't know that I'm making assumptions about her.

I decide she can't be older than twenty-two and could be a secretary or hairdresser. She obviously takes pride in her appearance, as her long, dark hair extensions are glossy and neat. She has a boyfriend, I decide, and he is someone who looks out for her financially and emotionally. Of course, I could have all this completely wrong, but I like to think I've got at least something right about her.

I'm in the middle of deciding what her parents are like when Nick comes back with her gin and tonic. He places it in front of her and she thanks him without looking up from her phone.

'Please will you tell me what's going on?' I stare at both of them, my question needing to be answered by someone. Anyone.

Nick nudges Gabby and she slips her phone back in her bag but still doesn't speak.

'Gabby knows Lucas,' he says, turning back to me. 'And I think you need to hear this.' Facing Gabby once more, he pats her arm. 'It's okay, you can speak freely. There's nothing to worry about.'

'Except judgement,' she says, looking straight at me. 'You tell her, I can't do it.'

Nick takes a deep breath. 'I know this will be hard for you to hear because you and Lucas go way back, but I'm begging you to keep an open mind. And I need you to help me decide what we should tell Hannah.'

I nod. 'Of course. You have to remember that I haven't seen Lucas for years. Haven't spoken to him either, we totally lost touch. And I want to help Hannah as much as you do.' I hope I'm not overdoing this; I don't want Nick to get suspicious of me.

'Okay,' Nick says. 'Well, Gabby was attacked by Lucas. Recently.'

Confused, I glance at her face and her arms. There is no sign of any bruising. 'What do you mean "attacked"? What happened?' But the minute my question is out there I already know the answer.

Nick lowers his voice. 'He forced her to … to have sex with him. That's what I mean.'

I cannot keep a gasp from escaping and Gabby finally looks up. This time her eyes are glassy. Instinctively I reach for her arm, but she pulls away. 'That's awful … I'm so sorry. So the police are looking for him?'

Gabby rolls her eyes. 'The police? Do you think I could go to them? Who would believe me? I'm just some stripper who was asking for it, aren't I?'

I am surprised by her revelation, but it doesn't change anything. When I don't react, she continues. 'I mean, anyone who

works in the sex industry is just asking to be raped, aren't they?'
She fires her words at me, making me feel as if I am the one who
has caused her harm.

Although I want to tell her to stop being defensive, I understand it. I know from stories I've covered before that she will be
used to negative reactions from the people she tells about her
work. Ignoring her dig, I ask her what happened.

Her anger dissipates as she begins to tell her story. 'He used to
come into the club a lot, usually Saturday nights, but he'd always
be alone and would keep himself to himself. He never asked for
private dances or tried to grab any of the girls. In fact we used to
call him The Gentleman. Because that's what it seemed he was,
despite being a regular in a strip club.' She pauses and reaches for
her drink, taking a long sip and keeping hold of the glass. 'He
was good-looking, too. For an older guy.'

From the corner of my eye I see Nick's eyes narrow. He and
Lucas seem to be a similar age.

'But I wasn't interested in him, if that's what you think,' Gabby continues. 'I have a boyfriend.'

I am pleased to hear this; to know there is someone looking
out for the young girl.

'I didn't lead him on in any way, I swear I never even spoke to him
till that night. Two weeks ago. I was leaving for home and he was
sitting in his car outside the club. It was a nice car. A black BMW I
think. I was impressed, I can't lie. But that didn't give him the right–'

''Course not. No man ever has a right to do what he did to
you.' I feel for this girl. She could be Helena. Or Grace.

'He offered me a lift home and I stupidly let him in to my
flat. He seemed kind of fun, and I'd had a huge row with my
boyfriend. Just felt like some company.'

'So he came to your flat?' I ask. 'He didn't take you anywhere?'
I don't know why it seems important I know this.

Gabby nods. 'We just spent the night drinking, I can't even tell you how many shots I had. But … ' She trails off, and I'm sure we all know what she is thinking.

'I know this is hard for you, just take your time.' I pat her arm, and this time she doesn't move it away.

'That's just it,' she says. 'I don't remember anything else. One minute we were drinking, the next I woke up alone.' She pours some more gin down her throat and waits for me to question her.

'But … I don't understand. When did he … attack you?'

Gabby puts down her glass and stares at her nails. 'That night. But I was so drunk I can't remember him actually doing it.'

I lean forward. 'Forgive me for saying this but I have to ask – how do you know for sure that … he did anything?'

Gabby's mouth twists. 'Are you a virgin, Hayley?'

'What? No.'

'Then you know what it feels like after you've had sex. You can just tell, can't you?'

'I don't know. I've never thought about it. Perhaps.'

'Well, believe me, *I* know. And there is no doubt in my mind that I had sex that night. Without my consent. As well as the soreness in my body, I woke up fully dressed, but my underwear was on inside out. How do you explain that?'

I think about this for a moment but she's right: there doesn't seem any rational explanation for it. 'So did you try to contact him after?' I ask.

Gabby tuts. 'How could I? I didn't even have his number. But there he was, the next Saturday, at the club as if nothing had happened. I jumped off the stage and confronted him. Told him I was going to the police, even though I knew I wouldn't. I'm not stupid, I know it would just be his word against mine.'

'And what did he do?'

'He just ignored me and walked out. But I could see fear in his eyes. I'm telling you, he was worried.'

Beside me, Nick shakes his head. He will already have heard all the details. 'I think Lucas has gone on the run. He's a successful business owner and will lose everything if this gets out. Even if he won in court, he would forever be tainted by the scandal.'

Gabby nods. 'Nick told me Lucas has disappeared. My threat has obviously scared him off.'

I look from Gabby to Nick and think about all I've heard tonight. I have to keep an open mind, but Nick's suggestion does make sense. I will see what Abbot thinks later.

'I'm sorry for what he did to you, Gabby, please let me know if I can do anything at all.'

She looks directly at me and smiles for the first time this evening. 'Just find him.'

'We'll try,' Nick says.

We still have our drinks to finish and I stay silent and listen to Gabby telling Nick about her younger brother's obsession with computer games. 'He'd love to meet you,' she says. 'Your games are his favourite.'

Nick tells her he's flattered and that he will definitely arrange something.

Sipping the last of her gin and tonic, Gabby stands up and announces she has to go to work. And when we say our goodbyes and she trots off, I admire her bravery in returning to work after what Lucas did to her.

'I'd better get back to Sienna,' Nick says. 'Make sure she's okay. But I really will try to help find Lucas. He needs to be held accountable for what he's done.'

'How did you find Gabby?' I ask, wondering why it is only now occurring to me to question him.

'It was a bit of luck really. I found out Lucas is a regular at The Paradise Club and went down there Sunday afternoon to see if anyone had seen him. Gabby was there helping with a stock check because they were short-staffed and she told me she knew him. And then she burst into tears and told me what had happened.'

'It won't be as easy to find him, though, will it?' I ask, hoping he will correct me.

Nick shakes his head. 'Not if he doesn't want to be found.'

We walk outside and I am shocked by how cold it has become since we've been sitting in the pub.

'Thanks for this,' I say. I want to ask him about Ginny but it would look suspicious. I am supposed to be a friend of Lucas's from university called Hayley, and even though there is a slim chance I could have met Ginny in the past, I can't risk Nick wondering about me.

'No problem. Look, I really don't think we should mention this to Hannah yet, not until I've done some more digging. I don't want to worry her yet, she's got enough to deal with. Is that okay with you?' he says.

I tell him I agree, that it would do more harm than good for her to know before we even find him.

Nick promises to be in touch, and as he walks away, I am grateful for his help, but feel as though we are no closer to the truth.

Back in my car, I decide to text Abbot to tell him I'll call him later instead of coming over. I have already spent enough time away from Matt, and his company is all I want right now. Even though I can't tell my husband any of this, his comforting arms around me will be enough.

But as I pull my phone from my bag, it beeps with a text message from Abbot.

Come over right now. Found something on laptop.

TWENTY

Leanne worked in Harry's bar and was older than us. I couldn't guess at her age then, and still can't now, but she was too old to be a student, yet young enough to get away with wearing the short skirts (belts, he would call them, mockingly) and clingy low cut tops she liked to parade around in at work.

One evening I went to the bar early. I wasn't due to meet him for a couple of hours, but I'd finished an exam and was sure I'd aced it, so I wanted to celebrate.

I ordered a vodka and tonic, staring at Leanne's cleavage as she leaned over the bar, forcing herself to be polite. I could tell she hated her job, detested serving students all evening, and that she dreamed of bigger things. I don't know how I knew this – perhaps it was just instinct, or maybe her disdain was etched on her face.

Normally she didn't say much more than the bare minimum needed to work out what I wanted, but tonight was different. 'Ooh, you're on the hard stuff tonight, then?' she said, smirking at me, but making no move to remove her breasts from my view.

I was sure she was mocking me, but perhaps it was an ineffectual attempt at flirting. Either way, I suddenly wanted to smack that condescending smile from her face. Who was she to look down on me? But I snapped this thought away and tried to focus on my impending drink, waiting for him to appear.

With her back to me, Leanne prepared my drink. I watched her recklessly flinging ice into the glass, and when she turned, I imagined ripping her tight skirt from her. I hadn't seen a naked body since Amanda, and felt sure that this time I would enjoy it. It had been so long, I was bound to, wasn't I?

Two hours later I was still sitting at the bar, watching Leanne as she served a flock of rowdy students. She had long ago given up talking to me, and was too busy to even glance in my direction, but I was glad he still hadn't shown up. Normally I would have stewed about his absence, and wondered what it meant, but Leanne distracted me from these thoughts.

'What time do you finish?' I asked, when she stopped to breathe.

I waited for sarcasm, or a straight rejection, but her face seemed to soften. 'About half an hour, why?'

I shrugged, trying to appear nonchalant. 'Do you live near here?'

'Yeah.' Her eyes narrowed, full of mistrust. 'Five minutes away. Why? What's with all the questions?'

'Just being friendly,' I said. 'You look like you could do with a break. You've been working hard all night. I could walk you home.' A shrug again.

She gave me a sideways look then, sizing me up, preparing her rejection. But then she surprised me. 'Sure. Why not? Nothing better to do.' She gave a brief chuckle, but we both knew she was telling the truth.

Her flat was a studio, with barely enough room for the bed. But I thought nothing of it then. I wasn't living in much better accommodation myself, so who was I to judge?

'Have a seat,' she said, pointing to the bed. And that broke the ice because we both started laughing. She had finally warmed towards me.

There were paintings covering the walls, mostly of faces and figures. I knew little about art but thought they were Expressionist, with their blurred, fluid lines. I could picture one of them hanging in my own bedroom so I asked her who the artist was.

'That would be me,' she said. There was no gloating or arrogance in her words, just a tinge of sadness. But her melancholy was no surprise – she was a talented artist being forced to work a low-paid job instead of making money from her passion.

'They're good,' I said. 'Bloody great in fact.'

She didn't smile or thank me, but poured us something from a clear bottle, without explaining what it was. I couldn't even identify it by the taste but I was already drunk, and the sharp sting of this liquid went straight to my head. I must have winced, because she laughed at me and downed her own drink without flinching.

We finished the bottle and started another one, and after a couple more drinks she let me kiss her. I could tell I was making all the effort, but she didn't push me away. Her unenthusiastic response turned me off, as well as the pink lipstick smeared across her lips which I could feel transferring to my own mouth. I wasn't hard beneath my jeans – I felt nothing.

I stopped kissing her and reached between her legs, hoping that would excite me.

'I think that's enough now,' she said, slapping my hand away. 'I'm really tired after my shift. Another time, though?'

She attempted to stand up but I pulled her back.

'Hey, get off me!' she said, trying to wriggle out of my grip. But her attempts were useless; she was inebriated from the nasty drink she'd given us.

I felt myself harden and blood rushed through me. I had never felt this before. All I knew was that I couldn't stop what I was doing.

It was frustrating that she squirmed so much, but I pinned down her arms and kept her still with the weight of my body. But then she screamed: a piercing sound I couldn't bear. So I covered her mouth, forced myself into her, and let myself get lost. And it was like nothing I'd ever felt before.

She was semi-unconscious by the time I'd finished, and I left her lying there and closed the door on her grotty flat.

Only on the walk home did the panic set in. What had I done? It was one thing to have those thoughts in my head, but now I had crossed a line. She would report me, that was inevitable, and then what? Prison? My life would be over.

There was only one person I could turn to.

TWENTY-ONE

As soon as he opens the door, Abbot pulls me into the flat and ushers me to the sofa. 'You're not going to believe this,' he says. The excitement in his voice is contagious, and I immediately feel my spirits lift.

On the coffee table sits Lucas Hall's laptop, open and displaying his Internet browser. 'What is it?' I say. 'What have you found?'

Abbot's smile spreads even further across his face, but he stays standing. 'Something that will help us find Lucas.'

I lean forward to peer at the screen, but it is only the Google homepage.

'No, that's not it, let me show you.' Abbot joins me on the sofa and places the laptop on his knees before tapping away. 'There's nothing dodgy like porn or anything, but I checked through all his emails and this thread disturbed me. Be prepared for a shock.'

I stare at the email message but it takes me a moment to digest the name I am looking at.

Charlotte Bray.

Turning to Abbot, my mouth hangs open. 'Charlotte Bray? *Our* Charlotte Bray?'

'Yes. You need to read it.'

Looking at the screen again I begin to read the first email. It's dated 15th December at 11:13 a.m.

Hi Charlotte,
I can't stop thinking about you. Can we meet up? Anywhere you like. Sorry I can't text, email is safer. You know why.
Love, L

I turn back to Abbot, my brain trying to unscramble all the thoughts flooding through it. But I get no further than Charlotte Bray and Lucas Hall – they know each other. 'What the hell? How is this possible?'

Abbot, still excited, says, 'That's the first email, but from what he's said it's possible Charlotte texted him first. I don't know how or where they met. Keep reading.'

Charlotte's email shows that she replied within ten minutes.

Hey! It's so good to hear from you, I wasn't sure you liked me. I really want to see you. Anytime, anywhere, let me know.
PS emailing is fine, love Char xxxx

There are only two more emails: Lucas asking if she can meet him the next evening at the entrance to Hyde Park station at eight p.m., and a reply from Charlotte saying she'll be there.

'When did Charlotte go missing?' Abbot asks, as soon as I've finished reading and stare at him open-mouthed.

'4th January,' I say, the date carved into my brain. So judging by the emails she first met Lucas about two and a half weeks before that. But what does it mean? Did Lucas have something to do with her disappearance? But she's safely back at home now with her parents, and Lucas is still missing, so it makes no sense. I know coincidences happen every minute of the day, but it seems unfathomable that Helena is somehow linked to Charlotte Bray. The Brays were a story I was working on, not meant to be part of Grace's life. I manage to communicate this to Abbot, even though my mind is now a mess.

'I know, it's crazy,' Abbot says, 'but at least now we have some-one we can question about Lucas, don't we?'

I think of Gabby, and her story, and wonder if it's possible that Lucas has done the same thing to Charlotte. The journalist in me knows I shouldn't jump to conclusions, but I recall the last time I visited the Brays, and my futile attempt to get Charlotte to talk; her catatonic state would be consistent with such an attack. It would make sense that Lucas had something to do with this so it's worth trying to speak to her again. 'Okay, I'll call Tamsin and tell her I'd like to try talking to Charlotte again. But I've got to be careful. Charlotte wouldn't speak a word to me yesterday, so what hope do I have now? Especially if I bring up Lucas. We don't know what happened between them, and if he's raped her she won't want to even hear his name.' And then I remember that in all the excitement of the laptop, I haven't yet filled Abbot in on my meeting with Nick. I tell him what happened now, and what I learnt from Gabby, and he shakes his head.

'All the more reason we need to speak to Charlotte,' he says. 'If there's a chance Lucas has hurt her too then we need to help her.'

Without hesitation I call Tamsin Bray. She sounds pleased to hear from me but tells me Charlotte still hasn't spoken to them properly. Although she mumbles the odd word, she won't speak about where she's been all these weeks.

I tell Tamsin I've had some thoughts about how I might get through to her – the whole time swallowing my guilt like a pill – and ask if I can see her tomorrow morning. I have already decided to take the day off work for the first time since I joined News 24.

'Please do come, Simone, we really appreciate all you're doing for us,' Tamsin says.

When I've ended the call, Abbot agrees that it's a good idea I take the day off tomorrow. 'This is enough for you to deal with,' he says. 'But remember I'm here if you need me. I kind of feel like we're in this together. Even though ... well, I know it's Matt who should be helping you.'

'I know. I feel awful every time I think of how I'm excluding him, but it's too late. I've been keeping it from him for days, so how can I involve him now?' I wait for an answer and when it doesn't come, say, 'No, it's best if he's just focusing on his work.' *And I can sort this out for both of us.*

'Well, at least go and be with him now,' Abbot says. 'There's nothing more you can do tonight.'

I stand up, but then remember Abbot was also looking into Chris Harding's sister. 'Did you find anything out about Mel Harding?' I ask.

Abbot says he checked with a friend of his who works for the police, and apparently the Hardings did file a missing persons report, but their initial investigations came to nothing. 'The police seem to think she might have deliberately left her life behind.'

Remembering Chris's anxiety, and his determination to track down Lucas, I doubt this is true. It is no wonder he has taken matters into his own hands. 'So do you think we should help him? I mean, he could be tied up in this just as the Brays are.'

Abbot nods. 'It looks that way. This Lucas, whoever he is, clearly has a history of ... this kind of thing.' I am surprised Abbot doesn't say the word; both of us are used to it from our work.

'I'll keep him updated,' I say. 'And maybe he'll find Lucas before we do.'

At the door, I ask Abbot what he will do now.

'I think it's time I pay Ginny a proper visit. I've been thinking about this. Now that Hannah has basically given us an excuse to approach Lucas's friends – why not Ginny?'

'But she wasn't on the list, was she?'

'No, but she doesn't know that, does she? I don't know why I didn't do it before. It just feels like time is running out, and she must know something about Lucas.'

I picture the scene: Abbot turning up on her doorstep, flashing a smile. Ginny will be putty in his hands. 'Do it,' I say. 'But just be careful.' I don't know why I add this, but we are mixed up in something we don't understand, with people we know nothing about. All I can say for sure is that it involves rape and possibly child abduction. And Ginny is the key to all this, I can feel it.

'How was your meeting?' Matt says, pouring us each a glass of wine.

'Quite productive,' I say, moving across to him and wrapping my arms around his waist. He has his back to me and the solid feel of him reminds me of when we first lost Helena. How the firmness of his body comforted me, let me know that somehow we would get through it together.

'Mrs Craig died tonight,' he says, turning to me, his eyes swollen and red. 'You know, the lady with cancer? She was only in her late forties.'

'I'm sorry,' I say.

'I just feel bad for her husband. Nice guy, he was always there for every appointment.' He hands me a glass. 'I just keep thinking, what if that happens to one of us? We've already lost our daughter, how would it be without each other?'

I am surprised to hear Matt saying this, he is normally a man of few words.

Keeping one arm wrapped around him, I tell him to think of everything we've already been through. That if someone had told us before we had Helena that we would lose her we would never have believed we could survive that.

'You're right,' he says, taking a sip of wine.

'I know it was touch and go,' I say, remembering the months – years – when we could barely function, the strained silences between us and our parents, nobody knowing what to say. Particularly Miriam. But counselling eventually helped, and we both threw ourselves into studying and then our careers, filling a void.

'But we stuck together, didn't we, even though there were times we could barely speak to each other. And look at us now.' As I say this, I know the words come more easily because I may be close to finding our daughter.

'You're right. I never would have got through this without you. Never would have finished my medical training.' He rubs my arm. 'Are you okay? I'm just worried. You've been quite distant lately and I know Grace turning up shocked us, but is there something else? You're normally so …'

'Talkative?'

'Well, yeah.'

We take our wine to the table, and I remember one week ago Grace sitting exactly where Matt is now. 'I'm just caught up in work, that's all. I'm sorry. What I'm working on will be finished soon, and then I'll have a bit more time to annoy you with my ramblings.'

'I miss it,' Matt says, the sadness visible in his eyes. I know he must be thinking of his patient again. Of us. Of our mortality.

'Let's watch a film,' I say. 'You can choose it. What do you think?' If anything has a chance of lifting his mood, it's watching a film.

Matt perks up. 'You mean you'll actually sit through a sci-fi film with me?'

'Yeah, as long as it's got *Star Wars* in the title.'

We both smile at this and I know, for the time being at least, I have distracted Matt from his melancholy.

* * *

After the film, I leave him to watch another one while I go up-stairs to bed. I haven't been able to focus on anything, my mind wondering how Abbot is getting on with Ginny. I have texted him three times already, but he hasn't replied, and now my anxi-ety increases. I try to call his mobile, but again, there is no re-sponse, only Abbot's cheery voice telling me to leave a message.

The next thing I do is text Chris Harding to let him know I've found someone who may have been in a relationship with Lucas. I don't give him any more details, but it will be enough to let him know we're making progress.

His reply is instant: a short *thank you*, and I wonder what he is doing at this moment; if, like me, he cannot switch off from this.

It is cold under the sheets, but I am too frozen to get out and turn on the heating. Instead, I email work to let them know I need an emergency day off, then I stare at the phone, willing it to ring.

I think of Grace and hope she is safe, wherever she is.

By the time Matt comes to bed, I have still not heard from Abbot.

TWENTY-TWO

I sit in the car outside the Brays' house and call Abbot. It is ten to nine so I've got a few minutes before I speak to Charlotte, a few minutes to get straight how I will begin. Once again, Abbot's voicemail kicks in, and I hang up without leaving a message. He will know from the number of missed calls that I am desperate to speak to him.

Through the car window I stare at the house and wonder what activity is taking place behind the walls. I imagine Charlotte will be in her bedroom, with her mother downstairs fussing over her, cooking a breakfast she won't eat, doing what any mother would do. And all Charlotte will want is to be left alone.

But things are about to get worse for her because in a few minutes I have to question her about Lucas Hall.

Tamsin greets me at the front door, her hair still wet from her shower and a huge white bathrobe swamping her thin frame. 'Sorry, I'm running a bit late this morning.' She pulls the belt of her dressing gown tighter around her waist. 'Elliott forgot to wake me. I was tempted to call him and make a fuss but I know he'll just say I'm exhausted and needed the rest.' She pulls me inside and closes the door. 'I know I should be ecstatic, after all, my girl's back, but …'

'I know,' I say. 'She's not herself.' I don't add that this is only just the beginning of the Brays' nightmare, or that I am about to make things a whole lot worse. 'It will take time, but you'll get there.' As I say this I am swamped with guilt for not talking to Tamsin about Lucas Hall first. She has the right to know what questions I'm about to ask her daughter. But I can't take the chance she will stop me. Charlotte is somehow mixed up with Lucas Hall and that means there is a link between her and Grace.

Tamsin takes my hand. 'I'm so sorry, listen to me. I'm complaining when you ... your baby ...'

'It's okay,' I say. 'Please don't apologise.'

'Thank you for doing this, offering to try again, after last time. I can't tell you what it means to us.'

I warn her that I still can't guarantee anything, but it's worth another shot.

Tamsin says she will make coffee, and I head upstairs to Charlotte's room, my body weighed down with guilt and anxiety. The chances of her talking to me are slim, but if she does then what could I be about to find out?

Her room smells musty, although at least now the curtains are slightly open, casting a slim rectangle of light onto the carpet. Charlotte sits on the floor with her back against the side of the bed, white iPod headphones protruding from her ears. She glances up as I walk in, but quickly stares down at her lap, twisting the white cable around her pale finger.

'Hi Charlotte, remember me? Simone Porter? Is it okay if we have a quick chat?' I move closer towards her.

There is no reaction, just a blank face, as if my words have bounced off her and dissolved in the air. I try to remember if Tamsin has ever mentioned Charlotte having any interests, but nothing springs to mind. She must be fond of dogs, though, as she helps out in the family business. It's worth a try.

'So you like dogs?' I say, joining her on the floor, but keeping a distance between us. It feels as though I'm talking to a young child, and I hope I'm not patronising her. But nothing I say is working, so I decide to change tack and get straight to the point.

'Charlotte, I'm here about a serious issue and I really need your help.'

A flick of her eyebrow.

'I don't want to scare you, but lives could be in danger.'

This time her leg shifts to the right, but she's too good at this game to give in so easily.

'I'm looking for someone and I think you might know him.' Still silence. 'His name is Lucas Hall.'

This time she turns her head and stares at me, her eyes widening as her brain catches up with what she's heard. I wait, but she remains silent.

'Charlotte? Do you know where Lucas is? Has he hurt you? Please talk to me. I wouldn't ask if it wasn't important. I know you've been through a lot, but this is an emergency.'

She twists her whole body towards me and one of her earphones slips out, emitting the tinny sound of her music into the room. Ignoring it, her eyes bore into me, but then finally she speaks. 'No. I ... I don't know who you're talking about.'

Surprised she's finally spoken, I move a bit closer towards her. 'Charlotte, please, listen to me. Did he ... hurt you? Did he have anything to do with your disappearance?'

She shakes her head. 'No, I told you. I don't know who you're talking about.'

I wait for her to tell me to leave but she doesn't. I know I am making her uncomfortable but I have no choice. 'Charlotte. I saw the emails you sent each other. I know you were seeing each other.'

'That's not true,' she says. 'Please, can you just go? I've got nothing to say. To anyone. I just want to be left alone.'

I move back. 'I know, Charlotte. I totally understand that. But Lucas has … hurt someone. A young woman. And now he's missing and I need to know where he is. Do you have any idea where he could be?'

She shakes her head. 'You've got it wrong. He wouldn't hurt anyone. He wouldn't.'

Finally, a breakthrough. But her words must mean he wasn't responsible for her absence. 'So you do know him?'

She gives a barely perceptible nod.

'Then if you think he wouldn't hurt anyone, help me prove that. Please.'

Her face softens as she contemplates her choices, but it is short-lived. The next moment, her eyes turn cold once more and she shakes her head.

'I've told you. He wouldn't hurt anyone. And I don't know where he is.' She turns away and pops her earphone back in, but the music has stopped now.

I am fighting a losing battle here. 'Can I give you my number?'

She gives me a *do what you want* shrug and turns away as I fish in my bag for my notebook. Scribbling down my mobile number, I stand up and hand her the sheet of paper. She doesn't take it, but I loosen my grip and watch it float to the carpet.

Defeated, I head to the door and am nearly through it and in the hall when she calls me back.

'Please, Simone. Don't tell my mum.'

Offering her a smile that is neither agreement nor refusal, I say goodbye and click the door shut behind me.

Tamsin is waiting at the bottom of the stairs. 'That was quick,' she says. 'No luck, then?'

'I think she just needs more time. Actually, I'm really sorry, Tamsin, but I need to rush off. Emergency at work. But I'll call

you later, okay?' I feel bad doing this to her but I need to find
Abbot and tell him Charlotte won't talk. I also need to know why
he hasn't been answering his phone.

Tamsin's eyes widen. 'Oh, okay. But please come back soon.
Don't give up on her.'

Outside in the car I try Abbot again. When he actually answers, it is all I can do not to shout at him.

'I know, I know,' he says. 'My battery died and I left my charger at home. I've been out all night. Sim, I've got so much to tell
you. Where are you?'

I tell him I'm just about to leave the Brays' house and that
Charlotte was no help.

'Meet me in Richmond Park,' he says. 'I've been cooped up
in the car all night and I need some air. We can have a walk and
talk properly then.'

Abbot is standing outside the park entrance when I get there,
wearing his scarf, gloves and thick padded coat. I half-register the
peaceful scenery, but we might as well be in an alleyway because
I am too jittery to appreciate it.

'I was worried about you,' I say, punching his arm. But I will
save my lecture for later; there are more important things to discuss.

As we walk, I fill him in on my conversation with Charlotte.
'We won't get anywhere with her, and I don't want to upset Tamsin, but she definitely had something going on with Lucas. I
could tell by her reaction to hearing his name.'

'Did she seem upset when you said he was missing?' Abbot
asks.

I think back. 'Not visibly.'

'Then do you think she's lying? Covering for him?'

'It's possible, but there's no way to get the truth out of her. We can't forget what she's been through. But it seems unlikely that Lucas was responsible if she's defending him like this.'

Abbot reminds me that we have no idea what she's been through, only that she disappeared. And it is still possible she was with Lucas, so that puts doubt on her being a traumatised victim.

'So another dead end,' I say, pulling the belt of my coat tighter around me. The wool offers me little protection against the harsh wind, and I long to be inside somewhere. 'What about you? What happened with Ginny?'

Abbot stops walking and looks around. Spotting a bench, he suggests we sit down.

'Is it that bad?' I ask, wondering if I'm about to hear that Grace was there and has admitted her claim to be Helena has been a cruel deception.

'Just come and sit,' he says, already heading towards the bench.

'Abbot, you're scaring me. What happened?'

A look I've never seen before crosses his face and he remains silent. The warmth has gone from his eyes, their brightness faded by something. Is it fear? Guilt? Whatever he needs to tell me, he is finding it hard. Finally he begins speaking, and I listen as he fills me in on his night.

When Ginny answered her door, Abbot gave her the story about helping Hannah Hall find Lucas. She immediately let him in, and they sat at the kitchen table – just as I had done only days ago – and drank coffee while they talked, as if they had known each other for years rather than minutes.

Something stirs within me when he explains this part. I know Abbot was only doing what he had to, but is it resentment I feel that he is bonding with the woman who could have stolen my baby? I force aside my irrational thoughts and focus on what he is saying.

Ginny was disturbed that Lucas has disappeared, and told Abbot the last time she saw him was a couple of weeks ago, when he'd popped over to check she was okay after her brother's death. 'But then I got called to work,' she says, 'and left him with Grace. He was gone by the time I got home.'

When Abbot asked if Grace had told her what she and Lucas talked about, she shook her head, telling him it couldn't have been important as Grace shared everything with her.

Then an idea occurred to him and Abbot asked Ginny if she'd mind texting Grace, just to double check, watching her phone as she sent the message.

'It was definitely to Grace's phone,' he says, before I can ask if he's sure the text was actually sent to anyone.

Within five minutes, Grace had replied, saying she hadn't seen him and ending the text with a *love you* and four kisses.

'I'm sorry, but I saw it,' Abbot says.

It is bad enough hearing all this, but what he says next causes a bomb to explode in my head.

'Sim, listen. I really don't think she abducted Helena. I've been going over and over it all night and I think we've got it wrong.'

I swallow the anger rising in my throat. 'Why? Why are you so sure?'

'Sim, how long have you known me? Wouldn't you say I'm a pretty good judge of character?'

This is true. Whatever story he's covering at work, Abbot instantly gets the measure of people, even when he's in the minority, even when he's fighting a battle to be heard. But nobody is infallible.

I nod and he continues.

'I spent ages talking to the woman and I hardly had to ask about Grace. It quickly became clear that she loves her daughter. I couldn't get her off the subject.'

'That doesn't mean anything! Of course, she loves her. She's been her mother for eighteen years. But that doesn't mean she didn't—'

'I just think we need to be sure before we approach her. The evidence we've got is weak. And what's made you so sure? At first you were keeping an open mind about Grace, but now it seems you're convinced she's Helena.'

I think about this for a moment. I don't know when it crept up on me, this overwhelming feeling that Grace is my daughter. I don't even think until this moment I have fully believed it, but I do now. Despite Abbot's opinion.

'A mother's instinct,' I say. It is the only answer I can give, even though I know Abbot won't understand it. 'And I don't want to just dismiss the fact that Ginny might have had something to do with it. Not until we can be sure.'

'Sim, listen, I really think it's more likely that Grace was lying, we just don't know why.'

My phone rings from somewhere inside my bag, saving me from having to reply to Abbot. I fumble around and pull it out, thinking any minute the anonymous caller will hang up.

I don't recognise the voice on the other end, but the woman asks for Hayley, so I am immediately on alert. 'It's Hannah,' she says. 'Lucas's wife?'

I ask her how she's doing, my mind already expecting to hear something that will lead us to Lucas.

'Not good,' she says. 'Well, I mean, I've had some news, and I suppose I should feel better, but actually I don't.'

'What news?' I ask, 'Have you found him?'

'Yes, well, sort of. He texted me about five minutes ago, saying he's met someone else and he's in France now. With her.'

I am so stunned by this information that it takes me a few seconds to respond. 'I'm … oh, I'm sorry to hear that. Why France?'

'Apparently she's French and they're staying with her family for a bit.' Her voice becomes shaky and she pauses, making me wonder if she is forcing back tears. 'He'll be back, though, because he still has the business to run. No doubt he expects me to take care of it while he's off with his whore … Sorry.'

'Don't apologise. I understand. I'm just sorry you have to go through all this.'

She thanks me for all my help and hangs up, and now I have to tell Abbot we've got even more evidence to prove Grace was lying.

He takes my hand. 'I'm sorry, Sim. I know this hasn't turned out how you expected.'

I pull my hand away, hating myself for doing it. 'It's not over, though, is it? Not until I've spoken to Grace myself and found out why she lied. This is not the end.'

'It never will be for you, though, will it? Don't you see that? This isn't about Grace or Lucas or Ginny any more, this is about Helena and your need for answers.'

Trying to keep control of my voice, I say, 'I can't believe that after you've spent a bit of time with a stranger you forget everything we've been through over the last few days. What about Gabby? Lucas still attacked her. And if you don't care about me, you should at least care that this is a *story*.'

Abbot stands up, shaking his head. 'How can you say I don't care about you? You've been the only person I've cared about for years. More than cared about. Don't tell me you didn't know. Everyone at work knows. Hell, my next door neighbour even knows.'

I stare at him, my mouth hanging open. I wonder if I'm mistaking what he is saying, but I see the truth in his eyes. Perhaps I have always known, but didn't want to think about it. *Couldn't* let myself think about it.

'I'm sorry,' Abbot says, when I don't answer. He sits back down. 'I know you're with Matt, and he's a great guy. I'm not trying anything … I just want it out in the open. I need to breathe. But I can't help how I feel about you. You know we have a connection, don't we?'

I can no longer listen, because Abbot's words are terrifying me. He shouldn't be saying all this to me. Not now. Not ever. I love Matt, but if there is anyone who could make me question my feelings then it is Abbot. So I do the only thing I can do.

I walk away without another word.

TWENTY-THREE

I lie beside Matt and listen to his slow breaths. He is lying on his back so I can see his profile, reminding me how much I love the way his ski-slope nose turns up slightly at the end. I am lucky to have him.

Abbot should not have told me how he felt. Whether I like it or not, his words have disrupted my already muddled thoughts. How can we continue our friendship now? I cannot pretend I don't know how he feels. I know it is unreasonable, especially after everything he's done for me, but I can't seem to stop feeling angry with him.

But there are also other things causing my fitful night's sleep. The hope I had of finding Helena, the thin strand I was clinging to, has gone. Lucas is not missing, and certainly not dead, and the only way to find out what Grace was playing at is to confront her directly, in front of Ginny. But there is no way I can do it today – I am grieving all over again for Helena, and need to take time to fully do this before I approach Ginny and her daughter. I picture the blue rabbit, still in my bag, but still can't explain how Grace had it. This is what I've been going over through the night while I lie next to my peaceful husband, a man I have kept oblivious to all of this.

As I watch him, the gentle rise and fall of his chest, I know what it is I have to do right now. I edge closer to him and kiss his arm, knowing it will stir him. And I am right. He smiles before he slowly opens his eyes.

'Morning,' I say, burying my head in the crook of his arm.

He turns to face me, still half-asleep. 'Hey, what time is it?'

'Only five. Sorry for waking you.'

'It's okay,' he says, pulling me even closer towards him. 'I need to get an early start anyway.'

'Matt? I was thinking. You know we talked about getting away somewhere? Really soon? How about Cornwall for a few days? We could leave tonight if you can arrange cover at the surgery?' I know I'm asking a lot so I avoid eye contact, to give him time to think this through.

But within seconds a huge smile spreads across his face. 'Really? I think that's a great idea. But can *you* get the time off work?'

I tell him it won't be a problem and ask if he thinks he'll be able to as well.

'It will be tricky,' he says, 'but I should be able to get a locum in to cover the rest of the week. I don't like to do it but we do need to get away, don't we? I'll just say it's a family emergency. Which it sort of is, isn't it?'

I should feel good that we'll be getting out of London for a while, that my head will have the space and time it needs to unscramble my thoughts. But I can't shake the uneasiness that sits in the pit of my stomach, and has done since the day Grace found me.

After breakfast – a huge fry-up, which Matt takes delight in cooking for us – we pack two small suitcases and load them into the car. Matt has booked us a cottage in St. Ives. He took almost an hour this morning choosing the right place, while I showered and dressed, and I don't have the heart to tell him it wouldn't matter to me where we stay; I just need to get out of this house.

With my phone in my hand, I almost text Abbot to let him know I'm going away, but I slip it in my pocket before I can change my mind. It is better if I keep a distance from him for now. Again, a flash of anger that he has jeopardised our friendship overcomes me, even though I know it is selfish to feel this way.

Almost five hours later we are in St. Ives, driving through a small town called Downalong. Even drenched in rain, the place is beautiful, and I feel a million miles away from everything that has happened over the last week. We are lucky it is January; we would never have got a place at such short notice during the summer.

The white stone-fronted cottage Matt has picked is called Labour in Vain, and I smile at the irony. This is what I have done for the past week: tried to find a man who was never even missing, because of a girl who isn't my daughter. I need to snap out of this and put it all behind me now.

Inside, we leave our suitcases in the kitchen and check out the cottage. It is bright and spacious, and provides far too much room for only two of us. My mind tries to picture what it would be like to come here with a family, but I shut that thought down. I am not one for moping around.

'There's free Wi-Fi,' Matt says, 'but how about we stay away from technology for the next few days and have a proper break? Just the two of us and nothing else. No internet, no phones, no work stopping us really being together.'

My eyes flick to my suitcase but I decide not to mention I have brought my laptop. I'm not sure why I packed it; probably habit more than anything else as I have no plan for what I'm going to do while we're here, other than to enjoy spending time with my husband.

'Fancy a walk on the beach?' Matt says. 'It's only a few metres away.'

Although it is freezing, and we will have to trudge through rain-soaked sand, I readily agree. We haven't done anything like this for years now, both of us caught up in our jobs and trying to distract ourselves from what we have lost.

Matt holds my hand as we walk, and for a fleeting moment I feel as though I am seventeen again, before we had Helena. There is definitely a before and after, an impenetrable line dividing my life then and my life now. I walked weightlessly before. I had no idea what pain was.

'You've been distant lately,' Matt says, snapping me out of my thoughts. 'I didn't want to bring it up, but it's hard not to. I just feel like you're … I don't know … drifting away from me.' He shakes his head. 'That sounds so melodramatic, doesn't it? But it's just how I feel.'

I could say I don't know what he means, that of course I haven't been distant, he's got it all wrong, but he deserves better than that. 'You're right. I'm sorry, it's just all this Grace stuff really got to me.'

He squeezes my hand tighter. 'I know. I thought it might be that, but shouldn't that be even more reason to let me in? We're in it together, aren't we?'

He is right, and not for the first time I question my decision to keep things from him. 'I just let myself believe that she was Helena. And you were so sure she wasn't, I guess I just didn't want to push things.'

Matt stops walking, forcing me to stop too, as he still clutches my hand. 'Look, we often don't agree on things but we've always worked it out, haven't we?'

'I know. I'm sorry. But I'm moving on now, I really am. Onwards and upwards!'

Ignoring my attempt at joviality, Matt resumes walking. 'You know, I was thinking all kinds of things. That maybe you were fed up with our life together and wanted out.'

Now it is my turn to stop walking and I let go of his hand and stand in front of him, pulling him towards me. 'Never. You're the one thing that keeps me sane. But I'm sorry I've made you feel this way.' It must have been bad for Matt to bring this up; he has never worn his heart on his sleeve.

'You never have to apologise to me,' he says. 'Especially not about Helena.'

We walk some more in comfortable silence, listening to the waves sloshing against the sand.

'I know it's bloody cold and wet here, but it's so peaceful, isn't it? It's as if nothing else exists in the world except this place.'

How right he is, I think, as we make our way back towards the cottage. I don't even want to think about leaving in a couple of days.

That evening I cook us steak with peppercorn sauce and we don't clear away afterwards, but leave the kitchen in a mess and settle down on the sofa to watch TV.

'I thought you said no technology,' I say, giving Matt a playful nudge.

'TV doesn't count,' he says. 'Besides, we're not going to be watching much.'

And then he is kissing me, pulling my jumper over my head, and I am melting away, everything else temporarily forgotten.

Although I feel much better now, I am still unable to sleep. It is past midnight and the book I've been meaning to start for

months now sits face down on the bedside cabinet, open at
the first page. Despite my promise to Matt, I am not cut out
for living without technology, and the feeling of being disconnected from everything gnaws away at me. My whole job
involves the internet, so it makes me uncomfortable to steer
clear of it.

Unable to stand it any longer, I climb out of bed, careful not
to disturb Matt, and make my way downstairs.

I don't turn on any lights until I get to the kitchen, and then I
put only the oven light on. I warm up some milk in a pan for hot
chocolate so that I don't wake Matt with the kettle.

My bag is on the table where I left it and, offering a silent apology to my husband, I grab my phone from the inside
pocket and hold down the power button until it springs to life.
After a few seconds it pings with several messages, and I immediately realise I am hoping to hear from Abbot. I don't like
how we've left things, and feel as if I have lost my closest friend.

Most of the messages are emails – all work related or junk
mail – and there is only one text. But it's not from Abbot; it's an
unknown number.

I click on it and read the words.

*I know exactly who you are. We need to meet NOW. Please. I'm
worried about Grace and I need your help. I know that will mean
something to you.*
Ginny.

And in this moment I am thrown right back to what I've been
hoping to escape from. It feels as if my heart has stopped and I
struggle to comprehend the message. I reread it several times, but
there is no room for misinterpretation.

My first instinct is to call Abbot, but then I remember our
argument. No, I am alone in this now and need to deal with

it by myself. I hit reply and begin typing. There is no time for questions.

I'm in Cornwall but will drive back to London now. Will come to yours, but it will be early in the morning.

I stare at my phone as I wait for a reply and after a few seconds it comes.

Doesn't matter what time. Please just get here.

And then I am moving, grabbing my coat and bag and leaving my hot chocolate untouched on the table.

I almost don't want to wake Matt, but it wouldn't be fair to only leave a note. I shake him gently, knowing this is usually enough to rouse him. 'Matt, I'm so sorry, something's come up at work. An emergency. And I really need to get back.' I can only hope he is too full of sleep to question me about what exactly has happened; I have not had a chance to figure out a cover story yet.

He turns on his side but struggles to open his eyes. 'Wha –? What's going on?'

'I need to get back to London, and I need to take the car, but I'll be back as soon as I can.' But even as I say this I have no idea what the next day will hold for me.

Matt manages to force open his eyes slightly and squints into the darkness. 'Do you really have to? Can't Abbot take care of it?'

'No, not this time. You know I wouldn't go if I had a choice,' I say. And this is the truth.

He starts to raise his head. 'Then I'm coming with you. I don't want you driving at this ridiculous hour of the morning.'

I am prepared for him to say this. 'No, I really don't want to ruin this break for you. Look, I'll get back as soon as I can, okay?'

Matt opens his mouth, probably to try and protest, but quickly closes it again. He knows how futile it is to try and talk me out of something once I have made up my mind. He also knows how important my work is to me, and that he would do the same. My stubbornness might annoy him but I am sure it is what he also loves most about me. That I know my own mind.

'I really don't like this,' he says. 'But I understand you have to go. Just call me as soon as you get to London, okay? And please stop along the way, don't drive all that way without having a break.'

I agree to do all this and kiss him goodbye, my mind whirring and alert. Is it really possible I am about to find out the truth about Grace? And from Ginny, too. There are so many questions I have, not least of which is what she meant when she said she is worried about Grace. But it is pointless speculating now. I need to just drive, and get to Ewell as soon as possible.

I need to know why Ginny took my daughter.

TWENTY-FOUR

It must have been almost midnight by the time I reached his place, but he let me in, full of apologies for being so late to get to Harry's. He told me – with a huge grin on his face – that a couple of people had seen me leave with Leanne the barmaid, so he thought he'd leave me to it.

And that's when he must have noticed my pallor, because he stopped smiling and told me to sit down. He didn't make me take my shoes off, as he usually did, and I only hoped I hadn't trailed mud or anything else into his flat. Unlike mine, his wasn't a typical student flat. It had two double bedrooms and an open plan kitchen, which was wasted on him as all he did was order takeaways or grab a McDonalds or KFC. But his parents were taking care of the rent for him, so he could live in relative luxury.

'What's happened?' he asked. 'You don't look right.' He fetched me a glass of water, but I couldn't stomach drinking anything.

I sat on his couch and eventually – after several false starts – told him what I'd done to Leanne, explaining every detail while I stared at his spotless blue carpet.

He stood up when I'd finished and told me to stay put. 'I'll be right back,' he said, disappearing through the front door.

As I sat there waiting, with too much silence and too much time ticking by, I became terrified that he'd gone to the police. After all, I hadn't known him that long, so what had possessed me to believe I could trust him? But then why wouldn't he just call them? No, this had to be alcohol-fuelled paranoia kicking in – I knew he wouldn't do that to me. I just knew it. I trusted him, and he was the only person I could talk to about this, the only person who would understand.

So I continued waiting, staring at the blank television screen, not daring to move from my spot on the sofa, even though my bladder was about to burst. And, as fearful as I was, I couldn't stop thinking about how much I'd enjoyed what I'd done to Leanne.

Over an hour later, he came back, with no mention of where he'd been or why he'd been gone so long. 'It's sorted,' he said, sinking into the sofa. 'Leanne won't be reporting anything. You've got nothing to worry about.'

I looked at him, full of questions but no idea which one to ask first. 'But … but I raped her.'

His voice became slow and measured. 'No, you didn't,' he said. 'Got it? You walked her home and made sure she got in okay. Then you went for a long walk, you needed fresh air to clear your head before bed. That's it. Okay?'

'But what if—'

'That's it. Okay? He repeated.

I opened my mouth but quickly closed it again. There would be no point questioning him and I didn't think he would provide any satisfactory answers so I simply nodded my agreement, and finally reached for the glass of water he'd got me before he left.

'Don't bother with that,' he said, grabbing it from me. 'I've got something better for you.' He made me a strong black coffee and by the time I'd finished it I had pulled myself together.

'Did you like what you did to her?' he asked.

Perhaps I should have been shocked by his question, but in the short time I'd known him I'd learnt to expect the unexpected.

Even though I already knew the answer, it took me a while to say it out loud. 'Yes. That's sick, isn't it?' I had no idea how he would take my response, but he had already helped me out, so the least I could do was give him honesty.

Then it was his turn for silence. But when he spoke, once again he shocked me to my core.

'Why is it sick? Because society tells you it is? They do that to keep us under their control, don't you see that? She was a grown woman – a lot older than you – and she let you back into her flat. She knew what she was doing. So maybe she changed her mind at the last minute, but that's tough shit, isn't it? Don't let anyone tell you you're not normal. Or you've got a problem. Do what you have to do.'

We said no more about it that night, but something had started. I don't know whether it was me igniting something in him, or whether it was just chance that he'd come across someone so similar to him, but whatever it was, we never looked back.

And what I did to Leanne was kind in comparison to what came next.

TWENTY-FIVE

It is nearly five a.m. by the time I pull up at Ginny's house. The street is still asleep, shrouded in darkness, but behind her curtains light struggles to shine through her downstairs windows. She has been waiting for me.

I walk to the front door and send her a text to tell her I'm here. Although she is expecting me, I don't want to ring anyone's doorbell at this time in the morning.

A shadow appears through the glass and the door opens. Ginny is dressed in a long thick dressing grown and her feet are bare. 'Hello again,' she says. 'Simone, isn't it? Funny, that suits you better than Hayley.'

I feel my cheeks redden, even though she is the one who should feel ashamed. Her lie is far worse than mine.

'But thanks for coming,' she continues, stepping aside. 'Come in, there's a lot we need to talk about, isn't there?'

The second I am in her hallway again, the anger I've kept bottled up explodes within me. 'I need explanations and I need them now.'

If she is surprised by the firmness of my voice she doesn't show it. 'Yes, I know. There's so much to say and I don't know where to start. But, please, let me get you a drink. I bet you didn't stop at all on the way here – you must be dying of thirst.'

She is stalling, but I will let her have her way. I *am* thirsty, and at least I'm here now. I will find out what happened to Helena. I tell her water will be fine; accepting any other drink from her, as if we are friends having a chat, feels wrong.

She moves off to the kitchen but doesn't tell me to follow so I stay where I am, my anxiety increasing by the second. I haven't thought this through properly. This woman stole my daughter and now I'm alone in her house and nobody knows where I am. I think of Abbot, how he should be here with me, how if we hadn't argued I would have asked him to come. After all, he has been with me every step of this journey, until now.

But I cannot think of myself now; I am here for Helena and, whatever the risks, I am doing what I have to for my daughter. I can think of her as that now because surely that's why Ginny has asked me here. I am finally going to get the truth.

When she comes back with a glass of water she seems surprised to find me still in the hall. 'Shall we go in there?' she says, heading past me to the living room.

'So, you must have a million questions.' Ginny sits at one end of the sofa and I pick the furthest seat from her.

'I do. I—'

'You must have realised this by now but I know all about you, Simone Porter.'

I don't answer. This is all wrong. I am the one who should be interrogating her.

'I know your baby was abducted eighteen years ago. Sorry to be blunt.' Of course she knows this, when she is the one responsible for it happening.

'Okay, enough,' I say. 'This isn't about me, this is about you and what you've done.'

She stares at me for a moment, frowning, trying to work me out. 'Okay,' she says. 'You're right. But first let me tell you how I found out. You must want to know that?'

'Okay,' I agree, 'let's start there.' But I am becoming unnerved. The woman is too confident, too sure of herself considering she has committed such a heinous crime. Something feels wrong.

She leans forward and lowers her voice, even though we are alone. 'After your friend Abbot was here I got worried about Lucas. He was a good friend of Daniel's, you see, so I care about him too. Anyway, I contacted Hannah Hall and she told me how nice Hayley was. Hayley, the old friend of Lucas's from uni. Now I don't claim to know everything about Lucas – far from it – but Daniel and Lucas had a lot of the same friends, and I'd never heard either of them mention anyone called Hayley. And then I remembered the Hayley who came to see me. Grace's friend's mother. The one who was looking for a carer for her mum. Call me paranoid, but my instinct was screaming at me that something wasn't right.'

She pauses for breath and waits for my reaction. What I want to tell her is that of course she is suspicious of everyone. She stole a baby, so she's got to have spent her whole life expecting the walls to come crashing down on her. But I will save my admonishment until I hear her admit it.

'Anyway,' she says, when I don't respond. 'The first thing I did was call my agency. And as I expected, Cassandra said a woman called Hayley had been in to discuss me, but had never followed it up.' She smiles at me, proud of her detective work. 'Well, what was I supposed to think after that? So then I went to Grace's uni. And guess who I spoke to? Yes, Jasmine. You know – the Jasmine whose mother is Chinese?'

'Can you get to the point?' I say, fed up with her smugness.

She narrows her eyes. 'Well, I'm sure you can guess the rest. Jasmine told me my friend had been to see her, looking for Grace, and all my suspicions were confirmed.' She pauses again, and shakes her head. 'But, Simone, it's not even important now, because I need your help. I don't know where Grace is. She hasn't turned up for lectures all week and although I've had some texts from her, I now know it's not her sending them.'

My stomach flips. 'I thought she was visiting a friend? What do you mean the texts aren't from her?' But even as I say this, I'm not sure I truly believed that's what Grace was doing.

'When your friend was here I got a text message from her. But I know one hundred per cent that Grace didn't write it. You see, she signed it off, *love Gracie.*' She looks at me as if I should know what she's talking about. 'She never calls herself that,' she explains. 'Never. She only likes "Grace", no shortening or changing it in any way.'

'But—'

'Ever,' Ginny says. 'Even as a child she used to tell people off if they called her anything other than Grace.' Her reference to Grace as a child sends a chill through my body, but I try to focus on what she's telling me. 'Anyway, I've checked with all her friends and none of them have heard from her since last week. She definitely isn't staying with any of them. So, please, Simone, you've got to help me. I really think we're in this together.'

There is no doubt in my mind about what I need to do. 'Of course I'll help, but I need some answers. You must know that. Is Grace … my daughter?'

Ginny's face softens, the harsh angular lines becoming rounder somehow. 'I will tell you everything, Simone, but I need to ask – how did you find us? How did you know about Grace in the first place? I've been trying to work it out all day but I just can't.'

And now it is my turn to speak. I tell her about Grace approaching me in Oxford Street last week, and about Lucas having given her my name. I almost tell her what Grace told me he did to her, but leave this part out. No matter what has happened,

I made a promise to Grace and I doubt she will want Ginny to know the details.

Ginny remains silent the whole time I speak, but her eyes become glazed with sadness. She has been betrayed by someone she considered a friend.

Reaching into my bag, I pull out the velvet rabbit and hold it out to her. Staying silent, she takes it from me, examining every part of it. She makes no move to give it back but keeps it clutched in her palm as she faces me again.

'I get it now. Of course you suspected me of abducting your baby – it's the most obvious scenario, isn't it? But please believe me, that is not what happened. I would never do that. Never.' Her last word echoes through the house.

'Then what the hell happened? How did Grace end up with Helena's rabbit? Tell me now.' I lean across and grab the rabbit, pushing it back in my bag before she can object. Whatever has happened, Grace gave it to *me*.

Avoiding eye contact, Ginny clears her throat and begins to speak, each sentence she utters tearing into me like a bullet. 'I had cancer when I was twelve and I needed chemotherapy. Lots of it. It was a long journey to recovery, but I would have gone through it a thousand times over if there had been any way the doctors could have preserved my fertility.' She pauses and looks at me, but all she will see is my impassive expression. Although her story saddens me, whatever she has been through is no excuse for abducting a baby. My baby.

'Anyway, I gradually got better and for a long time didn't give much thought to not being able to have a baby. I mean, who would at that age? It's something that seems a million years away, isn't it?'

Again, I don't react but wait for her to get to the part about Helena. Anger boils inside me but I somehow manage to keep it down. For now.

Ginny continues talking. She tells me how suddenly in her mid-twenties she realised the extent of what the chemotherapy had done to her, how it had left her bereft of the chance to have a family. Which then became all she wanted.

I can no longer contain myself. 'That doesn't give you the right to take someone else's!' I scream. 'All you did was leave me with the same gaping hole you must have felt. In fact, no, it was worse, much worse. Because we already had our little girl. We had her for six months. And then you took her from us.'

Ginny remains calm. 'Please, Simone, hear me out, hear everything I've got to say and then you can say whatever you like to me.'

I fold my arms and lean forward to try and stop the cramps beginning in my stomach.

'I couldn't have relationships,' she continues. 'What was the point? If they were ever to turn into something long term then I'd only have to tell the person I couldn't have children. So I cut myself off from men, kept to myself, focused on caring for others instead. But the pain was always there, a constant reminder of what I would never have.'

She is acting as if I don't know what this is like, how the pain may dull but is a constant companion. 'Get to the point. You must understand that it's hard for me to sympathise with you?'

She nods. 'Anyway, when I was thirty, my brother Daniel came to me and said he had a female friend who had got pregnant by mistake. She was a young girl and just couldn't have looked after a baby, but she was too scared to have a termination. Daniel said she was so desperate she might have dumped the baby, or worse, so he told her that if she had it, I would raise the baby as my own. The girl didn't hesitate to agree. He had sorted it all out with her before he even came to me with the idea.'

It takes me a moment to realise what Ginny is telling me, and when it sinks in I struggle to believe her. Surely it is a convenient and far-fetched story? 'You mean you didn't take Helena? My baby?'

She looks directly at me and I only see sincerity in her expression. 'No, Simone. I swear to you I would never do that. '

'But … who was this girl? Did you ever meet her?'

She shakes her head. 'No. Daniel told me it was best to stay out of it. All I had to do was pretend to be pregnant, which was easy as I was quite overweight then. Plus, I kept myself to myself and only really saw the elderly people I cared for. Nobody suspected I was lying about being pregnant.' She stares at the floor; at least she has the decency to feel ashamed.

'I know how awful it sounds … how beyond belief even. But I was desperate. And I never stopped to question Daniel about the morality of what we were doing. I thought we were helping this girl, and helping me at the same time.'

There are tears in her eyes now, but it's still not enough to soften me. 'So you're saying Grace is not Helena? But why did Lucas tell her about me? I must have something to do with this.'

Ginny stares at the floor. 'I knew at the time a baby had been abducted, but I never for one second connected it with my baby. Why would I? My brother and I were so close, he would never have done that. But now I know different.' She wipes at her eyes. 'What I'm trying to say is that I think Lucas was telling the truth and Daniel took your baby. For me. And she came with that blue rabbit. There was no pregnant girl.'

TWENTY-SIX

I stare open-mouthed at Ginny, scanning her face for any signs of deceit. Her tears have stopped and now all I see is sadness. I have spent the last few days certain that if Grace was telling the truth then Ginny must be the one responsible for her abduction. It never occurred to me that she could be in any way innocent.

I have so many questions for her that I don't know where to begin. 'So ... you think your brother abducted my daughter? Are you sure? And where do you think she is now?'

She offers a thin smile. 'I can't be completely sure, not without proof, but it looks that way. Otherwise, why would his best friend tell Grace about you? But whatever Daniel did, I really think he did it for me. I'm not saying his actions are in any way excusable, but he just wanted me to be happy.'

My blood boils. 'There are other things you could have done. Legal things. Adoption. Fostering. IVF. And no matter how close the two of you were, why would he do this? Break the law for you?'

'I know it's awful, but we were really close. Our parents died when Daniel had only just left school, so all we had was each other. I think he couldn't bear to see me in pain.'

I can't respond to this; I have too many other questions to ask Ginny. 'But Helena was six months old. If this girl didn't want to keep her baby why did she only give her up after that time?'

Ginny doesn't hesitate to respond. 'Daniel had an answer for everything. He told me that once the baby was born the girl changed her mind but realised after six months she couldn't cope.'

'Do you know how that sounds? And you never thought to question him?'

'I was just too desperate. Perhaps, deep down, I didn't want to know too much. I'm so sorry.'

'But how did you get away with it with doctors and hospitals? You would have had no paperwork for her and no evidence you'd given birth.'

'Luckily Grace was a healthy baby and didn't need much medical attention, but if she ever did need anything Daniel took care of it. I just assumed he was getting help from the young mum.'

'You must see how appalling this is? It doesn't matter *why* he did it, only that he did.'

Ginny shakes her head. 'I know. I know. But please, can we just work together to find Grace? Then we can sort all this out. And if she is yours … well, I want to do the right thing.'

A mixture of anger and sadness threatens to overwhelm me but I have to put my feelings on hold. There are a million things I want to do: shout, scream, punch Ginny. But none of them will help us find Grace. I now know she is almost certainly Helena, but at the moment, perhaps because I'm in Ginny's presence, I can't help but think of her as Grace. 'Right,' I say. 'You need to tell me everything about Grace and where she could be. And Lucas too. I need to know everything about him. Could there be a connection? Is there any chance Grace is with him?'

Ginny stands up and begins pacing the room. 'I don't know. I doubt it. Why would she be?'

And now I have no choice but to tell her what Grace claimed Lucas did to her in his flat. Given the circumstances, she is in many ways more Ginny's daughter than mine, so I need to speak carefully. I have to keep in mind how hurt this woman will be when she realises what Lucas, a man she trusted, tried to do to a daughter she's only ever protected and loved.

She listens without interrupting and I see her shudder when I get to the part about Lucas attempting to rape Grace. 'But he's not dead,' I say. 'We checked the flat and there were no signs that there had ever been any sort of fight. Plus, we know from Hannah that Lucas is in France with another woman. So I have to ask – why do you think Grace might have lied about this? Because that's what it looks like now, doesn't it?'

Ginny pulls herself together to consider my question. 'Since childhood, Grace has always been honest. You know exactly where you stand with her. In fact, I'd say she's brutally honest, even if she thinks it's something you might not want to hear. She doesn't hesitate to tell me if I look awful in something I'm wearing.' She smiles, and I imagine she is picturing a specific incident. But these should be *my* memories, not Ginny's. 'Since she moved out to go to university I don't get to see as much of her. I know she's meeting new people, spreading her wings, that's natural, isn't it? But I don't believe she would make up such an awful story.'

I want to take Ginny's word for this, but there are too many question marks around Grace's claim. 'What if she wanted to hurt you? For lying to her all these years? That's got to have messed with her head, surely?'

Ginny rubs her chin. 'Simone, tell me this. Did Grace strike you as being out for revenge?'

I think back to our conversations in the café and at my house. 'No. She didn't. It seemed like she just wanted to know the truth.'

'Well, please just hang on to that. Let's assume she is telling the truth. Lucas obviously isn't the man I thought he was, so we have no idea what he's capable of.'

'Yes, we do,' I say, and I tell her about Gabby and her claim that Lucas raped her.

Ginny's face pales until she is almost the colour of paper and she finally stands still. 'Come on, we have to go now,' she says, leaning down to me.

'Where?'

'To my brother's house. I haven't had the heart to go there since he died, but I've got the keys and we might find something.'

I don't know what she's expecting, or hoping, to find, but I don't argue. I have no better ideas and we need to find Grace. Before it is too late.

Daniel's house is in Hayes, and it is nearly an hour before we turn onto his road. It's still fairly early so the traffic has been quiet, but Ginny drove slowly, despite the urgency of our situation. I would have preferred to drive us here in my own car, but my petrol is low, and Ginny didn't want to waste time filling up the tank.

We pull up outside an ugly mid-terraced house, and I silently compare it to Lucas's house in Notting Hill. The grey stone walls are dirty, and the flat roof makes it impossible to believe it is a home. I wonder how two such close friends could have lived such different lives, until I remember that they may not have been so different after all. Both of them have shown they are capable of carrying out horrendous acts.

'It's weird to think the last time I was here he was alive,' Ginny says, switching off the engine. 'This won't be easy. But if there's anything in there that will help us find out what's happened to Grace ...'

She trails off and I imagine her mind is exploring all sorts of scenarios – none of them pleasant – just as mine has done all the way here. 'Let's just focus on that,' I say, offering her a thin smile. For now I have to put on hold any negative thoughts I hold towards this woman. Grace is the only one that matters, and we need to do whatever it takes to find her.

The sun is only just beginning to rise, so the street is gloomy and deserted as we leave the warmth of the car and cross the road to Daniel's house.

'I'm expecting to find a mess,' Ginny says, slotting her key in the door.

And she is right. As soon as the door opens the stale stench of neglect assaults us, and Ginny bends down to scoop up the mail that has piled up on the floor. I hold my breath as I follow her in. Once I've become accustomed to the smell, I consider how strange it is that only days ago I was searching Ginny's house with Abbot, and now I'm doing the same at her brother's.

'He lived alone then?' I ask, already reaching that conclusion.

'Yeah,' she says, fumbling along the wall for the light. Then she tells me that he was married for a few years but they recently separated. 'Actually, his ex was supposed to come here after he died and get the place sorted because half her things are still here, but she hasn't bothered yet. I suppose that's lucky for us, though.'

I tell Ginny we should look for his computer or phone. Anything which might show contact with Lucas. Anything that might tell us the truth about Grace and lead us to her.

Suddenly I feel out of my depth here. It was one thing looking for Lucas with Abbot, but another to be with a stranger, whom I still don't know I can trust. I fight the urge to call him, instead forcing myself to focus on what we're doing. 'Let's start in the kitchen and search together.' I don't add that there is no way I am letting her out of my sight.

To my surprise, the kitchen is not too squalid. There are three tea-stained mugs by the sink, and a half-finished loaf of mouldy bread on the worktop, but other than that it's cleaner than some kitchens I've been in where the owners don't have the excuse of being dead to account for their messiness.

A heavy coat hangs over the back of one of the kitchen chairs and Ginny must spot it the moment I do because she heads over to it and rummages in the pockets. 'Nothing,' she says, pulling her hands out.

'So who arranged his funeral clothes?' I say. Both my parents are still alive so I have little experience of death, but I am quite sure it is up to the next of kin to pick clothes for their loved one to be buried in.

'Lucas took care of all that. I was too distraught.' A look I can't read flashes across her face and she quickly changes the subject. 'Can you help me check all the cupboards and drawers? I have no idea what Daniel kept anywhere – I didn't usually come here. He was always at my place instead. Said it felt more homely.' She looks around. 'You can see why he didn't want to spend much time here.'

The kitchen turns up nothing helpful and neither does the living room. It is clear how little time Daniel spent here, and I wonder what he was so busy doing when he wasn't with his sister.

'Did he work?' I ask, as we head upstairs.

Ginny's face brightens. 'He was a taxi driver. He lost interest in university after the first couple of years and left before he got his degree. But he loved driving, said it gave him freedom no other job could. Plus more money than people might imagine.'

Her eyes are filled with sadness once more so I remind her what he has done, why we are here.

'I know,' she says. 'But I'm still hoping I'm wrong about this; that he was telling the truth about how Grace came to be mine. I mean, how do we know Lucas wasn't lying to Grace?'

I feel like shaking her. 'Why would he do that to Daniel if they were such good friends?'

She has no reply to that, but this time the tears come hard and fast. 'Let's just remember why we're here.'

The bedroom is quite nicely decorated, and I am surprised to see plump and colourful cushions neatly arranged on the bed. Seeing my shock, Ginny tells me that this is how Daniel's ex-wife arranged everything. 'He was just too lazy to make any changes after she left,' she adds.

Something on the bedside table catches my eye. 'Is that Daniel's phone?' I ask, walking across to it. I pick it up and study it. It's an HTC phone and I hold it up to show Ginny.

She takes it from me and examines each side of it. 'I think so, but the battery must be dead. Is there a charger anywhere?'

I open the bedside table drawer and see we are in luck. The phone charger is here.

'Let's take that downstairs with us,' Ginny suggests. 'But we need to finish checking up here first. After this there's only one more room but that won't take long to check. It's got nothing in it but a sofa bed. And I doubt the bathroom will turn up anything useful.'

I stand and watch while Ginny checks the wardrobe, rummaging through her brother's clothes, but finding nothing useful. Several times I open my mouth to ask again what she hopes to find in his pockets, but I leave her to it. At least we've got his phone. If there is anything at all useful we will find it on there.

When Ginny checks the bathroom, I stand in the hallway and think of Grace. I picture her walking up these stairs, standing in the spot I stand in now. She is bound to have visited her uncle's house before.

She is my daughter, I am more convinced of that than I have been since I met her, and now I am even more desperate to find her. I have no idea how it will work out – Ginny clearly loves her – but I will deal with that when we find her.

Ginny joins me and shakes her head. 'Nothing. Let's go down and charge this phone.'

Being in the kitchen reminds me how hungry I am, but there is nothing to eat here, and I wouldn't risk it if there were.

Ginny plugs in the phone and stares at the screen as it comes to life. 'Do you know how to work these phones?' she asks, her face reddening. 'I'm used to my BlackBerry so don't have a clue about any other makes.'

'Some people at work have them, so I can have a good guess,' I say, thinking of Abbot and how much he loves his HTC. 'I just hope it's not password protected.'

While I fiddle around with the phone, I ask Ginny where Daniel's computer is.

'That's a good point. He does have a laptop, but it's not here, is it? I wonder if Christine did come after all and she's taken it. I know it was an expensive one.'

'Here we are,' I say, as I get straight into the phone without being asked for a password. I start tapping icons and I am straight into Daniel's message inbox. 'Why wouldn't he security-protect it?' I say.

'Probably laziness,' she says. 'He wouldn't have wanted the bother of having to type it in every time he wanted to check his phone.'

This is the second time Ginny has described her brother as lazy, and I find it odd. A man who would go to so much trouble to give his sister the baby she was desperate for is anything but lazy.

Ginny joins me and we both lean on the worktop, staring at the device. 'And it was never out of his sight,' she says. 'He was always on the damn thing, I used to have such a go at him about it. He'd come for dinner with us and wouldn't say a word, but he'd be engrossed in something or other on there.'

Grateful that Matt is nothing like this with his phone, I check Daniel's message inbox and scroll through his texts. None seem suspicious and I don't recognise any names other than Ginny's. Next I check the emails, but there are none to Grace, Lucas or even Ginny. The only ones he has saved seem to be online purchases.

The final thing I can check is his photo album, and it takes me a minute to work out how to get to it. When I do, there are only a few photos on there, all of a dark haired woman.

'That's Christine, his ex,' Ginny says. 'I wonder why he's bothered to keep them.' I click out of the photos and then notice there is also a video. I immediately press to play it and the side of a woman's face fills the screen. She is not Daniel's ex, she seems much younger, with blonde bobbed hair and high cheekbones covered in blusher. I ask Ginny who she is.

'I don't know,' she says, peering closer at the phone.

I continue to watch and then I realise something isn't right. Whoever is filming moves further back so now I can see the woman's eyes are closed and her head flops to the side. Within seconds the camera zooms out further and I am stunned to see there is a man on top of her, yanking her hair back and forcing himself into her from behind, while she is clearly unconscious.

Beside me, Ginny lets out a shriek. 'That's Daniel,' she says. 'What the—?' And then she realises what I have already understood and her face drains of blood.

I'm sure we both feel we shouldn't continue watching, but neither of us makes any move to stop the video. We have to know what's going on. Realising there has been no sound so far, I quickly turn up the volume, bringing to life Daniel's heavy grunts, and the woman's silence.

And then another voice shouts out. It is a male voice, and I can only assume it belongs to the person filming. 'Stupid whore. Fuck her till she takes her last breath.'

Hearing this, Ginny erupts into tears, while I feel as if my legs will give way beneath me.

'Do you recognise that voice, Ginny? Who is filming this?'

Through her tears she manages to speak. 'That's … Lucas.'

For a few moments longer we watch, until Daniel forces the girl onto her back and rams his fist into her face, a sickening thud the last thing we hear before the screen becomes black.

Ginny falls to the floor and I scoop her up and lead her to a chair. I fill a glass with tap water and coax her into drinking some. 'You need this. And then we've got to get out of here. We have to find Lucas, now – and I know who can help us.'

TWENTY-SEVEN

Parked up outside the Brays' house, I feel as if I'm going around in circles. I have no idea if my plan will work, but there is no other option. I called Hannah Hall from Daniel's house, but her phone went straight to voicemail, so for now at least she won't be able to help us. Part of me is relieved I couldn't get through to her; I am dreading telling her what we've found. But I will have to do it. Lucas knows where Grace is. I'm sure of that.

We stopped at Ginny's to pick up my car, and on the drive here she begged me not to go to the police with Daniel's phone yet. Against my better judgement I agreed. At least for now. I know they will be able to help track down Lucas, but by the time we've gone through everything, and they've verified that the voice on the tape belongs to him, valuable time will have been wasted. But if this last shot doesn't work then I will go straight to the police; something I'm beginning to wish I'd done at the very beginning.

I turn to Ginny. 'So you're certain that's Lucas's voice in that video?'

'Definitely. I'd know it anywhere. It's him, Simone. Do you think he's got Grace?' Her voice trembles.

I have thought of little else for the whole drive here. After receiving his text, Hannah thinks he is in France, but that could just be his cover story. Although he's nervous about Gabby going to the police, escaping to France, especially if he has Grace with him, seems risky. It is a possibility, but I also need to consider that he is still here. And only one person can help me find that out.

'So this woman knows Lucas?' Ginny says, unbuckling her seatbelt. She seems distracted now; the shock of realising what Daniel is capable of must be making her question her whole life. And neither of us has dared to mention that we fear Grace ending up in the same situation as the woman in the video.

I have filled Ginny in on what happened to Charlotte, but it's difficult to know how much she is taking in.

'Yes, Charlotte definitely knows him. She tried to deny it but accidentally let it slip out. I think they were sleeping together. Look, do you have a recent photo of Grace on your phone?'

Ginny frowns. 'I think so, why?'

'Can you text it to me? I'll explain everything later. After I've been in there.' I flick my head towards the house.

Ginny does as I ask and after a few seconds my phone pings with a text message. I open it and Grace stares back at me, smiling and fresh-faced. Before her world was shaken to its core.

It is nine o'clock now and I'm sure Elliott will be in the shop, but I doubt Tamsin will have left Charlotte alone. This is good; if Charlotte is on her own the chances of her letting me in after our last conversation are slim. Tamsin, on the other hand, will just think I'm here to try and help her daughter again. I feel no guilt for taking advantage; I am here for Grace.

'I'm going in, but you should wait here,' I tell Ginny. 'It's … difficult with Charlotte, and I don't want to have to explain who you are to her mother.'

Ginny looks as if she's about to object but changes her mind. 'Okay. But please hurry.'

The last person I expect to open the door is Charlotte herself. She looks different somehow, neater and more together, and it takes me a moment to realise it's because she's dressed, her hair freshly washed.

'Oh,' she says, her forehead creasing. 'My parents aren't here. They're at the shop.' She begins closing the door.

'Wait, it's you I need to see. Just for a minute. I wouldn't ask if it wasn't so important.' I produce a large smile, even though after our last meeting, being friendly to Charlotte is the last thing I want to do.

'Look, if this is about Lucas then I've got nothing to say.'

To give her the impression it's not about Lucas, I shake my head. 'Just two minutes. Please, Charlotte.'

After considering my plea for a moment, she finally steps back and lets me in, and I glance briefly at Ginny before I shut the door.

'Can we sit down?' I say, when Charlotte makes no move to leave the hall.

She shrugs and heads to the living room, and I know the task ahead will not be easy. 'I know it was a bit awkward when I was here a couple of days ago, but I kept my word, Charlotte. I didn't mention anything to your mum about you and Lucas.'

She nods. 'I know. Thanks.'

'But I've still not been able to find him and it's even more important now that I do.'

'I've already told you, I don't know—'

'Do you know his wife got a text message from him saying he'd run off to France with some French woman?' I throw this out there – Charlotte's reaction will tell me what I need to know.

'What?' She screws up her face. 'That's rubbish. He's not … he wouldn't … Why are you saying this? You're lying!' Her voice rises and she starts scratching at her arms. It's not concrete evidence, but she seems to be concerned about what I've said.

Which can only mean she might be telling the truth about not knowing where he is. But even so, she can still help us.

'So you really don't know where he is?' I ask.

'Why?' she says, folding her arms. 'Why are you looking for him?'

'Actually, the person I'm looking for is a girl. This girl.' I bring up the picture of Grace on my mobile and show it to Charlotte.

'She's pretty,' she says. 'Who is she?'

This is the exact question I've been trying to answer for over a week now 'Her name's Grace,' I say. 'She's only eighteen and is missing, just like you were.'

Charlotte passes my phone back to me. 'Well, I'm sorry. But what's this got to do with Lucas?'

'Listen, Charlotte. I know you have feelings for him and want to protect him, but I believe he knows where Grace is.'

'No.' she shakes her head, her hair fanning out as she does so. 'Why would he? You've got it wrong.'

This is exactly how she reacted last time, but now I am prepared for it. From my pocket I pull out Daniel's phone and bring up the video, every frame of which is still ingrained in my memory. But I instantly reconsider. How can I let Charlotte see this? It is cruel and I can only imagine what it will do to her. I hesitate and almost turn it off again, but then I think of Grace and how I must do this for her.

'I'm sorry to show you this, Charlotte, but I have to.' Full of guilt, I press play and hold the phone in front of her.

Her eyes widen as she takes in what she is seeing, but it is only when she hears Lucas's voice that she looks away.

'That's him, isn't it? You recognise his voice, don't you? Please, Charlotte, you must see now how important this is?'

'I ... I don't understand. That's not Lucas. It can't be.' She avoids looking at me and I'm sure it's because she knows the truth.

'Yes, Charlotte, it is. And you can help me find him.'

There are tears in her eyes now, and she tries to wipe them away, but it is too late. I have seen the effect the video has had on her. But I don't say anything. If she is a decent human being she will come to the right conclusion. I just have to give her a minute. And right now, that is all I can spare.

Eventually, perhaps weighed down by the silence, she speaks. 'Do … do you really think that's him? That he's hurt that woman?'

I move closer to her and take her hand. 'I'm sorry, but yes. I know the other man was actually … you know … but they were in it together. He's just as guilty, and I happen to know he's done this to another woman.'

'But … he was so nice to me,' Charlotte says. 'I don't understand it.'

'Neither do I.' I think of Hannah and how Lucas must have been good to her for her to end up married to him, so it's possible he was kind to Charlotte. This reminds me that I still don't know why she went missing. But now is not the time to ask. 'Charlotte, please will you help?'

She looks at me directly and gives a hint of a nod. 'But how?'

Finally I have made progress. 'Okay, I need you to tell me everything you can about Lucas. Where you met. The kind of places he took you. Anything you can think of.'

Silence again, and I wonder if I will ever get through to her.

'Um … we just used to go to his place mostly.' Her cheeks redden and I assume she realises the significance of this. 'But the first time we met in a bar. In Soho. I'd never been there before. It was nice.'

I don't have time for Charlotte's reminiscing. 'So you mostly went to his flat in Embankment?' I say.

She shakes her head. 'No. His place is in Wood Green. But I can't remember the road name. I know where it is, though.'

This is better than I could have expected. Lucas has another property that we knew nothing about. I have no idea what we'll find there but at least it's something to go on. 'Right, grab your coat, Charlotte. I need you to show me where this place is.'

She opens her mouth, probably to protest, but shuts it again and stands up. 'But if he's not there, what are you going to do?'

'Get in somehow,' I say. 'See if my friend's daughter is there.'

'But how do you think we'll get in?'

This is a good point – I haven't thought this far ahead. 'I'll worry about that when we get there,' I say.

'Well, we might need these, then,' Charlotte says, reaching in her pocket and pulling out a set of keys. There are so many dangling from her purple heart key ring that it takes her a moment to find the ones she's looking for. 'These are Lucas's spare keys. He gave them to me so I could just let myself in to wait for him.'

This surprises me. Lucas must have liked Charlotte a lot to give her a set of keys. But then again, if this flat in Wood Green is anything like the one in Embankment then there would be nothing to trust her with. It could all just be for his convenience. To have her there waiting whenever he wanted.

Before we leave, Charlotte scribbles a note to her mum, telling her she's gone to a friend's house and will be back soon. 'I don't want her to worry if she comes home and finds me gone,' she explains.

Once we are in the car, I introduce Charlotte to Ginny, explaining that she is Grace's mother. She seems shocked to find someone in the passenger seat, but quickly recovers.

'I don't think he'll be there,' she says, and I wonder if this is what she's hoping.

It's been a long time since I was in north London, but I don't have time to set the Sat Nav. I have a vague idea how to get to Wood Green station, and thankfully I am right.

When we pass the station on our left, Charlotte calls out that I'm going the wrong way. 'I used to turn right out of the station,' she says. So I make an illegal U-turn and follow her directions.

We head along Green Lanes, back the way we have just come, and I wonder if Charlotte is lying and has no intention of leading us to Lucas. 'But we've just come this way,' I say, trying to keep my annoyance at bay.

'I know, but I'm not used to it from that way,' she says, staring out of the window. 'Here, take this left.'

Her warning comes so late that I have to slam on the brakes to avoid missing the turning. Ginny clutches the dashboard but doesn't say anything. She has been almost silent since Charlotte joined us.

'Sorry,' Charlotte says, 'I'm not great with directions.'

'Are you sure this is it?' I ask.

'Yep. I remember because it's the turning just before the betting shop. Just keep going up to the end.'

'It's Belsize Avenue,' Ginny says, as we pass the road sign.

I wonder why Lucas would have a property in this area. It's run down and grotty; nothing like his house in Notting Hill, or even the flat in Embankment.

When we reach the end of the road I realise it is a no-through road, cut off with bollards and a steep pavement. I turn the car around and slot it into a parking space.

'Which house is it?' I ask Charlotte, as she undoes her seatbelt.

'Over there. The one with the blue door.'

We all turn to our left and see the house she is talking about. It is mid-terrace, and is in need of maintenance.

'Why would Lucas have a house here?' Ginny asks, finally finding her voice.

Charlotte huffs. 'To get away from his wife, maybe? I dunno. But I'm not lying. That's his place.' She turns to me.

'So, should I go and knock first? And what am I supposed to say to him?'

'No,' I say. 'Let's think about this. We need to be careful. The main thing is that we find Grace, and there's a chance he knows where she is. That's all that matters for now. The police will have to deal with whatever else he's done.'

In the passenger seat, Ginny unclicks her seatbelt and leans forward. 'I feel sick,' she says, and there is no need to ask why.

'Right,' I say. 'I'll go and knock on the door. If there's no answer then both of you join me and Charlotte can let us in.' It's not exactly a master plan, but it's all I can think of.

I take their silence for agreement, and leaving them in the car, cross the road to Lucas's house. The paint on the blue door is peeling and there is a huge dent in the lower panel. It is only when I see there are two buzzers that I realise the house has been split into two flats. I turn to the car and wave my arms to get someone's attention. Charlotte rolls down the window and shouts out that it's flat B. Turning back to the door, I press the buzzer and wait.

I can feel their eyes on me as the seconds tick by with no sign of life from inside. Stepping onto the grass, I check the window, but the curtains are drawn. I don't even know if flat B is the downstairs or upstairs property. Leaving it a few moments longer, I head back to the car. As I cross the road I glance back and see that the upstairs curtains are also closed.

Before I reach the car, both Ginny and Charlotte clamber out, the slam of the doors echoing into the silent street.

'Okay, we'll need your key,' I say, holding my hand out to Charlotte.

'What if he's in there?' Ginny says. She wraps her arms around her body but it doesn't stop her shivering. I have only just noticed that her coat is too thin for this weather.

'Let's just be prepared for anything,' I say, leading the way to the house. I don't know what I feel at this moment, but it's closer to anger than fear. Since I heard Ginny's story I am even more desperate to find Grace, so nothing will keep me out of that house. Once we've found her we can all deal with the mess our lives will be in. Thinking of this reminds me of Chris Harding and his missing sister, and how he should know I have managed to track down another property of Lucas's. I also need to tell him about the video so I will text him once we've searched inside.

Charlotte tells me the gold key is for the main door, and I open it and step into a communal corridor, with one door to the right and a set of stairs leading to the first floor.

'It's the upstairs one,' Charlotte says, and I let her walk ahead.

Surprisingly, the seagrass carpet looks fairly new and is out of place against the yellowing woodchip walls. As I stare at Charlotte's back, and Ginny follows behind me, I can't help but let out a stifled laugh. In the last week I have found myself searching so many houses I have lost count. But my levity quickly evaporates when I remember why we are here.

Lucas's front door seems in better condition than the main one downstairs, and I knock on it three times, just in case the buzzer isn't working. But again there is silence.

'Do you realise we're breaking the law?' Charlotte says, as I'm about to slot the other key in the lock.

Ginny answers before I have a chance. 'No we're not. You have the keys. That means you can come here anytime, doesn't it?'

Charlotte's face creases in concentration as she thinks about what Ginny has said. 'I suppose,' she says, shrugging. 'But what if he's in? What will I say? He'll know I've betrayed him and—'

'Charlotte, remember what he's done?' I say, finding it hard to keep my voice from rising. 'Betraying him should be the least of your worries.'

'But how will I explain—'

'Just leave that to me.' I push the key into the door, but it doesn't open.

I turn to Charlotte and she takes it from me and tries herself. 'It's a bit awkward. There's a way to do it.'

Seconds later, she has got the door open and, with a deep breath, I step inside.

With the curtains shut and no window in the hall, the flat is shrouded in darkness, so it takes my eyes a minute to adjust. And when I finally take in my surroundings and peer into the living room, I realise there is nothing to see but a tattered sofa. There is no television, or even a stand where one might have been. Much like his flat in Embankment, there are no paintings or personal possessions and not even a mirror hanging on a wall. But this flat is not like a show home. It's as if nobody has bothered with it at all.

I turn to Charlotte, who is clearly more familiar with this place than Ginny or I. 'Where is everything? Why isn't there anything in here?'

'He doesn't exactly *live* here,' Charlotte says, her frustrated tone screaming out that I should already know this.

'Then why did he bring you here?' As soon as the question leaves my mouth I know the answer.

Charlotte flushes red. 'Because he's married, isn't he? We had to keep our love a secret.'

I flinch at the word *love*. I'm about to ask if she knows he has at least one other property like this but decide to save her the pain. She is already deluded about her relationship with Lucas, so I don't need to make it worse. Besides, what could be more horrifying than knowing he is a rapist?

'What's through there?' Ginny asks, pointing to a closed door ahead of us.

'The kitchen,' Charlotte says, leading the way. 'And next to it is the bedroom.' But she stops short before she reaches the kitchen door. 'What if ... what am I supposed to say to him? I mean, if that's really his voice in that video—'

'It *is* his voice,' Ginny says. 'I know his voice.' She raises her own voice, seeming to have found her strength again.

Charlotte nods. 'Well, what are we supposed to do now?'

'Find my daughter,' Ginny says, turning to me with an apologetic shrug.

Even though I am glad Charlotte seems to be facing up to what a monster Lucas is, there isn't time for this. I stride past them both and fling open the kitchen door, only to be greeted by an empty, dark room.

This leaves only one other room to try. 'But where's the bathroom?' I ask, turning back to Charlotte, who has remained in the hall.

'You get to it through the bedroom. Bit weird, I know.'

'Come on then,' I say. There is very little chance Grace is here, or anything that will lead us to her, and I feel myself flagging, all the hope I had before we got here evaporating into the oppressive air.

I am first through the bedroom door, with Ginny so close behind me I can feel her breath on the back of my neck. Once again the room is pitch black, but it's somehow a darker blackness than the other rooms.

And just as my eyes begin to adjust, and focus on the upside down Converse trainer that's lying on the floor, I am shoved to the floor, and barely have a chance to register the slam of the door, and a key turning in the lock on the other side.

TWENTY-EIGHT

For months I was distracted and I let my studies slip. I was so consumed with what we were doing and spent every moment waiting for the next buzz. Oh, don't get me wrong – I know this is far worse than a drug or alcohol addiction, but I was just as powerless to stop it, especially when I knew there were no boundaries, no limits to what we could do.

My night with Leanne had opened the floodgates for us, and now we were in it together. We picked the girls together, and then once we got back to their places, they were helpless to stop us doing whatever we wanted to them. We used alcohol at first, to numb them and keep them quiet, but he decided we'd need something stronger.

We travelled all across London, spending our nights in unfamiliar bars, but it was safer this way; we couldn't risk doing it locally.

When he first suggested the others join us, I was disappointed. Until then, it had been something just for us, and now he wanted to open it up. Although they had become friendlier towards me, I still didn't like it. But once he explained the potential, the things we could do to these women with all of us there, I came around to the idea.

I'm not sure which one of us suggested filming, but it brought in an added element. I could watch back the videos, once I was alone, and relive the moments, even if I had been just a bystander on that particular occasion.

The girls knew nothing of their experience, they were so drugged up, and we always needed a way to find new highs, once the buzz began to wane. But we chose the girls together. That was the deal.

Those months were good. Does my saying that disgust you? Doesn't that make it even worse than just carrying out the acts?

But how long can you ride the high? Sooner or later you have to come down, and that's what happened when I met Becky. She was a literature student and had just transferred to our university. She would always sit in the same place in the canteen, and I began to join her at her table, hoping to spark up a conversation.

I know what you're thinking: it wasn't how we normally met girls but she must have been the next one on our list. But you've got it wrong. Becky was different. I can't say how, all I knew was that I couldn't let the others know about her. I was infatuated with her before she'd even opened her mouth to speak.

She was small and cute like a doll, with wild, curly red hair that fell down her back and bounced every time she moved her head. I wanted to nuzzle in it and breathe in her flowery scent. I was fascinated by her freckles. She hated them, but I found them endearing.

After sitting together a few times at lunch, we struck up a conversation. I don't remember who started it, or what we talked about, but it must have been casual talk to start with. Family. Studies. Music. Nothing deeper than that. And then we went for a drink. I can't remember whether it took days or weeks, but eventually we were together. We fell into place.

Being with Becky should have changed things, shouldn't it? She should have been a distraction from him, someone I could focus all my attention on – she was certainly deserving of that. And sex worked with us too. It was nice. Comfortable. Exciting even. So different from the acts I carried out with him. Acts I couldn't pull myself away from.

I should have known it couldn't work with Becky, that I couldn't change and definitely wouldn't be able to share her. He threw a party and I was supposed to take her, to introduce her to everyone, show her off, see if she met with their approval. But I wanted to keep her to myself. I didn't want her to become part of it. She made me feel decent, despite what I was doing when I wasn't with her.

I told myself she wasn't like the other ones, surely everyone would see that? Surely they would say she wasn't right. She was too perfect, too innocent. Her view of the world was yet to be corrupted or blackened by events out of her control. I badly wanted to keep it that way.

I wouldn't let them have Becky.

So I did the only thing I could to protect her. I told her I didn't want to see her again, and watched, frozen like ice, while tears streamed down her red, puffy face, obscuring her freckles. She was still cute in that state, and part of me wanted to tell her I'd made a mistake and changed my mind, and that we should just run away. Get away from there. From everyone and everything. But then she would ask what we were running from, and there was no way I could answer that question. And how can you run from yourself?

For weeks she'd turn up at my door, knocking repeatedly while I held my breath on the other side, hoping she didn't know I was there. She said she just needed to understand. To be able to move on. And why couldn't I just give her that? If she'd ever meant anything to me?

Then suddenly it stopped, and I never saw her around the university. I heard from someone that she had transferred to another campus; that she'd had a family emergency and needed to be near her parents.

I missed her for months, her absence feeling like a hole somewhere in my body, but at least I had kept her safe.

TWENTY-NINE

Something lands on top of me with a heavy thud, and it takes me a moment to realise it is Ginny.

'What the hell?' she says, easing herself off me and rubbing her arm.

Standing up, I rush to the door and pound on it until my knuckles are sore. 'Charlotte? Open this door. Now!'

But there is only silence on the other side, and after a few moments I hear the slamming of the front door and footsteps thudding down the stairs.

I scramble in my pocket for my phone, but it's not there. 'Ginny, your phone – where is it?'

Her hand crosses to her shoulder, but there is no bag hanging there. We are in trouble.

Ginny takes over the pounding, panic etched on her face. 'Open this fucking door, now!' She turns to me but her fists continue slamming against the door. 'She's taken our phones. She planned this whole thing. Got us here on purpose. But why?'

It is an important question, but I have just remembered what I saw when I first peered into the room. I reach down and pick up the Converse trainer. There is a dark stain on one side, which even in the darkness I can tell is blood. 'Ginny, is this … Grace's?'

Ginny stops pounding on the door and squints into the darkness, holding out her hand. I pass it to her and wait for her to tell me that of course it isn't. She turns it around and studies the stain, her eyes widening as she comes to the same conclusion I have.

'I … I don't know. It could be. She has got a pair of these, but they all look the same, don't they? I just don't know! But if it is hers, and that's blood …'

I nod. 'Just try to stay calm.' I say this but I'm having trouble doing it myself. I need to keep focused and not just assume the worst. 'We'll work this out, okay? First we need some light in here.' I survey the room to determine where the window is, but there isn't one. 'That's weird,' I say. 'How can there be no window? Try the light switch.'

Ginny locates it next to the door and flicks the switch, but nothing happens. I stare up at the ceiling and of course there is no light bulb hanging from it.

'Try the bathroom, that must be it,' Ginny suggests, pointing at the other door, and I head to it and peer inside. The room has a narrow slit for a window, and it is sealed shut, but leaving the door open should let in at least a sliver of light. There is a shower and a toilet in here, but nothing else. No toiletries, towels or bathmat. No signs of life.

Back in the bedroom, Ginny stands still, holding a red piece of material out to me. I take it and quickly realise it's a dress. I check the label and see it is a size eight Lipsy Dress. 'Grace's?' I ask, finding it hard to picture the casually dressed girl I met wearing this fitted dress.

Ginny shakes her head. 'No. I've never seen her wearing that and she usually shows me any new clothes she buys. And it's not really her style.'

I only feel slight relief at this. 'But it's someone's, isn't it?' I say. 'Maybe the girl in the video?' The image of the girl's face appears in my head, but she was dressed only in underwear so there's no way of knowing.

'I don't know. Could be,' Ginny says.

I think of Chris Harding again and wonder if the dress belongs to his sister. If only I had tried to text him before we entered the house. I would have realised my phone was missing and could have prevented this mess.

But there is no time for ifs and maybes. I need to think on my feet and find a way to get us out of here. Now my eyes have become more accustomed to the darkness, I look around the room. There is nothing in here but a bed with a sagging mattress and burgundy duvet and a wooden shelf on the wall opposite.

Ginny sinks to the floor. 'Why would Lucas do this? Why? Daniel was his best friend. I thought he was looking out for us. And what's he done with Grace?'

'I don't know, but we need to stay calm. Conserve our energy. We don't know how long we'll be here or what he's got planned. And I need to be able to think.'

With tears flooding from her eyes, Ginny nods and hunches up against the wall by the bedroom door, looking like a small child rather than a woman in her late forties.

'Someone will find us,' I say. I'm not sure if I believe this but I need to give Ginny some hope.

She perks up a bit and wipes her eyes. 'So that little bitch, she planned to get us here all along?'

I think about this for a moment. There was no way Charlotte could have known we would turn up at her house, but the idea must have come to her as soon as we talked about Lucas's flat in Wood Green, which means that she must have texted Lucas in the car. I was concentrating so much on driving us here that I didn't glance at her in the rear-view mirror, and Ginny wouldn't have noticed either. It's possible she was communicating with him for the whole journey, and he told her what to do once we got here.

Charlotte certainly put a good act on at her house; I was convinced she didn't know where he was, especially after I dropped the bomb about him being in France.

Ginny agrees when I tell her all this, and curses herself for not paying attention to Charlotte.

'We've just been so intent on finding Lucas,' I say, 'so that we can get to Grace, it's not surprising we didn't suspect Charlotte.' And this is also how she managed to get our phones, and Daniel's, without us noticing.

Knowing this doesn't make me feel any better, but I need to stay focused.

At least Ginny is calmer now. 'Do you have people?' she asks. 'You know, people who will miss you? Who might worry?'

I join her on the floor and lean against the bed. It smells damp, but that's no surprise given the likelihood that this room never sees fresh air. I long to smell even the heavy polluted smog outside; anything is better than this. 'Yes,' I tell Ginny. 'My husband.' But of course, Matt won't be looking for me. Not for a long while. He'll be drinking his morning coffee in that cottage in Cornwall, peaceful in his oblivion, planning how to fill the rest of the time until I return. And because we've always been so trusting of each other, he won't even worry if he can't get hold of me for a while. He will think I'm – once again – swamped with work and too busy to return his call. And by the time he realises something is wrong, that I have never taken quite that long to reply, it will be too late.

And then I realise something even worse: Charlotte could easily be texting him from my phone, pretending to be me, telling him all sorts of lies. Although I have a passcode for my phone, it's plausible that she could work around it, or knows someone who can do it for her, just like Abbot did with Lucas's laptop. Panic bubbles inside me, but I keep it smothered. I can't fall to pieces now.

'So he'll call the police, won't he?' Ginny asks, her reluctance to involve them apparently thrown out of the window.

'Yes, he will,' I say, keeping my fears to myself. 'But we'll be out of here before then. I just need time to think.' Saying this keeps me sane, allows me to believe I can save us both.

'I have nobody but Grace,' Ginny says. 'I mean, there was Daniel before, but it's always been just the two of us really. You know, even if I have to lose her, I don't care if it means we get her back safely.'

I fully understand what she is saying, because even if Grace is mine and I have to give her up all over again to keep her safe, I would do it in a shot.

'Sorry,' she says. 'We probably shouldn't talk about that now. I just ... miss her so much. I can't bear not knowing where she is. It's like someone's scraping out my insides, leaving me hollow inside.'

And with those words, it all comes flooding back to me; all the pain of losing Helena, not knowing where she was, whether she was alive or dead. That feeling of suffocation. I crawl across to Ginny and put my arm around her, pulling her into me so she can rest her head on my shoulder. It is strange to remember that she's a carer, used to taking charge and looking after others, but now she is the helpless one. Abbot was right. He is a good judge of character. There is no way this woman could have abducted a baby.

Ginny closes her eyes and after some time she appears to be asleep, a light whistling sound escaping from her mouth with each breath.

Keeping as still as possible, I try to think of a way out of here. But it is hopeless. There is no escape: the bathroom window is too small even for a child to climb through and the bedroom door is too sturdy to break down.

I search the room thoroughly but there is nothing in here we could use to even dent the wood.

Abbot was the one person I could have depended on to notice me missing and try to find me, but we haven't spoken since Tuesday. I'm not due in work, so nobody there will question my absence, and if Abbot does ask where I am, he will just hear that I am in Cornwall with Matt, and that will be the end of it.

I need to pull myself together. Nobody is coming. Not Matt, not Abbot, nobody except Lucas Hall. Whether it's in five minutes, five hours or five days, he will show his face. And that will have to be our chance. Because until somebody opens that door, we are not leaving this room alive.

I must fall asleep because my eyes snap open and I am sprawled on the floor next to Ginny. Her eyes are still closed and her head rests against the wall. When I check my watch I realise it is past midday, so we haven't been here that long.

My stomach grumbles, reminding me I haven't eaten since dinner with Matt yesterday evening. I am also thirsty. Careful not to disturb Ginny, I ease myself up and head to the bathroom, praying the tap will work.

I am in luck and a stream of cloudy water flows out. Cupping my hands I ravenously throw water down my throat, ignoring the metallic taste.

Back in the bedroom, Ginny stirs and opens her eyes. 'I can't believe I fell asleep,' she says, looking around the room.

I remind her that she waited up for me all night, so it's hardly surprising. 'What time is it? And what the hell are we going to do?'

The panic is back in her voice so I need to calm her again. 'We're going to wait. Sooner or later he'll show up, and then we take him by surprise.'

Her eyebrows knit together. 'But ... how? What do you mean?'

'Just trust me, okay? I've got an idea and I don't know if it will work, but it's worth a try.'

The lines disappear from her forehead. 'Okay. Look, sorry I'm panicking. It's not like me. I'm usually the rational one, the one sorting other people out. But when it's my own problem I seem to fall apart.'

'I think you're allowed to, given the circumstances.' I walk over to her and sit on the floor again. The bed would probably be more comfortable but I can't bear the thought of sitting on it, knowing what has happened on the mattress. 'Grace is ... well, you raised her, didn't you?' I try to keep the resentment from my voice. It is impossible not to feel anger, but I keep it under control. After all, Ginny and I are in this together now. And at least now, after eighteen years, I am close to knowing exactly what happened.

'She's a great daughter, you know,' Ginny says. 'And if we're right about Daniel lying, which I'm sure we are, then she will be to you too when we find her.'

I am glad she is finally being positive about our dire situation, and only hope I can pull off what I need to do.

'You know,' she says, 'perhaps I could talk to Lucas. When he gets here. I've known him a long time and he was Daniel's best friend, surely that counts for something?'

I open my mouth to tell her how unlikely it is that Lucas will care about her feelings, given what he did to Grace, but think better of it. Ginny has only just pulled herself together and I don't want her panicking again. Instead I tell her we should see what happens when the moment arrives.

'What's your husband like?' she asks. 'Sorry if I'm being nosy, but I can't stand this waiting, I need to take my mind off it.'

She is right, in the absence of anything else to do but wait, there is no harm talking about things. Perhaps it will help us both keep it together.

'Matt's great,' I say, and an image of him walking along the rain-soaked beach floats into my head. 'I mean, he's not perfect – who is? – but I can't imagine my life without him. We've been through so much together, losing Helena, and we met so young, so—'

'He's like the other part of you?'

I think about this for a moment. 'No, I don't believe in all that needing another person to complete you stuff. We're both so independent – we have our own careers and interests, but when we come together, it just works.'

Ginny chews her lower lip and takes a moment to answer. 'I would have loved to have met someone special. It just … never happened. I guess I'm not that lucky.'

Her words set off anger inside me I thought I had suppressed and I stare at her in disbelief. Does she want me to feel sorry for her? Now I can no longer keep my emotions hidden. 'Are you serious? I may have Matt but we lost our daughter. Our baby. And you're talking about not having anyone.'

'No, I didn't mean—'

The door is flung open and a shadow appears in the door-way. Before I have a chance to comprehend what's going on, a man steps in, grabbing Ginny and dragging her backwards by her hair. She lets out a piercing yelp and I shoot to my feet to try and help her, but I am too far away from the door. By the time I am up and ready, the door has banged shut, a key turning on the other side of the lock.

Ginny has gone.

But I recognise the man who has taken her.

I know exactly who he is.

THIRTY

I rush to the door. I am ready. My legs may be trembling beneath me, but I am ready for him. I will only get one chance to get this right.

On the other side of the door Ginny is screaming, but her shrieks soon become muffled and I can only assume he is smothering her mouth. A thud comes next, followed by several more, and then there is silence. The silence is more terrifying than the sounds.

He has attacked Ginny and I am next on his list. But I won't let that happen. I am Grace and Ginny's only hope now. Helena's only hope. And despite the blood on the shoe, I have to believe she is still alive.

I don't know how long I stand there, poised, waiting, but eventually I hear the key turn once more. The door opens and he steps inside, his face twisted, his slanted grin menacing.

Nick Gibbs.

'Hello again,' he says, edging towards me. 'Bet you weren't expecting me?'

I step back. 'What have you done to Ginny? And where's Grace?'

His lips turn into a snarl, and I marvel at how different he looks from the kind man who was helping us find Lucas. None of this makes sense.

'Ginny's taken care of. She won't be interfering again.'

I try not to think about what his words mean. 'So … this was you all along? You're in this with Lucas? And Ginny's brother?'

'Enough of the questions,' he says. 'I don't think you want to know the answers before you go.'

'Go where?' But I already know what he means. I need to act now, before it is too late. I slip my hand in my pocket and feel for what I already know is there. I clasp it in my fist; the cold metal reassuring against my skin.

He doesn't notice. 'It's a shame, you know. I actually quite liked you. Apart from your snooping around. But then I can't blame you. It was Lucas and his fucking mouth that started this. He caused all this mess. And now I'm the one who has to fix it. You should have all just kept out of it. Bet you wish you had now, don't you?'

I am still confused, but there is no time to try and work out what he's talking about. 'Where's Grace? Where's my daughter?'

He smirks. 'Your daughter? You're sure about that, are you? You're going to trust the word of a man like Lucas?'

'How are you any better?' I say. 'Doing this?' If I can just keep him talking a bit longer I will be more likely to catch him off guard.

Ignoring my question, he tells me how gullible I am, how easily I walked into this trap. 'Let's just hope you don't make too much of a mess,' he says, 'I don't have time to waste cleaning up. You should have just minded your own business and stayed out of mine.'

With a rush of adrenalin I lunge forward and plunge my car key deep into his neck, thrusting it in with as much force as I can muster. For a sickening moment I think it hasn't done anything as he just stands there, staring at me with shocked eyes. But then blood spurts from his neck and he clutches at it, reeling backwards. I bring up my knee and thrust it into his groin, with strength I didn't know I had.

And then I run for my life.

I don't look behind me but rush through the hall and twist the door handle. There is a trail of blood along the carpet but no sign of Ginny, and I can't risk looking; he might be coming after me any second. But I will get help for her.

It takes too long to thrust open the front door, the catch is slippery in my sweating, blood-soaked hand, and I can almost feel Nick's arms grabbing me.

But I get through with no sign of him, and stumble down the stairs, holding my breath until I am outside. I take in a huge gulp of frozen air, but there is no time to stop. With my bloodied car key still in my hand, I race across the road and almost crash into someone.

Abbot.

I blink, in case I am mistaken, but he is still there, looking just as confused as I feel. 'Sim? What's going on? Are you okay? What are you doing here?'

But there is no time to explain. 'Quick, we have to get out of here NOW!' I know I must sound hysterical but Abbot doesn't question me. Fumbling with my key, trying to force it into the car door, I end up dropping it instead. Abbot scoops it up, a frown on his face as he notices the blood, but he only grabs my arm and tells me his car is right behind mine.

Only when he has made a U-turn and we are back on Green Lanes do I dare to speak. I tell him to take the next left and stop the car.

He does as I ask but as soon as we're parked up he asks me what's going on.

'I need to call the police,' I say.

By the time I've disconnected the call, Abbot knows exactly what has happened. 'What the fuck?' he says. 'Nick Gibbs? I can't believe it. And why didn't you call me to go with you? You could be dead right now.'

Like Ginny.

I am too shaken to explain my reasons so only offer an apology. He takes my hand and we sit and wait until an ambulance and two police cars pass us, sirens blazing, and we know it is safe to head back to Belsize Avenue.

When we get there, a police officer, who tells me his name is PC Millbank, meets us at the car and peers into the passenger side window to ask me what happened. I quickly recount the details, watching as he rushes off and heads towards the house. His colleagues join him, and they have no need to break the front door down; it is wide open, exactly as I left it.

Two paramedics wait on the pavement, standing beside a stretcher and other equipment I can't name. My insides turn cold as I remember the noises Ginny made. How will I ever explain this to Grace when we find her? I am the one who led Ginny here. I am the one who trusted Charlotte Bray.

'Are you sure you're okay?' Abbot asks. 'Maybe you should get checked out at the hospital?' He has barely taken his eyes off me since I ran into him, but I don't feel uncomfortable.

I nod. 'He didn't have a chance to hurt me. But Ginny …'

Abbot pulls me into a hug and all the tension between us melts away. He is still my friend. 'And you think you injured him badly? That he's still in there?'

This is what I am hoping. He didn't come after me, so there's every chance he is. 'There was a lot of blood,' I tell Abbot.

We stay in the car, sitting in silence until, after some time, the police officer I spoke to a moment ago appears in the doorway, beckoning the paramedics to join him. They all disappear inside, and I relax a bit. This will soon be over. They will bring Nick Gibbs out, handcuffed, and then they will find Grace. And Chris Harding's sister.

'There's still so much I don't understand,' I say to Abbot. 'Is he in this with Lucas? And did he take part in those attacks too?'

Abbot frowns. 'It doesn't make sense at the moment, but we'll get our answers. Speaking of answers, I still don't understand what you were doing here with Ginny and Charlotte Bray. I mean, I know you were looking for Lucas, but how did it come about? They said at work you'd gone away with Matt. To Cornwall?'

For the next ten minutes I fill Abbot in on everything that led to me being here. He is open-mouthed when I've finished and takes a moment to piece it all together. 'So Grace *is* yours? She's Helena?'

'It looks that way.'

'How do you feel about that?'

I am about to tell him I can't answer that right now, when I realise I am not the only one with explaining to do. 'How did you find me? How did you know I was here?'

'When I was at Ginny's the other night, she was talking about Daniel quite a bit and wanted to show me photos of him. So we were going through her albums when I saw a picture of him and Lucas from university. There was another guy in the photo, but I didn't recognise him. He had longish hair and stubble covering half his face. Anyway, I took the photo while she wasn't looking and got my mate to run it through a facial recognition programme. I found out this morning it was Nick Gibbs, but I didn't recognise him at all; he looked completely different with facial hair. I tried to call you but your phone was off. I've left a ton of messages.'

'Charlotte Bray took it. And Ginny's. And Daniel's phone with the video. The evidence the police need.'

Abbot looks towards the house. 'Don't worry, I think they'll have plenty of that.' He shakes his head. 'Anyway, I went straight to his house and parked up, ready to confront him for lying about the extent of his friendship with Lucas, but then he came out and got in his car. So I followed him to Wood Green. I lost him a bit further back but spotted his car right on the corner back there.' He points towards the other end of the street, where Nick Gibbs's car is still parked. At least that must mean he's still in there. 'And then I saw your car,' Abbot continues, 'and was deciding what to do when you rushed from that house.'

Through the window I see the paramedics reappear, pulling the stretcher along with them. Without a word to Abbot, I fling open the car door and rush towards them.

When I get closer I see it is Ginny lying on the stretcher, but her face isn't covered with a sheet. She is alive. There is an oxygen mask attached to her mouth so she must be in a bad way, but I'm just relieved she's not dead.

'Is she okay?' I ask one of the paramedics. He is young, with a shaved head, and looks as if he's only just left school. 'We need to get her to hospital now. Are you family?'

'Not really,' I say, wondering what Grace makes us. 'But as good as.'

Abbot appears at my side, clutching my arm.

'You'll have to visit her later,' the paramedic says. 'North Middlesex University Hospital. The police will need to talk to you first.' He turns away, back to the job of saving Ginny's life.

We watch as they load her into the ambulance and drive away, the siren blaring as they disappear onto Green Lanes. I turn to Abbot to ask him whether he thinks we should talk to Tamsin and Elliott Bray, when the police officers emerge from the house.

With no sign of Nick Gibbs.

I rush over to them and PC Millbank steps towards me. In his hand is a clear plastic bag with the blood-stained converse trainer. 'There's nobody else in there. We've checked the whole flat and there's no sign of this Nicholas Gibbs.'

Despair washes over me. 'But his car's still parked at the end of the road.' I point towards it.

'He must have left on foot,' PC Millbank says. *And he will be coming after me*, I think. I couldn't have injured him as badly as I thought, and now he will try to find me. The thought makes me shudder. 'Anyway,' PC Millbank continues, 'let us worry about that. If you're up to it we need you to come down to the station and make a formal statement. The sooner the better, while everything's fresh in your mind.'

'Yes, of course,' I say. At least I will be safe there. And I do want to help the police, but I am not ready to tell them everything. I point to the bag in PC Millbank's hand. 'Will you test the blood on that shoe?'

He offers a vague smile. 'Yes. Look, try not to assume it's your friend's daughter's. There are millions of people who own Converse trainers.'

I know he is right, and I need to keep reminding myself of this. 'But without Grace here, how will you know it's hers?' I ask this, but I already know the answer. They will test the DNA against Ginny's.

PC Millbank confirms this before turning to Abbot. 'Sir, we'll need you to give a statement too. You're a witness.'

Abbot tells him that's no problem and we arrange to go immediately to Wood Green police station.

Four hours later I leave the police station with Abbot, grateful to be outside, breathing in a lungful of fresh air. I have been in many police stations before, covering stories, but never as a victim. I feel like my soul has been exposed.

'So they know almost everything now,' I say to Abbot. 'About Lucas, Charlotte, Daniel and Nick. I even told them about Gabby, because surely Nick must have paid her off or manipulated her into meeting me at that pub? It was just his way to ensure I focused on Lucas and didn't turn my attention to him. But I couldn't tell them anything about Grace being mine. They just think she's missing and that I'm a friend of Ginny's and was helping her out.'

Abbot's eyes widen. 'But how did you get away with that? Didn't they wonder why you hadn't reported her missing? And when they find her, how will they find out if Grace is Helena when they'll be testing her DNA against Ginny's?'

'Matt and I can sort out a DNA test, we don't need them for that. And yes, they did ask why we hadn't reported Grace missing, but I just told them we thought she was away with friends.' I try to ignore Abbot's frown. 'Look, I couldn't tell the truth and get Ginny in trouble. I told them about Daniel being in that video so she will already have to deal with that. But she's fighting for her life in hospital and they'd just arrest her until they have evidence she didn't know Helena was abducted. And what proof is there? I'm sure she'd still be in trouble either way, but Grace wouldn't want that, would she?'

Abbot sighs. 'I suppose you're right. But it's a dangerous game, Sim, lying to the police. And what are you going to do when they test Ginny's blood?' He shakes his head.

'Well, it just won't be a match, will it? They'll just say it's not Grace's.'

'But don't you want to know if it is?'

'I just have to believe they're going to find her, Abbot. And that bastard Nick Gibbs, then I'll deal with whatever I have to. I need to see Ginny as soon as possible to let her know what I've told them. Our stories need to match up. Look, the main thing is we're not on our own with it anymore, Abbot. We've got the police on our side.'

'Yeah, let's focus on that. They've got the resources to find Grace.' He smiles a thin smile. 'Does part of you feel relieved?'

'Not until they find Nick Gibbs and lock him up for the rest of his life. I mean, this goes way beyond rape, doesn't it? There's also child abduction and attempted murder. It makes my blood run cold.'

'But are they offering you protection or anything? Surely they realise he could be after you?'

I tell Abbot they've assured me patrol cars will make regular visits to the house, driving up and down the road to check everything is okay. And I've also been assigned a Family Liaison Officer called Sandra, who will keep me up to date with the investigation.

'That's good,' Abbot says, placing his arm on my shoulder as we walk towards the car park. We drove here separately, neither of us wanting to leave our cars on that road.

'Now what's the plan?' Abbot asks when we get to my car.

'I need to tell Matt everything. I just hope he understands why I kept it all from him.'

Abbot places his hand on my shoulder. 'He will. He loves you, Sim, and you've got through worse than this.'

I know he's right, but it's a lot to expect Matt to just accept everything. 'He's still in Cornwall, but I'm too shaken up to drive all that way now and I wouldn't get there till late, so I'll have to get him to come back. And that means him getting the train, which will take hours.'

'Do you want to stay at mine until he gets back? So you're not alone. Or I'll come to yours with you?'

Although his offer is tempting, I will not let fear of Nick Gibbs dictate what I do. I tell Abbot this, and that I'll be fine.

'I really don't think it's a good idea to be alone, Sim. Seriously. Think what you've been through today.'

'Let me try it and see how I get on. I can call you if I get worried about anything.'

Abbot reluctantly agrees. 'But make sure you call me later.'

With a promise to do this, I watch him drive off before I open my car door and slip inside, locking the door. I need to call Matt and I hunt for my mobile until I remember Charlotte stole it. I check my watch and realise the shops are still open. There is bound to be a phone shop in Wood Green, but I don't want to traipse the streets when Nick Gibbs could be anywhere. So instead I start the engine and head in the direction of the North Circular and Brent Cross shopping centre.

'Simone? I've been worried. I thought you'd be on your way back by now. I've been trying to call you. And what number is this?' Despite his concern, Matt's voice immediately soothes me.

'I'm sorry. I lost my phone and had to buy a new pay-as-you-go one. Just for now.'

'That's a pain. So where are you?'

The truth is I am sitting in Brent Cross car park, staring at row after row of cars, but I can't tell Matt the reason I am here. Not yet. I don't want him worrying all the way home. 'I'm just leaving work. Listen, I know I said I'd come back down there, but … something's … look, would you mind coming home on the train? Tonight? I wouldn't ask if it wasn't important. I just don't feel up to driving but I need to see you. We need to talk.'

Matt will know that I would never normally ask this of him. He will see that the situation demands his acceptance. 'Sure,' he says, after a moment. 'But I'm worried now. Are you okay?'

'I'll be fine. Just really not well. So you'll come back tonight?'

He sighs. 'I can't pretend I'm not disappointed. I was looking forward to a couple more days here with you, but, yes, of course I'll come home.'

He tells me he'll text me the train details so I'll know when to expect him back, and we hang up. That was the easy part. Telling him the truth will not be so straightforward.

THIRTY-ONE

The first thing I do when I get home is double lock the front door and check all the windows are secured. In winter we rarely step out of the back door, but I check it anyway, relieved to find everything as it should be.

I still haven't eaten so I make peanut butter on toast and take it upstairs, wolfing it down as I run a bath. My limbs are aching and I need to wash the day off my skin. I also need this time of serenity before I break the news to Matt.

His train gets into Paddington at 11:44 p.m., so I have a few hours to prepare. Everything will change after this. He will finally know, like I now do, what happened to Helena.

I don't bother getting dressed, but slip on my fluffy dressing gown and go downstairs to wait for Matt. The house is eerily quiet, but I don't want the television or radio on. I need to be alert, to listen for unfamiliar sounds.

Finding a half-finished bottle of wine in the cupboard, I pour myself a glass, relishing the strong dry taste as it slips down my throat. But it doesn't ease my edginess. I take my glass and the bottle to the living room and sit on the sofa, my feet curled beneath me. Sleep starts to catch up with me by the time I've finished my wine, and although I try to keep it at bay, I am powerless to stop my eyes closing.

A thud forces me awake. I can't tell where it's come from, or what it is, but I know I didn't dream it. This is confirmed when it happens again. It sounds like it's coming from the kitchen. Immediately I am alert, thrown back to my experience with Nick Gibbs earlier, ready to defend myself. I look around the room for something to use as a weapon, but the only suitable object is the wine bottle on the coffee table. Pouring what's left of the contents into my glass, I stand up, grip the bottle upside down by its neck, and slowly make my way into the hall.

The thuds grow louder as I reach the kitchen, and my grip on the bottle grows tighter. I don't turn the light on, but in the darkness my eyes are drawn to the back door.

Someone is out there. I clearly see a shadowy figure the closer I get, and although I can't make out his face, it can only be one person. Nick Gibbs.

But why isn't he trying to smash the glass? Is he just trying to scare me first? Taunt me with the threat of what he will do?

My eyes flick to the phone on the corner of the worktop and I make my way towards it, knowing his eyes will be on me. I try not to panic; there is still time to call 999 before he can smash the double-glazed glass. And even if I don't manage to tell the police what's going on before he gets in, I'm sure they trace any calls that are cut off. They will be here.

'Simone? Simone?'

The voice is muffled by the glass but it is not Nick Gibbs's voice. I have heard it before, but it's definitely not his. It's not a menacing voice, and sounds more desperate than anything else. Clutching the phone in one hand and the wine bottle in the other, I move closer towards the door. And then I realise the man peering in is Chris Harding.

'What are you doing out there?' I shout through the glass.

'I've been trying to call you all day but you haven't answered. I was worried. We said we'd keep each other updated.'

I place the wine bottle on the table and grab the back door key from its hook. It is fortuitous that Chris has turned up like this as I only have his number on my stolen phone, and there is no other way for either of us to contact each other.

'Why didn't you knock on the front door?' I ask, opening the door.

A draft of cold air follows him in. 'You said your husband didn't know anything, and I wasn't sure if he was here. Sorry it's so late. I thought if he came to the back door I'd just run.'

I tell him Matt's not here, but that he'll be back soon, and pull out a chair for him. 'You'd better sit down. I've got a lot to tell you.'

His expression becomes increasingly anxious as I fill him in. Several times he starts to ask questions, but I tell him to let me finish. We don't have much time before Matt gets home. I deliberately leave out the part about the video on Daniel's phone for now, because I need him to be prepared before I voice my suspicion that it is his sister being filmed.

'So the police are looking for this Nick Gibbs?' he says, when I've finished. 'But what about Lucas?'

'I think they're both in it together. I mean, they've been friends since university, so I'm sure finding Nick will lead them to him.'

Chris slams his hand on the table. 'They need to hurry up. Mel's been missing for months now, and they're only now doing something about it. They didn't take it seriously but—'

'They needed evidence, Chris. And now they've got it. Just focus on that.' I don't point out that it's not really Mel they're looking for, because it doesn't matter. Finding Lucas should provide all the answers.

'I just need to ask you something,' I say. 'Do you have any pictures of Mel?'

Chris reaches into his pocket and pulls out his phone. 'I've got some on here. Why?'

'Just show me,' I say. I can't tell him about the video until I've prepared him, and I want to be sure it's her first.

'Here she is.' He passes the phone to me, and I immediately know it's the same girl. Although her eyes were closed in the video, her hair is the same blonde bob as the girl in the photo, and her prominent cheekbones are clearly recognisable. The girl in the video is Chris Harding's sister.

I struggle to find the words to explain this to him. I study his eyes as I speak, and the change in them the moment realisation hits. 'But … are you sure? You said her eyes were closed, so how can you be sure it's Mel?'

I tell him I am, and he flings himself up, the chair sliding away behind him. 'Fuck! Fuck!' he cries, his palms crushing the sides of his head. 'No!'

'I'm so sorry, Chris. But Lucas is definitely connected to her disappearance, you know that for sure now, so you can go to the police again.'

'But we don't have the video!' he yells. 'Shit, I can't believe this. I was right all along and I've wasted all this time when I could have done more to find Mel. She could be anywhere now.'

'I know how distressing this is, but the police will look into it now.'

For several minutes he doesn't speak, but sits down again and buries his head in his hands, his elbows resting on the table.

'You're right,' he says, eventually, slowly raising his head. 'I'm going to the police station now. Thanks for telling me.' He walks towards the back door but stops before he walks out. 'What's your new number? So we can keep in touch. I mean, I know the police are investigating now, but it would be nice to hear from you. And hopefully they'll find your friend's daughter and Mel. Safe.'

We exchange numbers and I lock the door behind him. I was lucky it wasn't Nick Gibbs, but I'm not taking any chances.

Less than ten minutes later, Matt arrives home. I rush to the front door to greet him and he wraps his arms around me, the cold from outside emanating from his skin.

'Are you okay?' he asks, as I lead him to the living room. 'I've been worried about you.' He feels my forehead with the back of his hand. 'You're a bit hot.' He kisses my cheek.

We sit on the sofa, and I realise he still has his coat on. 'I'm okay really. It's not … well, it's not anything wrong with me. But can we talk? I know you've just got back and you must be shattered, but it's important.'

He leans forward. 'Simone, honey, you're worrying me. What's going on? What's happened?' He spots my wine glass on the coffee table and points to it. 'Let me just get one for myself and then you can tell me what's going on, okay?'

While he's gone, I sit up straight and pull my dressing gown tighter around me.

Matt comes back with a glass of wine and I notice he has taken off his coat.

'I'm sorry you had to come all the way back on the train,' I say. 'How was the journey?' I am stalling for time.

'Well, I finished the medical journal I was reading and almost a whole novel, so it wasn't bad. Anyway, are you going to tell me what's going on? I'm really worried, Simone.'

This is it. I take a deep breath and tell him everything that's happened since Grace disappeared. And this time I tell him about Lucas and what she thought she'd done to him.

Just like Chris Harding did earlier, Matt tries to interrupt a few times but I beg him to save his questions until I've finished, which he reluctantly does. And when he is up to date, I inhale deeply and wait for the bombardment.

But I have stunned him into silence. It feels like hours have ticked by when he finally speaks, and I turn away from his red face. 'Why wouldn't you tell me? I can't believe this. After everything we've been through? You could have been killed! What were you thinking? And how could you trust Abbot before me? You should have gone straight to the police!'

A thick vein appears on his forehead, but he falls silent again. No doubt he is tallying up all the lies I have told him, wondering if he'll ever be able to trust me again.

Eventually he speaks, and it's not to give me a lecture on my betrayal. 'So … it's possible Grace is our daughter?'

I nod. 'Ginny seems to think so. And it does look that way.'

'And this Ginny – she's had her all along?' His hand clenches into a fist.

'Yes, but she didn't know. She thought she was helping her brother's friend.'

Matt shakes his head. 'But we only have her word for that, don't we? I mean, what proof is there that she didn't know? She could be lying.'

'There isn't any proof yet. But I believe her. And you have to trust me, Matt. I'm usually good at reading people.' But as I say this I think of Nick Gibbs, how I got him so wrong. And Charlotte Bray. Since Helena's abduction I have learnt to mistrust everyone, but they both had me fooled.

Matt shakes his head. 'And now we don't know where she is. I can't believe we found her, only to lose her again. If only her DNA sample hadn't been contaminated.'

'The police are looking for her now,' I say. 'They'll find her.'

'They didn't last time, did they?'

I am surprised to hear Matt being so negative, but then he hasn't had time to get his head around it all. 'No, but she's eighteen, not a baby, so surely it will be easier for them to find her this time?'

He doesn't answer, but tears form in the corners of his eyes, something I haven't seen since Helena was abducted. 'But they don't know she's our daughter?'

I tell him it doesn't matter at the moment, that knowing this information won't make them search harder, but he doesn't look convinced.

'Why wouldn't you tell them? They know everything else now, so why not the whole truth?'

'I know it sounds strange, but I did it for Ginny. No matter what's happened, she's been Grace's mum for all these years, so unless I find out she did actually know about the abduction, how can I get her into trouble and put Grace through even more hell when she's found?'

But even as I say this, and mean every word, I wonder whether I did the right thing by omitting this detail from my statement. After all, isn't it all tied to Lucas, and now Nick? Would knowing all the facts about Helena's abduction help them? But I will speak to Ginny before I decide anything.

'Are we safe here?' Matt asks. 'I mean, does this Nick Gibbs know where we live?'

'I suppose he could find out, but with the police after him do you think he'd be stupid enough to turn up here?'

Matt stands up and crosses to the window, pulling the edge of the curtain back to peer into the dark street. 'Anything's possible. Look what he's done so far. I'm getting a knife to take up with us.'

I don't object, and he disappears to the kitchen and comes back with our largest carving knife, placing it on the arm of the sofa as he sits down again. 'Just in case,' he says, and I am in full agreement.

He pulls out his phone and begins tapping the screen. 'I need to know what Nick Gibbs looks like,' he explains. 'You say he owns a computer games company?' Seconds later he is showing me the screen, asking if this is the right man.

A shiver runs through me, but I manage a nod. The kind face smiling back at me does not resemble the man I saw today.

'I'm still angry you didn't tell me, but I'm also proud of you,' Matt says, when he's finished reading about Nick Gibbs. He slides his phone back in his pocket. 'You handled it so well. Not just today, but this whole week.'

I shake my head. 'No, I didn't. I should have told you. But I didn't want to get you tied up in anything ... you know ... if Grace had killed someone then ...'

'I do understand,' he says. 'I don't like it, but I get it. I think.'

We sit in silence for a while, finishing our wine, each of us alone with our thoughts, until Matt finally speaks again. 'I can't get my head around all this. I need time to process it. We both need some sleep so let's go to bed now and maybe things will seem clearer in the morning.'

Neither of us sleeps well, despite our exhaustion. The slightest of noises has Matt jumping up, reaching for the knife under his pillow. But they are all false alarms. Whatever Nick is planning, he isn't making an appearance here for now. Perhaps he thinks it's too soon, that the police may be watching the house, waiting for him. I try to let this thought comfort me, but I still can't sleep.

But more than worrying about Nick Gibbs turning up, what keeps me awake is the niggling thought I've had since Chris Harding was here earlier.

The thought that in the video, his sister didn't look unconscious. She looked dead.

THIRTY-TWO

Giving up Becky hit me hard. It should have made me resent him, turn my back on him and everything we'd done, but it didn't. Instead, I threw myself deeper into our depraved world, wanting and needing more of a buzz than ever.

And he needed something more too. It was just like he told me – we were truly cut from the same cloth.

We didn't plan what happened that night, and none of us had mentioned how far we would ever go, but there was something different that evening. A fever we would all catch.

The four of us sat in Harry's bar, discussing the end of term. Our exams were nearly over and the promise of a long, hot summer stretched out before us. Planning how to spend it was almost as exciting as experiencing it.

'We should go away somewhere,' he suggested. 'Like Greece or Turkey. Spain even? There're some hot girls over there. I'm getting a bit bored of the skanky ones here. They're no fun, they don't know how to enjoy themselves. Think what we could get up to out there.'

I disagreed with him about the girls over here, but kept quiet. Becky knew how to live; her idea of fun was just different, that was all. It didn't make her boring. I missed her more than ever, but tried to fling thoughts of her from my head and focus on the friends I was spending the evening with.

As a distraction, I offered to buy the next round, and headed to the bar, leaving them to continue the conversation.

Leanne hadn't worked at the bar since the night I'd gone to her flat, and I still didn't know what he had said to keep her quiet, but whatever it was had worked. Her replacement behind the bar was a guy called Stu. He claimed he was a gigging musician, but seemed to spend every night working at Harry's, so I wasn't quite sure when he was playing these gigs. His dark hair flopped across his face and he was constantly flicking it back, only for it to happen again. I wondered how he didn't tire of it and cut the whole lot off. But I suppose he had an image to keep up.

I liked Stu, and found him easy to talk to. He always asked how I was doing, and I was beginning to wonder how different my life would be if I hung around with him instead of the others. But that wouldn't change who I was inside, would it? It wouldn't stop my cravings.

Stu and I chatted a bit while he poured our pints, and I carried them back to the table, the glasses balancing precariously in my hands.

They fell silent when I reached them and it was obvious they'd been talking about me. 'What's going on?' I asked, not caring if their conversation had been private.

'Oh, nothing. We were just talking about that girl over there.' He flicked his head towards the bar. 'The one with the red top. Do you know her?'

I turned around to see who they were talking about, and there was only one girl dressed in red. She leaned across the bar, counting out change to hand to Stu, a skinny black girl with shiny skin and a thick plait falling down her back. I hadn't seen her before, but could understand their fascination. 'Nope, never seen her before. But she's cute.'

He chuckled. 'That's what I said. I knew you'd like her. I think you should go and talk to her. She's definitely one for you to get things started with. Don't think she's a student, though. Could be older than us.'

Excitement stirred within me. I tried hard to fight it, to think about Becky instead and wonder what she was doing at this moment, but all I could do was imagine the black girl naked, helpless, her head lolling around, unable to move and stop me doing whatever I wanted. Whatever we all wanted. My whole body felt as if it would burst from the anticipation.

'So what do you reckon?' he said, a grin spreading across his face. 'I've got what we need in here.' He patted his pocket.

Without another word, I walked over to the girl and introduced myself.

THIRTY-THREE

I get up at six a.m. and it is still dark outside. I don't know what time Matt finally fell asleep so I try not to disturb him as I ease myself out of bed. Although it is early, the drive to north London will take me a while, and I need to visit Ginny before the police do.

The thought of eating turns my stomach, so after a shower I have a quick cup of coffee, and then I am ready to face what lies ahead.

Despite my early start it is nearly nine a.m. by the time I arrive at the hospital and find Ginny's room, although, thankfully, visiting hours have only just started. I almost don't recognise her when I see the fragile state she is in. Drips feed into her arms and her left arm and leg are covered in casts. Her face is swollen and purple, battered beyond recognition.

The blinds are still drawn so it's dark in the room, but I can see Ginny has her eyes closed. I don't want to wake her, but the police could be here any minute and we need to get our story straight. I need to let her know I haven't told them about Grace being my daughter.

I sit on the chair beside her bed and lean across to gently touch her right arm. 'Ginny, are you awake?'

She begins to stir and gradually her eyes open. It takes her a moment to register who I am, but when she does, it is only relief I see in her expression. 'Simone, I'm glad to see you.' She turns her head to face me. 'I didn't know what had happened to you and nobody could tell me anything last night. I was out of it before that. Are you okay? What happened?'

I am touched by her concern when she is the one lying in the hospital bed, lucky to be alive, and I am fit and well. Perhaps it is tied up in her guilt over Grace. 'Don't worry,' I say. 'I'm fine. I got away from him before he could do anything. I needed to get help for you so I called the police.' I shove the memory away. 'I can't believe what's happened to you. What … what did he do to you?'

'It all happened so fast, I barely remember. I know that sounds crazy, but maybe I've blocked it out. I just remember him pounding his fists into me and … smashing me against the wall. I think I blacked out after that, but I'm sure he thought I was dead.'

'Oh, Ginny, I'm so sorry. I should never have dragged you there, I—'

'Don't you blame yourself. This is my mess to clean up, not yours. None of this is your fault. Anyway, my broken bones will heal. I'm alive, that's all that matters.'

When I tell her I admire her positivity, she says it's only thinking of Grace that is getting her through this.

This time hearing her words, I no longer feel a stab of jealousy. I can accept that Grace and Ginny have an eighteen-year relationship, no matter how it came about. We will find a way to work this all out.

Ginny asks what happened after she'd been dragged from the room and I repeat the story as quickly as I can. The police could be here any second. 'You know Nick Gibbs, don't you?'

'Yes. He was a friend of Daniel's. From university. Before the funeral I hadn't seen him for years.' She stares at the ceiling. 'But what's he got to do with that girl, Charlotte?'

I wish I knew this, because somehow it all leads to Grace, I just can't put all the pieces together. 'I don't know yet, but listen,

Ginny, we need to talk about the statement I gave the police. They'll be here soon.'

She closes her eyes. 'It's okay, I understand you had to tell them. I'll deal with the consequences. Finding Grace is all that matters.'

I take her hand. 'No, listen, I didn't tell them about that. Or about what Grace said she'd done to Lucas. It's not important right now. That's what I came here to tell you. As far as they know, Grace is your daughter and I'm a friend of yours. That's our connection.'

'You lied for me,' she says, struggling to smile. 'I can't believe you'd do that for me.'

I have to be honest with her. 'The truth is, Ginny, I mainly did it for Grace. I want them to focus on finding her, not arresting you for something you didn't do. But I did have to tell them about Daniel and the video. Please understand that.'

She closes her eyes for a moment and then manages to nod. 'I understand. But still, thank you.'

'I can't promise the truth about Grace won't come out in all this. I mean, Nick Gibbs surely knows, so when they find him, what's to stop him telling them? But we'll deal with that when it happens. Also, they'll be taking a blood sample from you to test against the Converse trainer, but obviously it won't come back a match. There's just no way around that without admitting the truth.'

Ginny nods and asks for some water. I refill her glass and hold the drink to her mouth so she can sip from the straw they have given her. With a broken arm and leg, I don't know how she will manage for the next few months. I make a silent vow to myself to help her as much as I can.

For the next half hour we try to come up with a cover, and de-cide the most convincing way we could have met is if Ginny contacted me to try to get some work experience for Grace. 'It would have to have been last summer,' I explain, 'but that's enough time for us to have struck up a friendship. We'll just have to say that I couldn't get Grace any work last summer but was hoping to this year, which is why you and I kept in contact.'

Ginny agrees and half closes her eyes. 'Do you know what hurts more than this physical pain? Aside from Grace being missing? It's the fact that my brother betrayed me. I mean, he must have known the truth could come out any time and that I'd suffer because of it, but that didn't stop him.' She takes a deep breath. 'I don't even care that he did it for me, because look what he did to that woman in the video.' Her voice is louder now, almost a shout, and I turn around to ensure nobody is coming in to check what's going on.

'Ginny, just try to stay calm. Grace is the only person that matters now, but you have to let the police find her. You just need to concentrate on getting better. Whatever Daniel's done, you need to put it behind you and try to move on.' She may think this is easy for me to say, but I'm speaking from experience. I had to make a life for myself without my baby, and she will have to say goodbye to her memories of her brother.

She opens her mouth to speak, but the door opens, stopping her in her tracks. Two police officers walk in, flashing their badges at us. I immediately stand and tell them I was just leaving, but before I head to the door I throw a quick smile at Ginny, hoping to convey to her that everything will be okay.

Outside the hospital, I sit in the car and start the engine, but don't drive away. I feel uneasy, and it's not just worry over how Ginny is doing with her statement. A car pulls up behind me, the driver gesturing towards the exit. I shake my head and hold up my parking ticket, even though he won't be able to read it from where he is. He says something I can't hear and drives off, revving his engine. 'Jerk,' I shout out, but I know he can't hear me.

Reaching into my coat pocket, I pull out my new mobile and call Abbot's work line. Thankfully it is a number I know by heart, as all my other ones are now lost with my old phone. No doubt Charlotte Bray has already hacked into it and snooped through it, reporting back to Nick Gibbs, wherever he is.

Abbot answers after two rings, his voice comforting and familiar. 'How are you doing?' he asks, when he realises it's me. 'You're not coming in, are you?'

'No, not today. I'm guessing the big story is Grace's disappearance, though?'

He sighs. 'Yeah, sorry. But nobody's connected it to Helena, so don't worry. Anyway, I'm not working on it, but I'll keep you up to date with what's happening.'

I thank him and tell him I need Tamsin Bray's number, holding my breath as I prepare for a lecture.

'Sim, what are you up to? I don't like the sound of this. You shouldn't contact her – just let the police deal with it all now.'

'I am, I just need to talk to her, explain what happened. Something about the whole Charlotte thing just isn't sitting right with me.'

'Of course it isn't – she set you up, didn't she? What more do you want to know?'

'I just think she knows something about Grace, and I want to know what that is. Look, I'll be careful, but I'll get Tamsin's number with or without your help, so please spare me the lecture.'

Abbot falls silent and I hear the muffled sound of him covering the receiver. When he speaks again it is to give me the number, along with a warning to be careful and to call him if I need any help.

That call was the easy one. Now I have to deal with Tamsin Bray, and I know she won't be happy to hear from me. I dial the number Abbot has given me, my heart thudding in my chest.

'Hello?' she says, sounding out of breath.

'Tamsin, please don't hang up – it's Simone.'

She says nothing but I can still hear her breathing so she hasn't cut me off yet.

'Tamsin, look, I really think we should talk. Can you meet me this morning? Somewhere like a coffee shop? I need to explain everything.' I hope she can't see through my lie, that she is the one I want to explain things.

'You shouldn't be calling me,' she says, her voice sharp and hard, a far cry from the softly spoken Tamsin Bray I've met before. 'I'm sure the police would be interested to know about this harassment.'

I knew this wouldn't be easy, but part of me hoped Tamsin would remember how much I supported her when Charlotte was missing. 'Just see me this one time, for five minutes, and I promise you'll never hear from me again if that's what you want. You have my word.'

Again I am faced with heavy silence, for so long this time that I almost give up and end the call myself. But then she finally speaks again. 'One hour. Caffè Nero on Kilburn High Street. Don't be late, I won't hang around.' She disconnects the call, leaving me staring at the phone, wondering whether I misheard her.

The North Circular has emptied out by the time I leave the hospital, so I make it to Kilburn with ten minutes to spare. But parking is another matter, and when I finally get to Caffè Nero it is already past eleven a.m.

I see Tamsin immediately, sitting at a table in the corner, cradling a large mug. She looks up and fixes me with a hard stare, but I ignore it and buy a bottle of water at the counter before joining her.

'I shouldn't be here,' she says, before I've even sat down. She avoids eye contact but vigorously stirs her drink, keeping the spoon in her cup as she lifts it to take a sip.

I have to approach this softly; she looks as if she is ready to dart for the door any second. 'Thank you for meeting me.'

'Well, what exactly is it you want? I thought you were helping our family but you forced Charlotte to take you to that house.'

'You've got it all wrong! I didn't make Charlotte do what she did. She locked us in that room and told Nick Gibbs where to find us. Do you realise there's a woman lying battered in a hospital bed because of this?'

Tamsin finally looks at me, her eyes narrowed. 'Well, Charlotte tells a different story. She said you forced her to tell you where this Lucas lived, and then once you got there she was lucky to get away from that man, whoever he is. And now she's disappeared again. Probably scared for her life.'

So this is the story Charlotte has told her parents. I find it hard to control my anger, but I can't let this situation get out of control; I need Tamsin to listen to me. 'Do you know where she's gone?'

'No, I don't. And why would I tell you if I did? You're the reason she's gone.'

I want to scream at her that the only reason Charlotte is missing again is because she's on the run from the police. 'Look, Tamsin, you've got this all wrong. Even after what she did, I would never wish any harm on your daughter. I just need to know if she's told you anything at all about Lucas Hall or Nick Gibbs.'

Tamsin pushes aside her empty cup. 'Lucas was her boyfriend, that's all I know. I didn't know about him until yesterday. But Charlotte said people would be after her and that she'd explain when it was safe to come home.'

More lies. And Tamsin has no idea what her daughter is involved in.

'But at least this time she texts me when she can,' Tamsin continues. 'From different numbers, so I know she's safe.' She picks up her cup, but then remembers it's empty and places it down again. 'I don't know why I'm telling you all this, after what you've done.'

Nick Gibbs must have warned Charlotte we'd got away and that the police would be looking for her. 'Tamsin, please listen to me. If you do have any idea where Charlotte is, you need to tell the police. I think she could be in danger, and I'm sure she knows something about my ... my friend's daughter. Her name's Grace and she's been missing for over a week now. We think Lucas took her, which means Charlotte could know something.'

I am expecting some empathy from Tamsin once I've said this but all I'm greeted with is a blank stare. 'Charlotte knows nothing about this girl. Why won't you just leave us alone? The police are already involved, and know she's missing again, so stop harassing us.'

'Tamsin, please listen; my friend Ginny is in hospital with serious injuries, her only daughter missing. You're a mother yourself, you know what that feels like, how can you have no compassion for her? Please, just tell the police if you know anything. You don't have to tell me.' I push my water aside, too angry to even open the bottle.

Across from me, Tamsin falls silent, spreading out her hand in front of her and studying it. 'I have to put *my* daughter first,' she says, her voice too loud. 'And I shouldn't be here talking to you.

You manipulated her, forced her to go with you to find Lucas. All you cared about was finding your friend's daughter, you certainly didn't spare a thought for mine.'

Several people turn to stare at us, but I don't care. Tamsin is being unreasonable, and I'm wasting my time. And now it is my turn to increase the volume. 'Firstly, Charlotte is not a child, she's a grown woman, capable of making her own decisions. And if anyone has manipulated her it's the man she got involved with, not me. Do what you want, Tamsin. Lie and keep things from the police if you like. I just hope you can live with yourself if anything happens to Grace.'

I stand up, shoving my chair aside and leaving my water on the table. I ignore the stares as I leave the café, and the woman I thought I had bonded with.

My anger hasn't diminished by the time I get home. I open the front door, ready to tell Matt what happened with Tamsin, desperate for some comforting words, but the second I step in the hallway I hear voices. One is Matt's and the other a female voice I don't recognise. The sounds are too muffled for me to make out any words, but perhaps it is a colleague of Matt's, stopping by to run something past him.

This is what I am prepared for. What I'm not expecting is to find Sienna Gibbs sitting at my kitchen table.

THIRTY-FOUR

I stare at Sienna. Her puffy eyes and red blotchy cheeks tell me she is not here to cause trouble. There is no hint of make-up on her face this time and her hair is pulled back in a messy ponytail, as if she left her house in a hurry.

Matt rushes over to me. 'Simone,' he says, his voice a whisper. 'She turned up a few minutes ago looking for you. I wasn't going to let her in but she didn't look in a good way. Are you okay to talk to her?'

'It's fine,' I say. Not knowing whether to sit or stand, I stay by the door, keeping my distance from her. After my earlier encounter with Tamsin I am ready for another attack.

Matt heads back to the table and sits down, turning to Sienna. 'Sorry, what did you say your name was?'

'Sienna.' She doesn't look at him while she answers, but keeps her eyes fixed on me. 'Simone, I'm so sorry.' She bursts into tears then, loud retching sobs, and buries her head in her hands, so I give up my position by the door and sit next to her.

'How did you find me?'

'I'm so sorry,' she says, trying to control her tears. 'I checked Nick's computer and he had all your details on there. I know it was wrong, but I needed to see you.'

It doesn't surprise me that Nick found out my address. He would have suspected me from the minute Abbot and I showed up at his door.

Sienna explains she had no idea what her husband was like. At first I want to shake her and demand to know how she could have been so oblivious, but then I picture her kids, and what a good father Nick Gibbs appeared to be, and I decide to go easy on her.

'Do the police know you're here?' I ask.

She wipes her eyes with her coat sleeve, but the sobbing continues. 'No. I probably shouldn't be, but I needed to see you. To say sorry for what he did. I can't believe …' She trails off, struggling to find the words.

At least she isn't one of those women who refuse to believe what their husbands are capable of, even if it's staring them in the face. 'This must be hard for you,' I say. 'But could you tell the police anything at all about where he might be?'

She shakes her head. 'I have no idea. I haven't seen or heard from him since he left the house in a hurry yesterday morning. I called and texted all day yesterday but he didn't reply to any of my messages.'

'And there's nowhere you can think of he might go?' Matt asks.

Sienna turns to him. 'I gave them details of all his friends and family, but they don't think he'll go anywhere he can be traced. They're checking his mobile records and credit cards, but he's not used anything since he went on the run. They've also checked all the hospitals and put an alert out in case anyone matching his description turns up with a stab wound.'

Once again I am relieved she has acknowledged what he has done. 'Did you know he was friends with Lucas Hall? And Daniel Rhodes?' I ask.

Again a shake of her head. 'No. Nick didn't socialise much – he was always working. Or with us.'

'Well, he found the time to attack women, didn't he? And try and kill people.' As I say this I think of Mel Harding in that horrific video on Daniel's phone.

'Simone!' Matt's voice cuts through the air. But I don't feel guilty about what I've said; it is only the truth.

'No, no, she's right,' Sienna says, her face hardening. 'I don't know how he's involved in the disappearance of this girl, but clearly he's got something to do with it. And why would he try to kill you and that poor woman? I've gone over and over it, but none of it adds up.'

I have been wondering this myself. The only thing I know for sure, because of the video evidence, is that Lucas and Daniel raped Chris Harding's sister. What they did with her after that, I have no idea. Only two voices could be heard on the video but it's likely Nick was involved too. And what about the stripper Nick introduced me to? How is she involved in all this?

I say all this to Sienna, and watch as her eyes widen in horror. She probably hasn't heard about the video from the police, as the evidence is missing, and she clearly doesn't know anything about Gabby.

'The police will find her,' I say, 'but all I could tell them was her name. If that's even her real one.' I think of Charlotte and the lengths she has gone to for Lucas. Both Nick and Lucas seem to be skilled at manipulating people, so why not Gabby?

'He was probably fucking her,' Sienna says, spitting her words out. Her tears have stopped now, replaced by anger. 'What the hell was I married to?'

'He had everyone fooled, not just you.' I try to offer comfort with my words, but I know nothing will ease her pain.

'Yes, but I was the one who should have known. Anyway, I'm washing my hands of him. I don't want to lay eyes on him again. And he will never see his children. Oh God, how can I explain this to them?'

Neither Matt nor I know what to say to this.

'What will you do now?' Matt asks, trying to get Sienna off the subject of her children. 'Are you worried he'll come back to your house?'

She huffs. 'He can try, the police are just waiting for him to do that. And I won't be there.' She tells us her plan is to leave for Brighton today with the kids. Her sister and her brother-in-law live there and have offered to take them all in for as long as necessary.

'Just be careful,' Matt says.

Sienna stands up. 'I will.' Turning to me, her lips curl into a thin, sad smile. 'Simone, I'm really sorry. I just want you to know I'll help the police in any way I can. And I'm sorry for what he tried to do to you at that flat.'

'I appreciate that,' I say. And I mean it. She could so easily have gone the other way and stood by her monster of a husband.

Once she's gone, Matt and I stand in the hallway, clinging to each other. 'That poor woman,' he says, keeping me pulled into him. 'What a fucking mess.'

It's not often Matt swears, so I know how affected he is by Sienna's visit. Perhaps seeing her has made this more real for him. It is different for me: I have been in it from the beginning, finding things out as I've gone along and dealing with it hour by hour, not just in a disturbing chunk like Matt has had to. I should have told him everything from the start.

'I miss Helena,' he says. 'I know that sounds crazy because she was only a baby, but I suppose I miss what could have been. The life we would have had.' Matt has said this before, so I know how much pain it's still causing him.

I ease back from him but keep hold of his arms. 'We've got a chance now, though, haven't we? We know who she is.'

He nods slowly. 'But not *where* she is. They just need to find her for us. Not like last time.'

We both fall silent, contemplating Matt's words.

'Listen, Simone,' he says, after a moment. 'Let's go to the park. Now. I know we usually only go on the anniversary, but something's telling me we should go today. I don't know, maybe it will make us feel closer to Helena.'

At the mention of the park, my heart aches with the familiar yearning for my daughter. But at least this time there is hope. 'I'd like that. But is it safe with Nick Gibbs out there somewhere?'

Matt grabs my hand and squeezes it. 'I won't let him or anyone else anywhere near you. I couldn't protect our daughter, but I won't let anyone destroy our family again.'

It is always gut-wrenching to visit the park where Helena was taken, even after so many years have passed. On those first visits, I would stand still, unable to move, only capable of imagining the scene as it took place, rewinding it over and over in my head, the frantic words of Matt's mother wringing in my ears.

The toilet block where she was snatched was modernised years ago, but it still turns my blood cold to see it. And I have not set foot inside it since the first time. I had to then. I had to see the place where she was stolen. But I had no idea then that we wouldn't find her. Beneath the grief I still had a kernel of hope.

Today the park is quiet, with only a few mothers pushing toddlers on swings, everyone wrapped up against the fierce wind. Ignoring the children's shrieks of joy, Matt takes my hand and we walk slowly along the path, just as we have done every year. But this time is different. This time we have some answers.

'Mum's never forgiven herself,' Matt says, as we approach the toilet block. I have already decided that today I don't want to stop and linger, I will keep walking, urge Matt to do the same, and pray that the search for Grace is making progress.

'I know. But we've never blamed her, have we? It wasn't her fault she got sick. I mean, it was only seconds she had her back turned for. Seconds.'

Matt squeezes my hand tighter and almost comes to a stop, but I keep walking, pulling him along with me. He turns to me and I see his eyes are glassy. 'I know I never said it at the time,' he says, 'and didn't know how to really, but I loved you even more for that. For not turning against her. I mean, I found it hard enough, and she's my mum.'

I remember Matt avoiding her calls, struggling to hear her voice or see her face, and the anguish and guilt it caused him was always visible, even though he didn't voice it.

My pace slows now that we have passed the toilet block. 'Have you told Miriam about Grace?' I say.

He shakes his head. 'Not yet, but I will. I just don't want to get her hopes up until the police have found her.'

Now that he's said this, I wonder if he's thinking the same as I am. That there's a chance they won't find her. Or won't find her alive. But I don't want to throw this thought out there, I want us to live in this moment of hope for as long as we can.

'We can tell her together,' I say. 'We're due for a visit.' Miriam lives in Luton now and it's been some time since we saw her. She rarely comes to us, and it takes a real emergency for her to leave her flat.

Matt agrees and we complete our circuit of the park in comfortable silence. As we head back to the car, his mobile rings, blaring out from his pocket. The moment he speaks I can tell it's the surgery, and they need him in.

Confirming my belief, Matt apologises the second he hangs up. 'I'm sorry, Simone, but the locum's had an emergency and needs to get home. I need to cover just for a couple of hours, until about half four, then I'll be back.'

I tell him it's fine, that I understand. Besides, there are several things I need to do when I get home, the first of which is to call Ginny at the hospital to see how she got on with the police.

Matt drops me at home and we kiss goodbye. 'Don't answer the door to anyone,' he says. 'I'll call you when I have a chance. And you call me if you hear anything at all from the police. Double lock the door too.'

He waits until I'm inside and the front door is closed before driving off. Checking the door is double locked, I peel off my coat and head towards the kitchen, imagining warming myself up with a hot chocolate. I also need some lunch.

But before I reach the kitchen I stop, frozen to the spot. Someone is behind me. I haven't heard footsteps but I can hear short, quick breaths.

This is it.

He has come for me.

THIRTY-FIVE

I spin around, ready to fight for my life. But it's not Nick Gibbs standing in my hallway. It's Charlotte Bray.

'What the hell are you doing here?' I cannot keep the shock from my voice. But at least she should be easier to fend off than Nick.

She takes a step back and holds out her palms. 'I … I'm … please – I'm not here to hurt you or do anything.' Her tone and expression seem genuine, but she has fooled me before and I won't let her again.

'How did you get in my house?'

'I'm sorry, Simone, I smashed your small top kitchen window and climbed through the larger one. It wasn't locked. I know it's terrible but I was desperate to talk to you and I promise I'll pay for the damage.'

Reaching in my pocket, I pull out my phone. 'I'm calling the police.'

'No, wait!' She rushes forward and tries to grab it, but I am too quick and snatch it away, holding it up in the air. I am taller than her so she can't quite reach high enough to get it now.

'Move away from me now, Charlotte or, I swear, you'll get hurt.' I don't know why I am warning her, after she led Nick to us. She is responsible for Ginny's injuries as much as he is.

She freezes. 'Please, Simone, just give me two minutes and I'll explain everything. And then if you still want to you can call the police.'

I shouldn't agree to this. She cannot be trusted and I'm alone here. How do I know Nick Gibbs isn't in the house, waiting for me to let down my guard? 'Give me your phone,' I say, holding out my hand.

Her forehead creases. 'What? Why?'

'If you want me to listen, just do it, Charlotte. And quickly.'

Her brown leather bag hangs across her body and she starts to open the zip.

'Wait,' I say. 'I've had a better idea. Give me your bag.'

Assuming she will protest, I already have my argument prepared, but she surprises me and pulls it over her head without a word, handing it to me. I snatch it from her then grab her arm, leading her to the kitchen. The damage to the small window is not as bad as I've expected, and after taping some cardboard to it, I decide I will explain it to Matt later. I will just have to make sure I'm back before him so he doesn't worry.

Pushing past Charlotte, I head to the front door, instructing her to follow me.

'Where are we going?' she asks, once we're back in the hall.

'Do you think I'm stupid, Charlotte?' I pull on my coat. 'We're getting out of this house now, and going somewhere public. That's the only choice you have if you want me to listen, so I suggest you come with me now.' I surprise myself with my confidence. I still can't trust her and don't know what she and Nick Gibbs have planned, but if there's any chance she's finally being honest then I need to hear her out. I need to find out what she knows about Grace.

Once we're outside, the door shut behind us, I walk as fast as I can in the direction of Fulham Palace Road. It will be busy there, and I will feel safer. I don't speak to Charlotte, but I have her bag clutched tightly in my hand and can hear her rasping breaths as she struggles to keep up. Several times, I turn back to check we're not being followed, but thankfully there is nobody suspicious behind us.

Only when we reach the bustling main road do I dare to slow down, but not before I check once more that Nick Gibbs isn't following. A bus pulls into the stop we are approaching and instinctively I grab Charlotte's arm and tell her we're getting on it. She doesn't protest and I feel her arm fall limp in my grasp.

I get my Oyster card ready and ask her if she has one. Thankfully, she pulls one out of her pocket and we step onto the bus. Once we've scanned our cards, I lead her to the empty back seat, and carefully assess all the passengers getting on. None of them are Nick Gibbs.

'Right,' I say, when the bus starts to move, 'now you can talk. But I'm warning you, I don't trust a thing that leaves your mouth.'

Charlotte looks around her and lowers her voice. 'What, here?'

'Yes, start talking. I'll tell you when we're getting off.' I must sound as if I have a plan because she quickly nods. The truth is I still have no idea where we're going, but am hoping my instincts won't let me down.

Her voice is almost a whisper when she begins talking, and I have to lean closer to hear her clearly. That's when I see the tears in her eyes.

'He lied to me,' she says. 'Nick Gibbs. He told me I'd see Lucas again if I just did as he asked. But it was all lies.'

I tell her to slow down and start from the beginning, that what she's saying is not making sense.

'Please, can we just get off this bus? I will tell you everything, but I can't talk here.' She swipes at her eyes, but fresh tears appear as quickly as she wipes them away.

I look around and a few people seated opposite us are look-ing at Charlotte, noticing her distress. While I do want to be out in public, I realise a bus probably isn't the best place for the conversation we need to have. Through the window, I see we are approaching Putney Bridge. 'Okay, we'll get off soon and talk then,' I say. But I don't tell her where I plan to get off. I am still not taking any chances.

For several minutes we sit in silence and once we've crossed Putney Bridge, I stand, ushering her up with me. 'We're getting off at the next stop,' I say, pressing the red button.

As soon as we are standing on Putney High Street I know this is the right place. With so many cars and people passing by, it will be difficult for Charlotte to try anything. Spotting a bench on the corner of the pavement, I lead Charlotte to it and we sit down. It faces the main road, so from here I have a good view of cars passing and pedestrians. And with all the traffic noise block-ing our voices from being heard, we can speak openly.

Charlotte appears at ease with my choice, and although her cheeks are stained with mascara, no fresh tears fall. 'Open my bag,' she says. 'There's something in there you should have.'

Tentatively, I lift the flap of her bag and slide the zip open, peering inside. It is crammed full of things: a purse, an umbrella, an iPod, but I don't see anything Charlotte might be referring to. I must look confused because she thrusts her hand in and feels around, eventually pulling out three mobile phones.

'I'm sorry,' she says, 'I should never have …' She trails off.

I take my phone and try to switch it on but the battery must be dead. Putting it, and Ginny's phone, in my bag, I realise some-thing is missing, because the third phone is Charlotte's. 'Where's Daniel's phone?' I ask. 'You took his from my bag as well, I know you did.'

She stares at her feet. 'I'm sorry. I got rid of it. I just didn't want to believe that voice was Lucas's. I didn't want him to get into trouble.'

Annoyed, I realise there is nothing I can do about this now. I turn back to Charlotte. 'Right, I think you need to start from the beginning. And you'd better tell me everything.'

She explains that she met Lucas around the beginning of December. She'd gone to a bar in Covent Garden with some friends to celebrate a birthday. 'I was pretty drunk,' she explains, 'but the second he walked in I thought he was hot.' Charlotte knew he was a lot older, but for her that was part of the attraction. She wanted something different, was fed up of meeting the same kind of people. He kept staring at her all evening, but only made his move towards the end of the night.

'Who was he with?' I ask, wondering if Daniel or Nick Gibbs were with him.

'No one. He was on his own. Said he was just having a quick drink after a long day of meetings.'

Lucas approached her when she visited the toilets, and they talked in the corridor, away from her friends. 'I was quite forward,' Charlotte admits. 'I just grabbed him and started kissing him and I don't think he was expecting it. But he didn't stop me. Then he asked for my email address.'

I already know why he wanted to communicate this way instead of by phone, and I'm sure Charlotte worked it out too. Hannah.

'When you kissed him did you know he was married?' I ask.

She stares at her feet again. 'Yes. I saw his ring. And I know I shouldn't have done it, but he was like a magnet and I couldn't stop myself. I can't even blame the alcohol – I probably would have still done it sober.'

Charlotte tells me they communicated by email a few times, and then met up in Hyde Park. 'That was the first time we … you know. It was freezing cold but I didn't care. And nobody could see us, we were hidden in the bushes.'

I don't want to hear this, but at least he didn't force her. 'What happened when you went missing, Charlotte? Where were you?'

The involuntary smile that has formed on her face since she started talking about Lucas suddenly vanishes. Charlotte bites her fingernail. 'We'd been seeing each other for a few weeks and one night I was waiting for Lucas at his flat. We'd arranged it, and I was going to tell him I wanted him to leave his wife.'

I almost interject that this is ridiculous. They had only known each other a few weeks and she was ready to wreck his marriage. But I remind myself Charlotte is young, and clearly naïve. I think of Mel Harding, and wonder if she felt the same as Charlotte? Did she also hope Lucas would leave Hannah for her? I hope I'm wrong about what I think has happened to her. I pray the police will find her alive.

'But he didn't show up,' Charlotte continues. 'I'd fallen asleep on the bed when I heard the door opening. It was dark and I couldn't see much but I knew straight away it wasn't him. It was Nick Gibbs.'

I shouldn't be surprised to hear this but I am. I'm also sceptical. Although I think what she's told me up to now seems genuine, I have no idea of her agenda.

Tears drop from her eyes again. 'I'd never met him before but he introduced himself and told me Lucas had sent him, and that they were friends. Then he … he locked me in that room and he …'

I know what she's going to say but I need her to confirm it. When she does, it is worse than I imagined. Nick Gibbs kept her in that bedroom for two weeks, tied up and gagged, raping her repeatedly, until she could barely move. 'The thing is, there were several times I thought it wasn't even him, but some new person doing it. But I couldn't see through the rag he blindfolded me with. I think he ... told someone else ... and they came and ...' She breaks down, her body shaking with the force of her sobs.

I reach out and hug her, even after what she's done, I doubt she could fake this much emotion. 'Why didn't you tell the police, Charlotte? How could you let him get away with that?'

'D'you know what got me though it?' she says, her voice shaking. 'The thought of seeing Lucas again. And Nick said that would only happen if I didn't make a fuss or try to run away. I was so desperate to see Lucas that I believed him. But he also threatened my family. Said he knew where Mum and Dad worked.'

And now – if Charlotte is telling the truth – things are starting to make sense.

'But you got away,' I say. 'Why did he let you go?'

'One day he just threw the keys at me and told me I could go. He knew I wouldn't tell anyone what he'd done because I was desperate to see Lucas again. They were best friends, he said, and if Lucas knew about this he would blame me, and say that I'd seduced Nick. Or he said the police would say that Lucas was involved and arrest him too. I just couldn't take that chance.'

I feel sorry for her in this moment. Her naïvety has got her into this mess, as well as her desperation for a man who doesn't even care about her. Because from what she has told me, I am sure Lucas was one of the other men raping her in that room. But I don't say this. I will spare her that, at least.

'Charlotte, did Nick ever film you? I mean when he ... you know.'

Her face pales. 'It's possible, I suppose. But I was blindfolded so I wouldn't have known. Oh God!'

'Sorry, I shouldn't have asked, but don't think about that. Look, I need to ask you something important. Do you know anything at all about Grace, the girl I showed you a picture of?'

'Your friend's daughter?' She shakes her head. 'No, I'm sorry, I've never seen her.'

'And did Lucas or Nick ever mention her?'

Again she shakes her head. 'I'm sorry, but no. Never.'

My disappointment threatens to crush me. Since sitting on this bench with Charlotte, I have allowed myself to believe she knows something that will help the police find Grace.

Trying to stay strong, I turn to Charlotte. There is something I've just remembered. 'But the police found your bag, Charlotte. In east London. Before you turned up. How is that possible when you would have had it with you when you went to Lucas's flat?'

'Nick took it,' she says, without hesitation. 'He must have dumped it, but I don't know why.'

It is hard to argue with this; it's perfectly plausible he dumped it miles away to throw the police off the scent.

'Now I understand why you wouldn't let anyone examine you when you were back home,' I say, remembering Tamsin's anguish at this.

'I couldn't. If Nick thought I was helping the police he would have kept me from Lucas.'

'So what happened when you saw Lucas again?' I ask.

She stares at me, her eyes glassy and wild. 'That's just it. I didn't see him again. He … he just disappeared. But then you were asking about him that day and Nick called me and said I had to help him get to you. He knew all about you, and said you'd try and talk to me again.'

It is clear to me now that the second Abbot and I turned up at Nick's house he knew we weren't who we claimed to be. And a man with that much money would have no trouble tracking me down and keeping tabs on me.

'How did he want you to help?' I ask. 'What did he tell you to do?'

'I swear I didn't want to help him,' Charlotte says, her eyes filling with tears. 'He just said to let him know if you asked about Lucas. It was just bad luck that you turned up that day wanting me to show you where his flat was. I was so confused and desperate to see Lucas that I didn't think about what I was doing. I texted Nick in the car and he told me what to do.' She grabs my arm. 'Simone, I'm so sorry. I had no idea what he was planning. If I'd thought about what he might do I never would have … even if it meant never seeing Lucas again.'

I tug my arm away and shake my head. Then I remember something. 'You knew the road name where Lucas's flat is all along, didn't you?' I should have realised at the time it was strange she wouldn't know it after seeing Lucas for weeks. But I was so focused on finding Grace, this detail slipped by me.

She nods. 'But I couldn't tell you, or you would have gone without me. I'm sorry.'

So I'll ask you one more time. Have you seen Lucas?' I am shouting now, but my voice is drowned out by the traffic. 'Why were you in my house? What the hell are you up to?'

Charlotte flinches. 'I'm sorry! I'm not up to anything. Nick was lying!'

I have known Nick was lying to her since she began her story. 'But what happened? How do you know that now?'

What she says next shocks me to my core.

'Because he's dead! Lucas is dead!'

THIRTY-SIX

Her name was Tia, and close up she looked even better than she had from our seats in the corner. I offered to buy her a drink, and her bright white smile told me this would be easier than I expected.

'A Malibu and Coke,' she said. Her tight curls sprang from her head as she flicked it back, and I caught a waft of coconut shampoo. She smelled fresh and clean, this girl, and I felt a frisson of excitement. But it was nothing compared to what came later.

We chatted for a while, and I could feel their eyes on me the whole time. I knew they would be anticipating this as much as I was. I asked her about herself, pretending to be interested that she was taking a year out to travel. Wasn't everyone? But girls liked to think you were listening, so I nodded and smiled at everything she said.

It took several drinks to get her tipsy; she was obviously used to drinking. But by closing time, she was unsteady on her feet, and gratefully accepted my offer to walk her home.

She said she lived only twenty minutes away, and while we walked I glanced around to check they were keeping up. She, of course, was oblivious, happy in her drunken stupor.

But it was nearer to forty-five minutes by the time we got to her flat, and I couldn't hide my irritation. She didn't notice I had grown quiet.

Although small, her flat was modern, clean and tidy; she obviously took as much pride in it as she did her appearance. She turned on the radio and lit some candles. 'I hate bright lights,' she said, but I knew she was doing it to make the place sexy.

But all her effort was pointless. I would not be kissing her slowly, undressing her carefully, and waking up with her in the morning.

She poured us both some vodka, but said she had nothing to go with it. That was fine with me: the stronger the better. She didn't notice me sipping mine slowly – taking one sip for every three of hers – because she was so intent on topping up her alcoholic high before it vanished.

We sat together on her cramped couch, and I tried to keep my hands off her. I was under strict instructions to wait. So instead I watched her while she giggled at nothing, expectation swelling within me. She got up and danced around, giggling when she tumbled to the floor. Then came the knock at the door. Tia was too busy rolling around on the floor to notice, so I got up and answered it.

And let them in.

She didn't react to the fact we had company, even when they were standing right over her, instead she continued giggling to herself, making no move to get up from the floor.

'You don't mind if my friends join us, do you?' I smiled down at her.

He stood at my side. 'How much have you given her? She's so wasted we probably don't even need this.' He held up the small bottle, waving it around.

'But isn't that risky? What if she remembers in the morning?'

He brushed off my concerns. 'You worry too much. Just enjoy this. Watch.' Standing over Tia, he grabbed the half-empty bottle of vodka and began pouring it over her face. I expected her to flinch, to roll out of the fountain, but she barely moved. 'See. Told you. Completely wasted.'

I looked at them and back at Tia, and knew I could relax. I had waited all evening for this, I wasn't going to waste it.

'You can go first,' he said. 'You did all the hard work.'

They sat watching as I tore off her clothes and forced myself into her, their cheers adding to my excitement. She wasn't protesting, but

I covered her mouth with my hand, enjoying her squirms beneath me.

'Hurt her,' he said, crouching down beside me. 'Really fucking hurt her.'

I rammed myself so hard into her that her body jolted and her head smacked against the TV stand, drawing blood.

And then his hand was around her throat, squeezing it, but I couldn't tell how tight. 'Hurt her like this,' he said. 'She'll like it, she won't know she does, but she will.'

I have often thought about what happened next, relived it over and over. But not for the reasons you may think.

He didn't remove his hands, and I began to panic. She was jolting violently now. What if he never let go? I moved off her and let him take my place. But he still didn't let go, in fact, now I could see she was struggling to breathe.

I shouted out, but he was oblivious, too caught up in what he was doing. And Daniel was no help – he was enjoying every second, filming it all. Perhaps he didn't quite realise what was happening, but either way he didn't care.

When he finally finished and released his grip, she lay motionless beneath him, her wide eyes staring at the ceiling.

I waited for panic to set in, but his face was calm, the pleasure he'd just experienced still visible.

And I knew then we would all be tied together forever.

THIRTY-SEVEN

It takes a moment for Charlotte's words to sink in. I've spent a lot of time looking for Lucas, and even after Grace's story, haven't truly considered the possibility that he is actually dead. Beside me on the bench, Charlotte is once again distraught.

'Charlotte, calm down and tell me what's happened.'

Through her tears she manages to speak. 'I ... after I locked you in the room I called Nick and told him what I'd done. He told me I'd done well, but when I asked him about Lucas he said he'd call me later.' She wipes her face with her sleeve and shakes her head. 'He didn't call, but he texted a few hours later telling me to disappear for a while. He said not to speak to anyone, but to go somewhere safe until he called. So I took a train to Portsmouth and got a hotel room. I waited for him to call but he didn't. I tried his mobile loads of times but he never answered.'

She doesn't acknowledge that this is probably because he was too busy trying to work out what to do after leaving Ginny for dead.

I want to ask her how she could have anything to do with the man who had repeatedly raped her but I already know and fear the answer. The pull of Lucas meant she would put up with anything, just to be with him.

Charlotte tells me that she finally got hold of Nick late that night and he was furious with her. 'He shouted and cursed down the phone, telling me to stop calling him. I was shocked. I mean,

I knew he was nasty and evil but he had always seemed so calm, so together. This time he was really flipping out. And it scared me even more.'

It's not hard to work out why Nick verbally attacked Charlotte. His plan had gone wrong, he was badly injured and the police were hunting for him. He'd got away with depraved acts, but now he knew his time had run out and he was in serious trouble. He also must know his family would want nothing more to do with him.

Charlotte begins to shake. 'I asked him about Lucas and he started laughing. His exact words were, "You stupid bitch, he's dead. You will never fucking see him again. And now you have to live with knowing he's been right under your nose the whole time." And then he cut me off. But not before he told me I'd end up the same way if I said anything to anyone or contacted him again.'

If this is true, Charlotte is taking a huge risk speaking to me. I think about what Nick told her about Lucas. It is an odd thing to say. 'What do you think he meant about Lucas being right under your nose?' I ask, reaching in my bag to pull out a tissue.

With a trembling hand, Charlotte takes it when I hand it to her, but only stares at it. 'I don't know,' she says. 'I just don't know. Unless …'

'Unless what?'

'Oh God, I think … I think I know where Lucas is!' She jumps up. 'We have to go to the police now. I was going to tell you that I'm turning myself in today, but they'll need to know … where he is.'

I think I understand what she's saying, but I have to be sure. 'Charlotte, are you saying you know where Lucas's body is?'

She breaks down again and I can barely understand her, but she manages a nod.

'Come on, try to keep it together. We need to go now.' I am closer than ever to finding Grace, of that I'm sure.

We sit in the waiting area of Wood Green police station. To save time we jumped on a tube at East Putney, but it still took us almost an hour to get here. On the journey I tried to get Charlotte to confirm where she thinks Lucas is, but I could get no sense out of her. It's almost as if she couldn't tell me the words, couldn't bear to think of it. I only hope she will be able to tell the police.

There are four others in here, all staring at their feet or the walls, avoiding eye contact, and I wonder what they are here for. Are they victims of crime or perpetrators? Perhaps it is better not to know. Charlotte joins them in staring at the floor, red-eyed and anxious. She will be considered an accessory for helping Nick, and that will undoubtedly mean a harsh sentence, years of her life wasted. I am still furious about what she did, but I've come to realise she too is a victim; she would have had no way of knowing exactly what Nick was planning, but proving that to the police would be another matter.

It is almost half an hour before Charlotte is called by a police officer. He isn't dressed in uniform, so must be quite high up in the investigation. This is a good sign. She turns to me before standing up, her eyes pleading, but I shake my head. 'They won't let me in there with you,' I whisper. 'Plus, I need to call my husband and tell him where I am. I need a car to follow the police; they'll never let me go to the crime scene and I have to be there. I have to see for myself.'

Charlotte seems about to protest, but then she nods, slowly following the officer.

'Don't worry, I'll be right here when you finish,' I say.

She offers a faint smile and then she is gone.

Outside, I call Matt's mobile, but there is no answer. I don't usually bother the receptionists at the practice when he doesn't pick up, but this is an emergency. My stomach is twisted into knots and I don't want to think about why. Dialling the surgery, I immediately recognise Abigail's voice.

'Oh, hi, Mrs Porter. Dr Porter's with a patient at the moment, I'm afraid, but I can give him a message as soon as he's finished? He's running late with his patients but I'm sure he'll be able to call you back as soon as he can.'

I tell her not to worry, and just to let him know that I'm fine and will try again later. There is only one option now, and somehow it feels right.

Abbot picks up immediately, as if he's been expecting the phone to ring. 'Sim, hey, how are you? Is everything all right?'

I tell him I'm fine and ask where he is.

'I just got home from work. Why? What's going on?'

He listens while I give him the briefest possible explanation, and by the time I've finished he is already in his car, ready to make his way to Wood Green.

For ten minutes I pace up and down the car park, too anxious and too cold to keep still. I will finally get answers about Lucas Hall today, and they are bound to lead us to Grace. When the fierce wind gets too much for me, I head inside to wait.

It is nearly an hour and a half before Abbot arrives, striding into the police station and making a beeline for me. 'She still in there?' he asks, keeping his voice low.

'Yep,' I say, wrapping him in a hug. 'Thanks for coming. I know it's asking a lot. You know, after everything.'

'Shhh,' he says, 'no, it's not.

I squeeze his hand but can't manage any words.

'So Charlotte's telling the police everything?' Abbot asks.

'Yes, let's hope so. Whatever she's done, she really fell for Lucas. But infatuation can feel like love to a young girl, and she just lost her head. Hearing Nick's words must have shocked her into action, though, because she's turned herself in.'

'But are you sure you can trust her? After everything she did?' A deep frown appears on Abbot's face.

'No. But what can she do here? Nick's hardly likely to stroll through those doors, is he?'

Abbot fetches us each a cup of water from the machine in the corner and when he comes back I can tell he has something on his mind. 'Um, does Matt know you're here?'

'I couldn't get hold of him. He's at the surgery seeing patients.'

'I see.' Abbot rubs his chin. 'Did you tell him … you know … what I said?'

With so much else going on I haven't even entertained the idea of telling Matt that Abbot has feelings for me. We both have enough to deal with at the moment and even if I felt the same I would never act on it. 'No. I won't tell him. There's no need, we haven't done anything, have we?'

Abbot leans forward in his chair. 'And I never would. You're married. I just … shouldn't have said anything.'

'Let's just—'

The inner door is flung open and Charlotte appears. Her eyes are more bloodshot than when she followed the officer, and she wraps her arms around herself in a defensive stance.

I stand up and rush towards her. 'Are you okay? What did they say?'

Spotting Abbot, she shrinks back. 'Who's that? Why is he here?'

I tell her not to panic, and explain that he is my friend, and is going to drive us.

She seems to accept this and as I make introductions she visibly relaxes. 'The police will be going there now. Are we going? Please, Simone, let's go now. I need to see. I need to know.'

'So they said you're free to go?' I ask. 'I thought they might be questioning you for longer.'

'They said they'll need to speak to me again, but were happy I came here today. They explained I was being interviewed as a witness about Lucas, not a suspect. But I'm not sure about the other stuff. You know, helping Nick.' She glances at Abbot again. 'Please, Simone, can we go now?'

From his seat Abbot nods, and the three of us head out of the police station.

When we get in the car, I turn to Charlotte and warn her she shouldn't expect to be let anywhere near Lucas when they find him. 'It's a crime scene,' I point out. 'They won't let us near in case we contaminate it.'

'I need to see Lucas. Let them try and stop me,' she says.

There is already a swarm of police officers – some in uniform, others in suits – on Belsize Avenue when we arrive, and crime scene tape surrounds the house. We stay in the car after Abbot parks up, all of us knowing we won't be allowed any closer than we already are. Thankfully, we are far enough down the road that nobody has noticed us.

Abbot is the first to speak. 'So what's the plan?'

In the back seat Charlotte whimpers and stares through the side window, her eyes wide and glassy.

'Hey,' he says, turning round to face her. 'We don't know for sure he's in there, do we? Nick Gibbs could have just been trying to get at you and he knew this would hurt. Let's just wait and see.'

Although his words seem to have little effect on Charlotte, I appreciate what he's trying to do. And I want him to be right because I'm still convinced Lucas can lead us to Grace. But if Lucas is dead, the question still remains whether Grace is responsible. After all, Nick Gibbs might have told Charlotte that Lucas was dead, but he didn't exactly admit he'd killed him. I struggle to believe Grace is responsible, but if she did kill him that night in his other flat, somebody else must have helped move him here, surely she couldn't have managed it alone?

'But I know he is,' Charlotte says. 'When the police were questioning me, they did a check on flat A and Lucas owns it. They told me.

'I don't know how I didn't think of it the other times I was here,' she continues. 'I just thought they were two completely separate flats with different owners. But I should have thought it was weird that I never saw anyone leaving or coming in. Why would he lie to me? Why did he have separate flats?'

Beside me Abbot opens his mouth to speak and I know without a doubt he's about to tell Charlotte the whole truth about Lucas and what he does to women.

'Let's just see what happens,' I say, before he can say anything. I still don't know why I am protecting her feelings, allowing her to keep thinking she meant something to Lucas, after what she did, but perhaps it's because she is close to Grace's age.

But Charlotte doesn't let it go. 'I did ask him about who lived there once. He just said he didn't know them. And I didn't think to question him.'

'This is London,' I remind her. 'How many people are friendly with their neighbours?'

She falls silent again, and we all go back to waiting.

For hours we sit there, all of us staring at the street – dark now from the setting sun – as more officers arrive. It is only when I see the crime scene officers arrive I know for sure they have found something.

Rubberneckers have gathered on the pavement, speaking in urgent whispers, their bodies shuffling with excitement. For them this could just be another television crime drama.

'I can't stand this anymore,' I say. 'I need to ask what's happening.' Without waiting for agreement or disapproval, I jump out of the car and head over to the officer standing by the crime scene tape. It is only when I get within a metre of him that I recognise him as the officer who came when I escaped from that bedroom. PC Millbank.

'Hi,' I say. 'Sorry, do you remember me?'

'Yes, Simone Porter, isn't it? You know I can't let you in there.'

I'm impressed and pleased he remembers my name, but he's clearly not going to make this easy for me. 'I know that, but I was hoping you'd be able to tell me what's going on. Please.'

'I can't do that, I'm afraid.' His voice is not unkind, but I am suddenly tempted to run past him, even though I know I wouldn't get very far.

'Okay, but do you think you could get the Detective Inspector? I try and remember the name of the man who interviewed me on Thursday, but it doesn't come to me.

PC Millbank sighs, but then beckons his uniformed colleague over from the front door. 'I just need to speak to DI Holbrook,' he tells him, and disappears inside.

Turning to the car, I see Abbot and Charlotte watching, both of them unable to hide their anxiety. Minutes tick by and I pace the pavement, trying to keep warm while I wait. Finally, after what seems like hours, but is probably only minutes, DI Holbrook comes out, and I am relieved to see he is the same officer who interviewed me.

'Mrs Porter,' he says. 'You know I can't give you any details at the moment, but you can call your Family Liaison Officer later and she'll give you an update.'

'Please, can you just tell me what you've found?'

DI Holbrook shakes his head but then his words surprise me. 'Actually, there is something you can help us with. I'm afraid we've found two bodies in there, one of which we can identify as Lucas Hall. The other has no ID on her.'

'Her?' I say, feeling my stomach clench.

'Yes. Now we don't like to do this but the sooner we can get an ID the better. I know your friend's daughter is missing, so would you mind helping us? I can't let you in there but I've got a photo I can show you.'

Bile rises to my throat and my legs weaken beneath me. An image of Grace flashes in front of me, her large eyes shining. It can't be.

I nod, unsure I can manage any words, but knowing I need to do this.

'Thank you,' he says. 'I'll be right back.'

Everything moves in slow motion when he comes back outside, a trick my mind is playing to delay the inevitable. And then I am staring at the photo he holds out to me on his phone.

And there is Grace. Helena. Her eyes wide and blank, her body battered and bruised.

Turning away, I lean over and lose the contents of my stomach.

THIRTY-EIGHT

Our house feels quieter than it's ever felt before. Even though Helena has never lived here with us, we always had the silent hope of finding her one day. And we did, too briefly, but now she has gone and we are once again consumed by our grief.

It is as if we are living that first day again, only worse this time because now there is certainty that we will never see our daughter again. How cruel it is that she was brought back into our lives for only a matter of hours. Our unspoken words to her will remain trapped, never to be heard. We now have finality. Closure. And rather than being any comfort, it's like being ripped apart.

It's been two days since I stood on Belsize Avenue, staring at a photo of my daughter's cold, lifeless body. After seeing her, after those first moments of shock and pain, I was on autopilot, numb, making a mental list of all the things I had to do, the most important of which was visit Ginny.

The police had already informed her before I got to the hospital, and I'm sure she could barely see me through her tears. It was doubtful she could hear me either through her sobs, but I promised her the police didn't know the truth, that they weren't going to come for her the second she was well enough to stand.

'It doesn't matter anymore,' she'd managed to say. 'What have I got left? Grace was everything to me.'

I had to let her have her time, and keep my heavy grief on the inside. We sat in silence for a while, holding hands, alone with our thoughts and memories.

But then she became inconsolable and had to be sedated, so it was time to leave. I told her I would be back, though, and I meant every word. I will not desert this woman.

Now I lie in bed, with Matt beside me, and it is far later than we have ever lain in before. Neither of us is asleep; we just don't have the energy to face anything yet. Matt knows everything now, including all about Charlotte breaking into the house, and it feels good to no longer be keeping things from him.

I know without him saying a word what is on Matt's mind, and he confirms this when he says, 'I wish I'd talked to Helena more that day she was here. Spent more time with her. Now it's too late.'

I reach for his arm and run my fingers across it. His skin is cold where he's rested his arm out of the duvet. 'I feel the same, but we can't have regrets, Matt. We only did what we thought was right at the time. There was no real evidence, was there? Apart from the rabbit. But like you said, there would have been thousands of those manufactured.'

He shakes his head. 'But you believed. You never doubted her, did you?'

This is not true. I didn't believe Grace at first. But the more time I spent with her, the more I just felt *something*. I can't explain what it was, but I felt that she was Helena. But despite that, I did give up when we went to Cornwall. I tell Matt this, but it does nothing to snap him out of his melancholy. Even my suggestion to cook bacon and eggs has no effect.

Leaving him in bed, I force myself up to make breakfast anyway; I'm not interested in eating it, but cooking distracts me from thoughts of Helena.

Matt comes downstairs when I call him, smelling of deodorant, his hair wet from the shower. 'I thought I'd better snap out of it,' he says. 'This is even worse for you after everything you've been through these last couple of weeks so I need to hold it together. Sorry for moping around.'

I serve our breakfast and we both sit at the table, pushing the food around our plates, letting it grow cold. 'Listen, I was thinking,' Matt says, placing down his knife and fork. 'Let's get out of here. You know the police still haven't found that lunatic, Nick Gibbs? Well, why don't we get out of here for a few days? At least until we can feel safe again.'

Although I haven't forgotten he's still evading capture, Grace has pushed everything else to the back of my mind. But Matt is right. He could just be biding his time before he comes to finish what he started. And now that the police are after him for murder he's got nothing to lose. 'Okay,' I say. 'But what about your work? You've only just got back from Cornwall.' My work will be easy enough to sort out, but Matt's is a lot trickier.

'I know we can't tell anyone the truth,' he says, 'but I can say there's been a death in the family and take bereavement leave. I'll say it's an aunt or something. Even if I have to take annual leave, I don't care. We need this time to ourselves.'

I nod my agreement.

'Remember the other day we talked about seeing Mum?' Matt continues. 'I think we should visit her now. She knows nothing of this but the sketchy details I gave her on the phone yesterday and I owe her a face-to-face visit to explain. She still feels responsible for all of it and I think we need to reassure her. Plus it's been too long since we went there.'

As soon as Matt's said it, I don't know why I haven't thought of it myself. My suggestion about visiting Miriam was quickly forgotten once I saw Helena's photo. But this is a perfect idea. Miriam lives in a top floor apartment and the whole building is surrounded by security gates. We would at least feel a bit safer there. 'I just need a few hours to get dressed and pack,' I say, already feeling better at the thought of getting out of here.

'And I'm guessing you want to check on Ginny,' Matt says. Sometimes I forget how well he knows me.

On the drive to Luton, Matt asks how Ginny is doing. There is no easy answer to this. Although when I called the nurse told me she was sleeping, and that she had calmed down, I could sense she didn't think it would last long.

'She just needs time, I suppose. Like we all do.'

'We just have to get through each hour,' he says, keeping his eyes fixed on the road. 'Anyway, I still don't quite know how I feel about the woman, after everything, but I imagine her suffering is awful. She raised Helena for eighteen years.'

We reach Luton by lunchtime and, stepping out of the car, I immediately feel better. Coming here was the right decision. Of course it will be difficult to explain things to Matt's mum, but the three of us can support each other.

Miriam greets us by the downstairs door and throws her arms around both of us, squeezing tightly. 'I just ... I'm so sorry,' she says, tears trickling down her cheeks. I have seen so many tears over the last few days I'm not sure I can handle any more.

She leads us inside and we trudge up the stairs, Miriam clinging to Matt's arm, almost dragging him down with her weight. She was always a slim woman, but in the last few years, her lifestyle of rarely venturing outside has meant she's piled on too many pounds.

Her flat has been decorated since we were last here, and I compliment her on her choice of colours. She has painted over the bland, neutral walls with a warm yellow shade. I tell her I love what she's done and she manages a smile.

'I had to do something to brighten the place up,' she says. 'It just gets so dark in here.' For the next few minutes she goes through all the changes she has made, and I know it's simply a distraction from having to talk about Helena.

'You must both be starving,' she says, forcing a smile. 'I've got some chicken in. How does that sound?' She doesn't wait for an answer, but heads to the kitchen, leaving us to stare after her.

Matt shrugs. 'She just needs time,' he whispers.

After lunch, Matt takes Miriam into town to get some things she needs. I know without him saying it that he will use it as an opportunity to talk to her alone, to tell her everything that's happened in more detail. She is obviously having trouble speaking about Helena, so maybe if it's just the two of them she might open up.

Once they've gone, I lie on the sofa and close my eyes. But instead of seeing darkness, Helena's face appears as the eighteen-year-old who called herself Grace. I let myself watch her for a while, but my eyes snap open when it becomes too painful.

I must drift off, though, because the next thing I know, someone is standing over me, peering down at me, but not speaking. My vision is blurred to start with but I am sure it is Nick Gibbs.

'Simone?'

Not Nick Gibbs, but Matt, speaking my name.

Relief washes over me and I clutch his arm, just to make sure it's really him.

'Sorry to wake you,' he says. Then he lowers his voice. 'I think I cheered Mum up a bit and reassured her that what happened to Helena is not her fault.'

I pull myself up to make room for him on the sofa. 'But what about you?' There is sadness in his eyes.

He plonks himself next to me and sighs. 'I'll be okay. We both will, we just need to give it time.'

Miriam enters the room and we fall silent. She is carrying a tray with three steaming mugs. 'Matt said you'll probably want tea, is that okay? If not I'll swap you for my coffee.'

I thank her and tell her tea is fine.

Matt suggests we put on the television, and I know it's not because there is anything interesting on, he simply wants to fill the silence. Miriam switches it on and the True Movies channel begins showing. With a gasp, she quickly flicks over when we realise the film that's playing is about an abducted child. So instead we opt for a sitcom that no one finds funny.

While we're watching, I flick through my phone, grateful to have it back from Charlotte. And that's when I notice a text from her.

They've found Nick Gibbs! He's been arrested!

I check the time of the message and see she sent it over an hour ago. 'They've got him!' I shriek into the room. 'Nick Gibbs. They've arrested him!'

Matt jumps up. 'What? How do you know?'

'Charlotte texted me.'

'But how does she know?'

'I guess the police would have told her. I don't know.'

'You shouldn't be talking to that girl,' Matt says.

I know he is probably right, but I feel sorry for her. She is now in a lot of trouble for the role she played in helping Nick Gibbs, and her future is uncertain.

'Shall I call the family liaison officer to confirm?' I say. 'She'll tell me.'

It takes me a while to get through to Sandra, but eventually she comes on the line and confirms what Charlotte has said. They have arrested Nick Gibbs.

I can hardly believe what I'm hearing. 'But how did they find him? Where?'

'He was desperate enough to try and see his kids. Somehow he found out they were in Brighton and he was arrested trying to take them from their mother.' I digest what she's telling me. Nick risked being caught so he could see his children. How is it that someone so fucked up, someone capable of such atrocities, can still have love in their hearts?

'So what will happen to him now?' I ask, half-dreading the answer. I know only too well, from the cases I've covered at work, how criminals are so often let loose on technicalities.

'Well, he's being interviewed as we speak and we can hold him for twenty-four hours while we gather all the evidence to charge him with murder.'

'Will there be enough? I mean, surely he covered his tracks?'

'Simone, please let us worry about that. If we need more time we can apply for it. Either thirty-six or ninety-six hours in fact. So don't panic. We *will* charge him.'

Reassured by Sandra's words, I thank her and she promises to be in touch soon with updates.

'That's great news,' Matt says, when I report the conversation, and I notice the colour returning to his cheeks. 'I hope he rots in jail for what he's done.'

I agree, but point out that we don't know yet who is responsible for killing Grace. It could have been Nick or Lucas. Or both of them together. There are still many questions remaining unanswered, but hopefully a police interrogation will get to the bottom of it.

'Well, whoever did it, they're both as guilty as each other,' Matt says, and Miriam and I both agree.

I text Abbot to tell him the news, and he replies with a promise to find out everything he can. Any moment now, this will be breaking news. The discovery of two bodies in a flat in Wood Green is already plastered over the television, radio and internet, all of which I try to avoid.

'Now you can both feel safe again,' Miriam says. 'You must have been petrified he'd come after you.'

Nodding, I keep to myself that this is only just the beginning. He could be allowed out on bail, or he could have acquaintances that will sort out any unresolved business for him. And his case will still have to go to court, which is a lengthy process. But I try to stay positive; they have caught him at least, and he will have to answer for what he's done.

We've had such a big lunch that none of us feel like dinner, even by eight o'clock. Despite the good news we've had about Nick, Matt soon sinks back into sadness, staring at the TV screen with blank and distant eyes. Every so often I notice Miriam glancing at him, lines creasing her forehead as she wonders what she can say to him. But there is nothing. We will both have to just get through this however we can.

'I was thinking,' Miriam says to Matt. 'Would you be able to put up a shelf for me in the spare room? There's not much storage space in there and I thought it would be nice for guests to have somewhere extra to put things. I've already got the shelf ready to go.' I remember the last time we stayed here I kept everything in my suitcase because there was nowhere to unpack. But I also know it is an attempt to distract Matt.

'Okay,' he says, leaning forward. 'Now?'

'If you wouldn't mind? I know it's getting late but—'

'It's fine,' Matt says. I know he will be grateful to spend some time on his own, carrying out a task which requires all his focus.

Miriam says she's borrowed a toolbox from Miles next door, and they both head off to the spare room.

'Come and see what I've done to the bedroom, Simone,' she calls, after a moment.

'I just need to make a quick call,' I tell her, remembering I need to update Chris Harding. No doubt he will already have heard about Grace and Lucas, but the news of Nick Gibbs being arrested will surely bring him some extra hope.

'But it doesn't look good, does it?' he says, once he's offered his condolences. 'If that man killed your friend's daughter and his own friend, then there's no way he spared Mel's life. Not after what he did to her in that video.'

'Let's just hope they get the truth out of him,' I say, knowing there is not much I can say to reassure him. I recall the certainty I had when I'd seen the video that she was taking her last breaths, but I don't speak aloud my fear.

'I'm going down there,' Chris says. 'To Wood Green police station. I need to remind them not to forget Mel in all this. I know you've already told them about the video but there are so many things they're investigating, I just don't want Mel to be forgotten. Not if there's the tiniest chance she's still alive. Sorry if that makes me sound callous. I know it's important they find out what happened to your friend's daughter.'

'Don't apologise,' I say. 'I understand. You've got to fight for Mel.'

After the call, I join Miriam in her bedroom and sit on the bed, closing the door slightly against the noise of Matt drilling.

'So, what do you think?' Miriam says, gesturing at the walls. She has done a good job. The walls, curtains and bed sheets are lilac, a soothing, peaceful colour I've heard is perfect for a tranquil night's sleep. I tell her it's lovely and she beams with pride.

'Oh, I almost forgot,' she says, pointing to a large cardboard box in the corner of the room. 'That's Matt's stuff. Things he kept in the loft at the old house, but now I've got nowhere to store it.

I'd completely forgotten I had it all. Would you mind having it? I mean, you don't have to take it now, of course—'

'That's fine, Miriam. And we will take it now. It shouldn't be clogging up your flat.' A vision of Miriam's huge old house – Matt's childhood home – flashes into my head. It was always too big, even when his dad was alive, so I understand why she sold it and moved here. But it wasn't just downsizing that brought her here; it was the need to run away. Helena's abduction changed her life as much as it did ours.

'Thanks, Simone. Anyway, I'll just see how Matt's getting on. Stay here and look through the box if you like. Get a glimpse of his childhood. I'll be back in a sec.'

When she's gone I make my way over to the box and lift up the flaps. Inside is a jumble of objects and books, and I dip my hand in and pull out the first thing I feel. It is a naked action man doll. Smiling, I make a note to myself to tease Matt about this later. He has never before mentioned that he owned one of these.

Peering in to see what else I can find, I pull out school books, a model train and a swimming trophy. I knew Matt was a strong swimmer at school but had no idea he'd won anything. But then again, he has never been one for bragging. There is also a dartboard in the box, but I can't see any darts. A large textbook catches my eye, and I pull it out. It's a biology book, and from the description on the back I see it is university level.

I'm about to put the book back when something slips from it and falls to the floor. At first I think it's a piece of paper, perhaps with some study notes on it, but I soon realise I'm staring at the plain white back of a photograph.

Scooping it up, I flip it over, and almost stop breathing. What I'm staring at makes no sense. There are four people in this photo, four young men, standing on some steps outside what looks like a university building, their arms draped over each other in camaraderie.

Nick Gibbs. Lucas Hall. Daniel Rhodes.

And Matt.

I freeze for a moment, but when my mind registers what this means I sink to the floor, unable to tear my eyes from the photograph, willing the faces to change before my eyes. But there is no doubt. It is definitely them.

Outside I hear drilling, and Miriam's voice. I have no idea what she's saying because I can't take in anything other than this photograph and what it means.

And then the doorbell rings, and footsteps patter along the tiled corridor. There are more muffled sounds before Miriam shouts out to Matt. 'The police are here. They want to talk to you,' she says.

Forcing myself to stand, I move closer to the bedroom door. And that's when I hear more clearly, and suddenly everything makes sense.

'Matthew Porter? We're arresting you on suspicion of rape and murder. You do not have to say anything but it may harm your defence if you do not mention when questioned something you later rely on in court. Anything you do say may be given in evidence.'

And that's when I scream.

THIRTY-NINE

Do you hate me, Simone? Has what I've done overshadowed your love for me? I expect it has, and I know I only have myself to blame for that. But I haven't finished my story. And you need to hear it all before you vanquish me from your life, because I know that is exactly what you'll do, never mind that we made vows to stick together through better or worse. Ironic isn't it – because there's nothing worse than this, is there?

I didn't know what would happen to Tia that night. That's not me staking a claim to innocence. I know I am far from that. After all, I helped them clean up the flat, remove any evidence that any of us had been there, and didn't say a word when we all walked out, leaving her lifeless body for someone else to deal with. And the things I had planned for her that night I can't even bring myself to mention. But I need you to know that her death was in no way something I wanted. I'm not even sure Nick intended to kill her, but after he did, he got a taste for it. He got off on it. Wanted to do it again and again. Especially as we got away with it. This is what I've told myself ever since, but there is, of course, another possibility. One I don't want to think about.

I was sickened by what we'd done, Simone (and I say we *because I was there too and did nothing to stop him. So were Lucas and Daniel, which makes us all guilty). I could barely leave my house, couldn't function, could barely live with it. I think Tia's death shocked me into despising who I was and what I was doing. And as well as that, I've had to live every day with the fear that we will get caught. Even after all these years.*

I cut them all off after Tia's death, ignored their calls, avoided them around the university campus, stopped going to Harry's. Lucas and Daniel didn't seem too bothered that I was no longer part of the group (I don't think they'd ever really wanted me there) but Nick would not let me go so easily. Don't get me wrong, I never fooled myself into believing it was because he missed my company. Oh no. There was only one reason he kept hounding me. I knew what he'd done, and he wanted me to stay close so he could keep an eye on me and make sure I didn't talk to anyone about it. I was a constant threat to him, even though I'd never given him reason to think I would open my mouth. And to be honest, I wouldn't have. I couldn't have. I was just as guilty as he was.

But I couldn't shake him off, Simone. I never went out with the three of them again, but he'd corner me in corridors and try his best to coax me into meeting up. I knew what meeting up *meant. Drugging girls and raping them, filming them while they took their last breath. That's what the experience with Tia had led them to. I wanted no part of that. What I'd already done was bad enough, but the three of them had no limits. And what would be next?*

It got easier in my third year at university because Nick finished his course and stopped harassing me. Daniel had dropped out a year early, and I had no idea how he was spending his days. I assumed Lucas just kept his head down and focused on getting his degree, because he would pass me in the corridors without a glance. I heard that Nick had done well, of course, he was always ambitious, wanted to be a success. He wouldn't let anything interfere with his studies, not even his sickening urges, though I'm still not sure how they didn't distract him.

And then, after graduation, my life changed again. Only it was for the better this time, because I met you. Do you remember? I still have the image of you in my head, and I often summon it now, when this place threatens to destroy me.

You were standing outside the Häagen-Dazs shop in Leicester Square with your friend Lily, stuffing ice-cream into your mouth as if you were scared it would disappear if you didn't gobble it up.

I couldn't take my eyes off you, Simone. I mean, you were beautiful of course, but it was more than that. I was drawn to you like I'd never been drawn to anyone, not even Becky, and it had nothing to do with depraved thoughts. Your smile lit up your entire face, and I just knew, even though you looked younger than me, that I could learn from you, that you could save me from myself. It sounds melodramatic, doesn't it? But that's exactly what you did. I need you to know that. That our marriage wasn't a waste. You kept me sane, kept me from ending up like them.

Do you remember I approached you and asked if your ice cream was nice? You simply nodded, while your friend giggled beside you. As beautiful as you are, you were probably used to being approached by strangers, but I didn't let that deter me. And then I did something I've never done before. I went and bought three more tubs of ice cream, came back and handed one each to you and Lily. 'You have to try the pistachio,' I said, tucking into mine. And then I said goodbye and walked off. That was it. Simple and effective, I hoped.

I didn't know whether you would notice that your ice cream contained a tiny scrap of paper with my phone number scrawled on it, but you did eventually because two days later you called me, asking if you could speak to the ice-cream man.

Things moved pretty quickly after that, didn't they? Even though you were determined not to rush anything. We progressed from phone calls to meeting up, and then you began to stay at mine more nights than you spent at your parents' home.

It never bothered me that you were three years younger than me and about to start university, while I had already finished. Every-

thing about you was just right for me. I learned who I really was in those first few months with you, I saw the decent person I could be. And it cemented the change I had already put in place.

Things were going well for us. Even Nick's calls couldn't bother me. But then we had an accident, Simone, and it was the start of our ending, wasn't it?

I knew you were on the pill, I'd seen you take it enough times, panicking if you were even five minutes late remembering. But you still got pregnant. What were the chances? We'd known each other less than six months, and I won't lie: I was terrified. I was only twenty-one, and had just started medical school. Ironic isn't it, that after hurting so many people, I chose a healing profession? Perhaps I was trying to atone for my sins? But whatever the reason, my future was all mapped out in my head, and although it did include you, babies were not even a dot on the horizon. I had rarely given a thought to whether I would ever want a family. I supposed I did perhaps one day, far into the future, but not then. Definitely not then.

But I knew the second you told me that there was only one option for you. You were having this baby, even if it meant putting your life on hold, making huge sacrifices. You could never consider the alternative. This was right for you. I remember you telling me that I didn't have to be a part of it, that you would never force me into anything, but you were doing this, no matter what.

I would never have turned my back on you, so I accepted what had happened and tried to get my head around it. Maybe I could be a good father? And my mum and your parents would certainly help us. We would manage somehow.

When Helena arrived, all smooth and new, I loved her, Simone, I really did. But it was hard. Life was different, we barely had time to breathe, and I felt my grasp on things slipping away. I could hardly focus on studying, and the cramped flat we rented was like a prison. And there was no escape. I felt my life slowly slipping away.

But then Nick called one evening. He said he would leave me alone if I just met him for a quick drink. Nothing else, just a chat and a beer. I remember the exact moment; my eyes flicked to you as I stood with the phone clutched to my ear. You were stressed because Helena wouldn't settle, and no matter what you did she continued bawling, a deafening sound the whole building could probably hear.

I needed to get out, even just for half an hour, so I agreed to Nick's request. I had no idea what he wanted, and I didn't believe that he was prepared to leave me alone, but I assumed he just wanted to threaten me into maintaining my silence. Still, even an evening with Nick was preferable to the claustrophobia of the flat and the baby's screaming.

You didn't ask which friend I was meeting, but even if you had I would have lied. You knew nothing about them and that was the way it had to stay.

I met Nick in the Wetherspoons in Ealing, and he wasn't alone. Daniel was with him, but there was no sign of Lucas. I didn't want to think about how he might be spending his evening.

We all offered strained nods to each other but I could tell they were relieved I'd turned up. 'What's going on?' I said.

And that's when they told me about Daniel's sister, Ginny. How she was desperate for a baby but could never have one of her own because she'd had chemotherapy as a child. I couldn't understand her urge, but I continued to listen, wondering where this would go.

'I'd do anything for my friends,' Nick said. 'I believe in loyalty, and quite frankly, Matt, you've let me down.'

I tried to say I hadn't, that I would never breathe a word of what had happened in Tia's flat, or anything else, but he shook his head.

'I just can't take that chance. There's too much at stake. Things need to be evened out.' There was menace in his voice and I wondered if it had always been there, or was I only now seeing the true man? Either way, the threat was clear.

I tried to assure him. 'I swear to you, I won't breathe a word.'

And that's when he told me that he knew I wouldn't, and that I was going to make a sacrifice to prove it.

'You're too young to have a baby,' he said. 'You're twenty-one and you have a ball and chain around your ankle. What kind of life is that?' I had never spoken of you, or Helena, but he knew all about you both anyway.

I wanted to argue that this was nonsense, but I couldn't. He was right.

'She's trapped you, that girlfriend of yours. But there's a way out. It's not much different than if she'd had an abortion. Just think of it like that. That will make it easier.'

I wasn't sure what he meant at first. Surely he wasn't talking about harming my baby? No, even for Nick that would be abhorrent. Then Daniel piped up and it all became clear. 'We want you to give your baby to my sister. It kills three birds with one stone. First, you escape from the hell you're in, second, you help Ginny out, and third, you prove your loyalty to Nick.'

The laugh escaped without me realising it was coming. But when they didn't reciprocate, I knew they were serious. Standing up, I scraped my chair back and turned away, leaving my drink unfinished.

'Wait,' Nick said, his loud voice stopping me in my tracks. 'Perhaps we gave you the impression that you have a choice here. Well, let me just clarify. You don't. Not unless you want to go to prison for murder. I can make it so all the evidence of everything we've ever done points to you alone. And remember Leanne?'

I'm sorry, Simone. I should have carried on walking. I should have gone to the police and told them everything. That was the moment to finally do it. Yes, I would have gone to prison for a long time, but you and Helena would have been safe.

You will by now have realised that I was part of our daughter's abduction, that I arranged it all with the others and have known for eighteen years exactly where she was. It was simply their luck that

Mum was sick that day, but even if she hadn't been, they would have still taken Helena.

But what's even worse is that I saw our baby a few times after that. Any time Ginny was worried about anything medical, Daniel brought Helena to me to check over. And I didn't breathe a word to you. Not once. I never even came close. I closed that chapter of my life and never reopened it.

Not until I was forced to.

The others left me alone after that and I didn't hear from Nick again until the night Lucas attacked Helena in one of his flats. He called me in a panic, and reminded me again of the time he'd helped me clear up the mess I'd made with Leanne the barmaid. Then when that didn't work, he used the old threat, only this time he could add child abduction to the list of crimes. He said he knew a lot of people, that he could easily keep his hands clean, but I was not so lucky.

I went to the flat in Embankment, Simone. Helena was no longer there, but Lucas's body was. And it wasn't a lamp that killed him. Nick had battered him over and over until barely a patch of skin was free of blood or bruises.

'He was out of control,' Nick said. 'Talking to her about your wife. Who knows what else he would have said?'

'How did you know he was here?' I asked, still confused.

'Because the drunk fool called me and told me what happened. I told him to wait here for me, and that we'd sort the little bitch out together.' He didn't even flinch when he called Helena that word, as if he'd forgotten she was my daughter.

I knew then I was right to fear him. That if he could do that to Lucas, then he would have no trouble ending my life. Whatever friendship we'd ever had was nowhere near as strong as theirs had been, I always knew that. So I did the only thing I thought I could do. I spent the next few hours helping him move Lucas's body to his flat in Wood Green. Then we came back and cleaned up the mess. By the time we were finished there wasn't a speck of blood or anything else anywhere.

And then I went home to you, Simone, and fell exhausted into bed. You didn't even stir, and I was grateful for that.

I didn't know he'd taken Helena a few days later. Or that he had her phone and must have been using it to text Ginny and Helena's friend. I really thought she'd run off somewhere, like some teenagers do. And I had no idea you had made any contact with Ginny or Nick. If I had, I could have done something about it. I would have done something about it. Please believe that. And then maybe I could have salvaged something from the mess I have made. Nick tried to contact me several times after I helped him with Lucas's body, and I can only assume now it was to tell me about you finding him. But I avoided his calls and deleted his messages without reading them.

Yes, I am a monster. But I love you, Simone. I won't even bother trying to apologise again because that is an insult to you. What I have done goes way beyond any kind of apology. But know that I am sorry, and that I will die sorry.

You have probably guessed by now that I never submitted Helena's DNA for testing. How could I? The truth would have come out and Nick would have killed us all. I know my fear is no excuse for the lies and deceit. I am a coward.

Before I go, there is one more thing you should know. One more thing that will cement in your head what a horrific human being I am. Remember that private detective? Mark Hunter? I had to tell Nick about him. I swear to you I don't know how he dealt with it, probably the same way he dealt with Leanne, but it is just one more thing I have on my conscience.

It won't make any difference to you that I've now confessed every one of my crimes to the police. It is too little, too late.

Move on with your life, Simone, and don't give me another thought.

EPILOGUE

One Year Later

The sun streaming through the window wakes me up, warming my skin with a smooth kiss. I love these brief moments before I am fully awake, before I remember. It is getting easier, though, and I am quicker at pushing anything negative away.

But I won't forget Helena. Ever.

I reach across the bed and stroke his smooth chest. 'Good morning,' he mumbles, slowly coming around. And then he smiles, just as he always does, his blue eyes shining. 'What are your plans for today?'

'I thought I'd go and see Ginny. Maybe take her shopping or something.'

Abbot stretches and turns onto his front. 'Good idea.' He drapes his arm over me. 'Have you heard from him again?'

'Yep. Another visiting order came yesterday morning. I threw it in the bin.'

Abbot does not seem surprised to hear this. I have been doing the same thing for a year now. When he was first arrested, I read Matt's letter because I wanted an explanation, but now I want nothing more to do with him. It's funny how twenty years with someone can be erased in seconds. As if it never existed. Perhaps he needs closure, but I don't care. I got mine the second I saw that photo and the police pounded on Miriam's door. Matt no longer exists for me.

It wasn't a hard decision to sell the house in Fulham and buy my own flat in Putney. In fact, it was the easiest thing I've ever done. There is nothing of Matt in my new home, no memories tainting the atmosphere.

Everything is still fairly new for Abbot and me, but we have a solid foundation of friendship to build on.

'Do you want me to come with you?' Abbot says. 'I don't mind. I've grown fond of Ginny.'

'Maybe not this time,' I say, and he does me the courtesy of not asking why. 'We're meeting up with Hannah too. Just for a coffee.' I have come to view both Ginny and Hannah Hall as friends, despite the horrendous circumstances that brought us together.

Even Chris Harding and I keep in regular contact. Things have been hard for him since the police found his sister's body a few months ago buried in a wood near another of Lucas Hall's flats in Cockfosters.

'But I'll come to your place this evening if you're not doing anything?' I tell Abbot.

He smiles and tells me we can get a takeaway. We are in my flat this morning, but he offers to make breakfast. I immediately agree; he may not be a master chef but he's an expert when it comes to fry-ups.

While he's in the kitchen I shower and dress, and then I stare at myself in the mirror. I can already see the subtle changes, and I run my hands over my distended stomach. To the side of the mirror, on the chest of drawers, the blue velvet rabbit catches my eye. I pick it up and clutch it against my chest. A tear rolls down my cheek but then I remind myself that I need to stay positive for the new life growing inside me.

Putting the rabbit back in its place, I comfort myself with the thought that a piece of Helena will always live on.

LETTER FROM KATHRYN

Thank you for choosing to read my fourth book, *The Girl You Lost*. I very much hope you enjoyed the journey the book takes you on.

Your support is very much appreciated and if you did enjoy the book then I would be extremely grateful if you could take a moment to post a quick review on Amazon and let others know what you thought. Word of mouth is a lifeline for authors so any recommendations to friends and family would be very welcome!

One of the best parts of my job is hearing from readers so please feel free to let me know what you thought via Twitter or my Facebook page. You can even contact me directly through my website.

To make sure you don't miss out on my forthcoming releases you can sign up to my mailing list at my website link below.

Thank you again for all your support – it is greatly appreciated.

Kathryn x

www.bookouture.com
www.kathryncroft.com
www.twitter.com/katcroft
www.facebook.com/authorkathryncroft

THE GIRL WITH NO PAST

The No. 1 Bestseller

Fourteen years running from your past. Today it catches up.

A gripping psychological thriller for fans of
***Gone Girl* and *The Girl on the Train*.**

Leah Mills lives a life of a fugitive – kept on the run by one terrible day from her past. It is a lonely life, without a social life or friends until – longing for a connection – she meets Julian. For the first time she dares to believe she can live a normal life.

Then, on the fourteenth anniversary of *that* day, she receives a card. **Someone knows the truth about what happened.** Someone who won't stop until they've destroyed the life Leah has created.

But is Leah all she seems? Or does she deserve everything she gets?

Everyone has secrets. But some are deadly.

'Couldn't turn the pages fast enough … one of the best books I've read this year.' *The Book Review Café*

'From the first chapter, the book keeps you guessing … an amazingly thrilling and gripping story … even better than *The Girl on the Train*.' *More Delight*